HAPPILY NEVER AFTER

PHOEBE MACLEOD

Boldwood

First published in Great Britain in 2025 by Boldwood Books Ltd.

Copyright © Phoebe MacLeod, 2025

Cover Design by Head Design Ltd

Cover Images: Shutterstock

Every effort has been made to obtain the necessary permissions with reference to copyright material, both illustrative and quoted. We apologise for any omissions in this respect and will be pleased to make the appropriate acknowledgements in any future edition.

A CIP catalogue record for this book is available from the British Library.

Paperback ISBN 978-1-83533-380-8

Large Print ISBN 978-1-83533-381-5

Hardback ISBN 978-1-83533-379-2

Trade Paperback ISBN 978-1-80656-030-1

Ebook ISBN 978-1-83533-382-2

Kindle ISBN 978-1-83533-383-9

Audio CD ISBN 978-1-83533-374-7

MP3 CD ISBN 978-1-83533-375-4

Digital audio download ISBN 978-1-83533-378-5

This book is printed on certified sustainable paper. Boldwood Books is dedicated to putting sustainability at the heart of our business. For more information please visit https://www.boldwoodbooks.com/about-us/sustainability/

Boldwood Books Ltd, 23 Bowerdean Street, London, SW6 3TN

www.boldwoodbooks.com

To Tara.

PROLOGUE

TWO YEARS AGO

'So, that went well then,' I say to Angus with a smile as he carefully negotiates the farm track.

'What do you mean?'

'All the research we did about how to choose a puppy. You know, don't just pick the cutest-looking one, assess their personality by whether they're curious or fearful.'

'She didn't seem fearful to me, and we did do most of the things the books told us. We met the mother and I didn't spot any of the signs that would have indicated it was a puppy farm.'

'I'm not convinced she's all Border Collie,' I observe.

'Me neither. I reckon she might be a bit of a Heinz 57, but that can make for a healthier dog. Some of the Kennel Club-approved breeds have all sorts of issues.'

I sigh contentedly. 'She is very cute though, isn't she?'

Angus turns to me and grins. 'You've got it just as bad as I have.'

'What are we going to call her?'

'I was reading in one of the puppy books that it's best to go for a short name with hard consonants in it, because dogs find those easier to learn.'

'Oh, that's a pity,' I say with a smile. 'I was planning on calling her Josephine, or Evangelina.'

He laughs. 'No, you weren't.'

'Hermione? Amethyst?' I add, joining in with his laughter.

'Stop it.'

'What about Tabitha?'

'Better, but maybe a bit long.'

He's so transparent, it's all I can do not to laugh out loud. 'You've already decided on a name, haven't you?' I tell him. 'Come on, spit it out.'

'Not at all. She's going to be spending more time with you than me, so I think it's only fair you name her.'

'But you have a suggestion.'

He does have the decency to look a little guilty now. 'I was wondering whether Meg would work. I mean, we can totally choose something else if you hate it, but—'

'It's fine,' I interrupt him. 'Meg it is.'

A comfortable silence descends as we reach the main road and Angus turns towards home.

'It's a big thing, taking on a puppy,' he observes after a few miles. 'You know what they say about how getting a pet is merely a precursor to having a baby?'

'Whoa!' I cut in with a laugh. 'One step at a time.'

He pats my thigh reassuringly. 'Don't worry. I'm sure Meg will keep us both busy enough. Shall we call into the pet store on the way home and see about getting some bits and pieces for her?'

'I think that's an excellent idea.'

I lean back in my seat and close my eyes. Yes, getting a puppy is a big deal, but I think we're ready for it, and it's another sign of our commitment to one another that we're taking on dog parenthood. I may have feigned alarm when Angus started talking about babies, but I'd be lying if I said the thought hadn't crossed my mind too. He'd be a great dad, I reckon.

I'm jolted out of my reverie by my phone ringing in my pocket. The caller ID shows that it's my agent, Tamara.

'Laura, I've got fabulous news,' she says before I even have a chance to say hello. 'The publisher called. They're really excited by the concept for your next book, to the extent that they're offering a substantial advance.' She names a sum that makes me inhale sharply.

'Is everything OK?' Angus mouths.

I nod. Tamara is still speaking, telling me about contracts and so on, but

I'm no longer listening. This is the biggest advance I've ever been offered, and a real sign that the publisher has faith in me. As soon as the call ends, I turn to Angus.

'We need to make another stop on the way home,' I tell him.

'Oh, yes?' His expression is curious.

'The publisher bought my concept. We need champagne.'

He laughs. 'I don't know why this always surprises you. You're a bestselling author. You'd have to come up with something truly dreadful for them not to buy it. You really need to learn to ditch the impostor syndrome.'

'I know, but I think it comes with the territory,' I tell him.

'Yeah. And now you'll agonise over whether the book is shit right up until the point that everyone buys it and loves it because you're actually very good at what you do. And we know that this book is going to be brilliant, because in a couple of weeks Meg will be there to give you inspiration.'

I lean over to kiss him on the cheek. Angus has been my most vocal supporter from the beginning, and I love him to bits for it. I truly don't know what I'd do without him.

1

PRESENT DAY

'Claire, that guy over there is totally checking you out. Have you noticed?'

Claire flipped the tab to stop the flow of lager into the pint glass she was filling and followed her friend's gaze. It was a typically busy night in the Pig and Whistle, so it took her a moment to locate the object of Pauline's attention.

'The one sitting to the right of the dartboard?' she asked, having clocked a pair of dark eyes under full brows.

'That's him. He's barely stopped looking at you all night.'

'Eeuww, Pauline. He's way too old.'

'I don't know. You're nineteen. What's he? Twenty-six? Twenty-seven? Perfect for someone like you. Unlike boys your age, he's probably got a job, his own car, maybe even a house or flat. He's not bad looking either, is he? You could do a lot worse, I reckon. Go over and say hello.'

'Are you out of your mind? I might as well just chuck my knickers at him and tell him I'm desperate. No, if he's interested, he's got to make the first move, and I'm still not convinced about his age. My dad would freak.'

'Your dad needs to realise that you're an adult now. Time to start dating men instead of boys. There are loads of empty glasses nearby. Why don't you do a collection run and see if he says anything? Go on. I'll finish this order for you.'

Claire knew well enough that there was no point in arguing with Pauline when she was like this. With a sigh, she picked up a tray, making her way slowly across the room to the table where the man was sitting. Now that Pauline had pointed him out, she was acutely aware of his eyes on her as she moved.

'Can I take these empties for you?' she asked when she finally reached his table.

'Thanks.' He looked up at her and smiled. He had a nice smile, she had to admit, and Pauline was right. He was good-looking in a swarthy kind of way.

'I don't think I've seen you in here before,' she remarked.

'I've only just moved into the area,' he explained. 'I'm Darren, by the way. Darren Enticknap.'

'Pleased to meet you, Darren. I'm Claire.'

I sigh and lift my eyes from the laptop screen to look out of the window. Normally, I have no trouble slipping into the zone when I'm writing, but the last few paragraphs have taken over two hours. What's more, the text feels bland and clunky as I cast my eyes over it. Ever since Angus left, writing has felt more like a chore than a pleasure and I can't deny that it's showing in the quality of my work.

If real life were anything like one of my books, I'd have seen Angus's sudden departure coming. However, a month has passed since he decided – quite out of the blue – that he needed to be as far away from me as possible, and I still haven't fully come to terms with it.

'You're not going to cry again. We're moving on, Laura,' I tell myself forcefully as I prepare to recite the mantra my best friend Olivia gave me when I was still raw and bewildered in the early days after he walked out. 'Angus left because, well, I still don't really know why he left if I'm honest, but it's definitely more to do with him than me.'

I shift my gaze to the dog basket beside my desk, unsurprised to see Meg's chocolate eyes staring reproachfully at me. I may be the one who normally walks and feeds her, but she's always been more Angus's dog than mine and, if anything, she's moped even more than me since he left. To be fair, a lot of that has probably just been her picking up on my misery.

'Don't look at me like that,' I chide her gently. 'Us girls have got to stick together at times like this. For all we know, it might be you he suddenly decided he couldn't stand any more and I was just collateral damage.'

I try to focus back on my work, but Meg has evidently decided that the fact I've spoken to her means something good is going to happen. She stands and shakes herself before resting her head on my thigh and staring at me, wagging her tail hopefully.

'You've already had a walk today,' I remind her. 'Plus, the weather outside is filthy.'

The wagging only intensifies. I try hard to ignore her, but she ups the ante by nudging my elbow with her nose.

'Fine,' I say exasperatedly. 'It's not as if I'm achieving anything useful. Do you want me to see if Auntie Liv is around?'

The mention of one of Meg's favourite human beings increases the tail wagging to such a frenzied level that her whole bottom is now swinging from side to side with the force of it. It's impossible not to smile at such simple joy as I dial Olivia's number.

'Hi, Laura,' she says breathlessly when the call connects. 'What's up?'

'I feel like I should be asking you the same question!' I reply. 'You sound like you're in the middle of running a marathon.'

'I think that would be easier than the truth. Do you remember that yoga channel on YouTube I mentioned last week?'

'Umm, no.'

'I definitely told you about it. Anyway, I decided to give it a go. I thought yoga was supposed to be gentle, but I swear this woman is trying to kill me. Anyway, are you all right? How's the book?'

'The book's fine but Meg's hassling to see you. I'll tell her you're busy, don't worry.'

Liv's laughter is rich and full. 'Translation,' she replies. 'You're distracted and struggling to concentrate, so you're using my favourite dog as an excuse to scrounge a cup of tea and a madeleine off me.'

'OK, OK. You've got me.'

'Have you seen the weather though? You'll get soaked.'

'I'll come round to the back door so we don't drip all over your hallway.'

'Good plan. The garden gate is open so just let yourselves in. I'll have a towel ready for Meg and I'm putting the kettle on now.'

'I'll see you in ten minutes.'

Liv was one of the first people I met when Angus and I moved from his home city of Glasgow to Margate four years ago. She's one of those people that, on paper, are easy to hate. Born to idiotically wealthy parents, she coasted through various exclusive private schools, barely scraping passes at GCSE before getting herself expelled just before her A levels for 'bringing the establishment into disrepute'. The way Liv tells it, she was caught in a compromising position with a boy, but her father told a different story after a few glasses of wine one evening. According to him, the incident with the boy was definitely instrumental, but the straw that broke the camel's back was when she was found wandering through the town, drunk as a lord, one Saturday afternoon. Any attempts to cajole her back to her room where she could sober up out of sight were met with bellowed, albeit beautifully enunciated, streams of such obscenity that the school allegedly felt the need to publish an apology in the local paper.

Whichever it was, she never sat her exams, deciding instead to gain 'life experience' through travel, to her parents' horror. At thirty-two, she may only be three years older than me, but she's certainly crammed an awful lot more experience into her life than most people our age could manage. In the time I've known her, she's told me various stories of terrible jobs she did to keep herself afloat during that time, including one in a Thai brothel where she assures me – not entirely convincingly – that she wasn't servicing clients, just making sure the rooms were kept well equipped with condoms, lube and the other accoutrements of the sex trade. The one that captured her imagination, though, was a job in a pâtisserie on the outskirts of Paris. She discovered a talent and passion for pastry that she retains to this day, and her long-suffering parents were so relieved when she came home and told them what she wanted to do that they had no hesitation about handing over her substantial trust fund so she could set up the coffee shop and pâtisserie that she still runs. Which is how I met her; I applied for a job when we first moved south and spent a happy year working there before my writing career finally took off.

'Fucking hell, look at the state of you,' she drawls affectionately as Meg and I let ourselves in through the back door and I start to remove my dripping raincoat. 'Did the rain do all of that or did you take a wrong turn through the car wash on your way over? Oh, Meg, no!'

It's too late. Meg may be delighted to see her, but getting the excess water out of her coat onto the floor, up the walls and into the fabric of Liv's clothes is obviously a higher priority than greeting one of her favourite people.

'Come here, you idiotic animal, and let me dry you properly,' Liv says as she wraps an excitedly wriggling Meg in a towel. 'Look at the mess you've made of Auntie Liv's special yoga leggings. I only bought them this morning.'

'I'm sorry,' I say as she releases my dog, who promptly rushes over to the corner of the kitchen where she knows Liv keeps the treats. 'I should have wiped her down outside.'

'Don't worry about it. To be honest, I'm really not sure Spandex is a good look on me.' She rises to her feet and gives me a twirl. 'What do you think?'

'They certainly hug your figure.'

'Very diplomatic. They don't leave anything to the imagination, do they? You could probably count my pubes through them if you looked carefully enough. Trevor would have loved them, dirty bastard.'

'And how is Trevor?'

'No idea. We parted ways a couple of days ago, around five minutes after he mistakenly decided that having access to my knickers gave him the right to mansplain my business to me.'

'Oops.'

'Yeah. I don't think he'll be making that mistake again. Criticise me all you like – Lord knows I'm not perfect – but come for Maison Olivia and I'll take your head off.'

'Noted. Not that I'd have dared anyway.'

'I still miss you in the shop. I know you're a super-duper novelist these days, but are you sure you can't fit in a few hours per week behind the counter? We did have some laughs, didn't we?'

This is a familiar refrain from her, and one that I normally shut down swiftly. Before Angus left, I'd have told her that I absolutely loved the freedom that being a full-time writer gives me. However, I have to confess that I am struggling with being on my own all the time, and the idea of the odd shift at Maison Olivia is becoming more appealing. There's just one problem.

'What would I do with Meg?' I ask as Liv hands her a chew from the tin.

'She might be a selling point, like the cat in that bookshop you spend so many hours in. As long as she stays in the customer area and out of the kitchen, I don't see a problem.'

'Yeah. Good luck explaining the no-go zones to her,' I remark wryly as Meg jumps up, placing her front paws on the kitchen counter and giving Liv the full puppy-dog eye treatment in the evident hope of securing a second treat. 'Plus, I'd only need to turn my back for a minute and she'd be gone.'

'You wouldn't run off, would you, darling,' Liv coos as she hands Meg another chew.

'You'd have to set up a treat dispenser to keep her occupied, and then she'd be so fat she wouldn't be able to wander off.' I lean over to push Meg's feet off the counter, to her evident disappointment. 'That's enough, Meg,' I tell her firmly. 'Stop hassling.'

'Darjeeling OK?' Liv asks as she diverts her attention from the dog to the teapot. She's fastidious about the process of making tea, warming the pot before adding loose leaves and hot water. In the shop, every pot of tea is accompanied by a sand timer so customers know precisely how long to infuse each blend for. She roundly condemns teabags as 'common' and, to my amusement, she actively recoiled on the one occasion Angus offered her a mug of a well-known supermarket brand.

'I stole these from the shop,' she says with a smile as she opens a container to reveal beautifully golden madeleines, placing them on a china plate.

'I'm not sure you can steal from yourself,' I observe as I take one and bite into it. 'Mm. This is seriously good, Liv.'

'Of course it is. I'm the best pâtissière in Margate, as you well know.' She brings delicate china cups and saucers out of the cupboard, along with a silver tea strainer. 'So, what's up? Still missing knobhead?'

I sigh. 'I don't know if "missing" is the right word. I just wish I could under-stand why he didn't feel he could talk to me before he left. How am I supposed to get closure when I don't know what was making him so unhappy? I'm also starting to wonder if his sudden burning desire to work on a cruise ship was because he knew I wouldn't be able to track him down or contact him.' I can feel tears pricking the back of my eyes and I swallow to try to suppress them. I'm really bored of crying.

'Laura.' Liv's voice is soft. 'You can't torture yourself with this. That's the path to madness. What's the mantra?'

'I'm not sure the mantra is working,' I tell her ruefully as she starts to pour out the tea.

'Hmm. OK, let's turn this on its head and assume the breakup is all your fault. Why?'

'I'm not saying it was *all* my fault. But I must be partly to blame. These things are never simple.'

'Nonsense. He's a man and they're not capable of being complex. If a man is being complicated—'

'He's hiding something simple,' I finish for her. Liv has a seemingly never-ending stock of *bons mots* like this. She calls them her 'lessons for life' and trots them out with total conviction.

'I do have another theory, if you're interested,' she says once we've settled ourselves in her enormous, squishy sofa and she's taken an appreciative sip from her cup.

'Go on.'

'Insecurity.'

'What? Angus may be many things, but I wouldn't describe him as insecure.'

'He's a man, isn't he? They're all insecure, trust me. I reckon it comes with the penis. As soon as they discover they have one, they have to compare it to everyone else's and boom. Insecurity. Before you know it, they're buying some enormous car or a houseful of shiny man gadgets to compensate. That's why I prefer women, on the whole.'

Unlike her opinions, Liv's sexuality is best described as 'fluid'. In the time I've known her, she's dated both sexes but never found 'the one'. Her current attitude to men is completely normal given that she's just broken up with one. If her last relationship had been with a woman, she'd be complaining about how complex their needs are, and saying she just wants the simplicity of dating a guy.

'I'll bite,' I tell her. 'What's he insecure about?'

She takes a chunk out of her madeleine before answering and, when she does, her tone is thoughtful.

'I'll answer that with a question of my own. Were you earning more than him, do you think?'

This isn't something that I've ever thought about, and it takes me a while to do the sums in my head. Liv watches me, sipping her tea and absentmindedly stroking Meg, who has climbed onto the sofa and is resting her head adoringly in her lap.

'Not to begin with,' I tell her. 'I mean, the publisher can't have had as much faith in the first book as they said they did, as the advance was tiny. But of course that meant the royalties kicked in quickly when it surprised us all by becoming a bestseller. Advances on books two and three were much better but so were sales. I guess I probably do earn more than him. Why?'

'Think about it. All the time he's earning more than you, he's Mr Bread-winner providing for his woman. That's going to stroke his ego and make him feel manly. Then you overtake him and he's no longer Mr Big. Bitter pill to swallow. Maybe he couldn't, and that's why he left. It would also explain why he couldn't tell you what the problem was, because he knew it would make him sound petty.'

'Angus isn't that shallow.'

'I refer you to my earlier point. He's a man. They're all that shallow. Trevor certainly was.'

'I'm sensing some transference here. Angus is nothing like Trevor.'

'Maybe not on the surface, but deep down they're all the same, trust me. Another madeleine?'

As Meg and I make our way back through the pouring rain a couple of hours later, Liv's words are echoing round my head. Angus wouldn't have walked out over something as silly as me earning more than him, would he? I mean, I never mentioned it and it certainly never occurred to me that he might be struggling. I did pay for more than my fair share of dinners out, I suppose, and I liked to buy him gifts, but that's what you do when you love someone.

Did he secretly have an issue about my income and resent my generosity? If so, what kind of person does that make him?

2

Unlike Liv, who meets most of her conquests online, Angus and I met in real life, during freshers' week at Edinburgh university. Having made my bid for independence by deliberately choosing to study about as far away as I could get from my parents' home in Kent, I was determined to immerse myself in all things Scottish. I wouldn't have noticed Angus on the Economics Society stall had he not been wearing the most ridiculously garish kilt, and I couldn't help stopping to ask if that was his clan's tartan. It wasn't; he was wearing it specifically to get attention but, before I knew it, he'd invited me to join him and the other new society recruits for a drink that evening. I made it clear that, as an English literature undergraduate, I had no interest in joining the Economics Society, but he was undeterred and suggested it would be a great way to broaden my horizons and meet people from other courses. In the end, he wore me down and I have to admit it was a very pleasant evening. He walked me back to my hall of residence at the end and, somewhere along the way, I seem to have agreed to go on a date with him.

The weird thing is that he really wasn't my type, physically at least. He wore his long, dark hair in a ponytail, which has always given me the ick on men, and his wardrobe appeared to consist solely of black ripped jeans and a selection of black T-shirts advertising various thrash metal bands that I'd never heard of. To complete the cliché, he had an electric guitar that he used to try to serenade me with. I'm no princess, but even I struggled to find the screeches and feedback howls romantic. He was, however, enormous fun to spend time with and I slowly found myself succumbing to his charms. By the time he graduated, a year before me, we'd mapped out our future in Scotland together. He was going to secure a job in the Scottish parliament, and I'd offer private tuition so I could have flexibility to write the novel that I hoped would launch my literary career.

Of course, life never works out the way we plan, does it? Not only did the Scottish parliament fail to spot that Angus was indispensable and offer him a job, none of the other companies in Edinburgh he applied to were interested in him either. By the time I graduated, a year after him, he'd been forced to move back home to Glasgow, where his father had given him a role in the family carpet business as a fitter. Although it was reasonably well paid, it wasn't really making use of his talents and he spent a fair amount of time complaining to me about how boring it was. Undeterred and in love, I relocated to Glasgow as well, where his mother welcomed me like a long-lost daughter, much to Angus and his brother's amusement. However, my own search for work was also fruitless. Although nobody said it out loud, my Englishness definitely counted against me and I ended up working a number of zero-hours waitressing jobs while my writing went nowhere.

Thankfully, Angus never stopped applying, progressively widening his search until it pretty much encompassed the whole country. Ironically, his chance of escape from his father's sphere of influence came when he was offered a job as an employment coach in Margate, just over thirty miles from my own parents. I was surprised how relieved I felt when he decided to accept it; although I'd been made very welcome by his family and still look back on my years in Scotland with affection, Kent has always been my home and I was ready to return. It felt like this was going to be the fresh start we needed and I was delighted to see Angus throwing himself wholeheartedly into his new life.

And then, of course, I met Liv.

* * *

'I've been thinking,' she says as I don one of the dark blue aprons with the Maison Olivia logo embroidered in white. It's a week or so after my visit and I've left Meg at the flat to do a trial two-hour shift.

'Always dangerous,' I quip. 'Dare I ask what about?'

'You, actually. Well, you and me, to be precise.'

'Are you propositioning me? I mean, I love you to bits and everything, but—'

'Of course I'm not propositioning you. Apart from the fact that you're totally not my type, you're my best friend, and I wouldn't want to risk messing that up.'

'Now I don't know whether to be relieved or offended!' I reply with a laugh. 'What's wrong with me?'

'Nothing. You're beautiful, even if I sometimes worry about some of the dark stuff that comes out of your mind when you're writing. I just prefer curvy women, that's all.'

'You know what they say: crime writers are safe because they let all their dark thoughts out onto the page. It's the romance writers you need to worry about.'

She laughs. 'I'll have to add that to my lessons for life.'

Our conversation has obviously distracted her from the train of thought that started it, as she turns her attention back to glazing some strawberry tarts. This gives me a dilemma. On one hand, Liv's thoughts can often be direct to the point of brutality and they're sometimes best left unexpressed, but how am I meant to know whether this is one of those unless she shares it?

I sigh. 'So, this thought...' I prompt.

'Oh, yes! You got me so far off topic I completely forgot. Here's the thing. You and Meg are rattling around in that flat without Angus and, not to put too fine a point on it, I think you're lonely.'

This is one of the more brutal ones then. To be fair, she has got a point. The whole reason for me doing this trial shift is to give me time away from being on my own. Meg is lovely, but I miss conversation and I've probably leaned on Liv more than usual since Angus left.

'I see,' I tell her.

'Don't be cross. You know it's true. Anyway, my spare room is massive, as you know, so I thought...' She tails off.

'You thought...' I prompt again.

'I thought you and Meg might like to move in,' she says hurriedly. 'Think about it before you shoot me down. You'd have your own space, with company on tap when you wanted it. Meg and I already love each other and, unlike your flat, I have a secure garden she can use. I'd charge you rent, obviously, but it would be a fraction of what you're paying now so you'd be quids in. I'd also have a bit of extra income, so it's a win-win. Don't answer now. Think about it for a while.'

This kind of generosity is typical of Liv, but she knows me too well. My initial reaction is immediately to say no. It just seems like a retrograde step; I may be a bit lonely, but at least I'm fully independent. If I move in with her, I lose a little bit of that and I'm not sure I want to.

* * *

'What can I get you?' I ask the waiting customer as I take my place behind the counter. I may not have worked here for years, but everything is instantly familiar. Even the forbidding-looking coffee machine doesn't frighten me; I learned early on in my waitressing career that, despite each machine having its own set of foibles, they're all much of a muchness underneath.

'Umm, I'd like an espresso and a bottle of sparkling water, please, but I can't decide on a pastry, I'm afraid. They all look so delicious.'

This is a familiar complaint and I smile at the man. He's wearing a pink jumper over a stripy blue shirt, and a pair of light grey trousers. His thick head of hair is silvery-white, contrasting nicely with his deep blue eyes. He's either naturally fastidious or he's made an effort for someone, as everything about him is spotless and I can just detect the faint woody aroma of his aftershave. I'd guess him to be in his early seventies, but he's in good shape for his age.

'That's not a problem,' I reassure him. 'Have you been here before?'

'No. I'm, er, not local. I'm just here for the day, actually.'

'OK. What flavours do you prefer, something fruity or more creamy?'

He smiles, revealing even white teeth. I'd be willing to bet they've had work done on them. 'I like both,' he replies. 'Sorry.'

'Don't worry. If you were having tea, I'd recommend one of our fruit tarts to go with it. The strawberry ones are lovely, but I'll confess that the *Tarte Normande* apple one is my absolute favourite. Coffee and fruit isn't such a happy mix though, so I'm going to recommend a slice of our *Flan Pâtissier*. It's a French custard tart, absolutely delicious, and will go beautifully with your espresso.'

'I'll happily accept your recommendation,' the man says, handing over his card to pay.

'Take a seat and I'll bring it over as soon as it's ready,' I tell him, noting that he's heading for one of the tables near the door.

'He's meeting someone,' Bella, who's working the counter with me, remarks as I place a slice of *Flan Pâtissier* on a plate and set about making his espresso.

'What makes you say that?'

'Obvious. Look at the clues. He's here on a day trip but he's by himself. He's made an effort to look his best without going over the top. Aftershave. No wedding ring. Sitting by the door so he can keep an eye on the pavement outside. He's got first date written all over him.'

'Blimey. Are you this forensic with all the customers?'

'Oh, no. Only the interesting ones. See that lady over there?' She nods in the direction of a woman about my age, who is savouring a macaron with her cup of tea.

'Yes?'

'She's enjoying a bit of much-needed peace while her toddler is at nursery. I'm guessing the father doesn't live with them and has pissed her off in some way.'

'And you're basing this on?'

'Again, simple. She paid using her phone and I couldn't help noticing that her lock screen image was her and the kiddie. No sign of Dad in the photo and no wedding ring, so she's not married. Before she started drinking her tea, there was a bit of a messaging flurry and she didn't look happy. I reckon Dad's a dickhead. Ah, here we go.'

As if on cue, the door opens and a smartly dressed older woman walks in. The man immediately gets to his feet, smiling warmly as he shakes her hand and pulls out a seat for her.

'Boo-ya,' Bella murmurs. 'Definitely first date. Sweet. Would you like me to take the order over, or do you want to wow him some more with your product knowledge?'

'I'll do it. You carry on your psychoanalysis.'

By the time I've delivered the man's order, taken one from her for a pot of Earl Grey and a *Tarte aux Fraises*, and handed that over as well, I am in full agreement with Bella. This is obviously a first date and, if the way she loops her arm through his when they leave is anything to go by, it's going rather well. Bella turns and grins at me when they're gone.

'You know what?' she says softly. 'If I'm still up for meeting someone new at that age, I'll be amazed. Good luck to them, that's what I say.'

Although I'm impressed by her powers of observation, I can't help feeling a bit depressed. It seems like everyone in here apart from Liv and me is either embarking on or already in a relationship. Bella wasted no time on filling me in about her new boyfriend in a rare lull between customers. Even the woman in the corner – who absolutely made Bella's day by having a tense conversation on the phone that she swears ended with the phrase, 'Oh, fuck off, Jason. You don't get to shag around like you did and then come for me because I've moved on. Pete's twice the man you were' – is evidently in some kind of relationship, even if her ex doesn't seem that happy about it. It all brings my newly single status into sharp focus.

By the time my trial shift comes to an end, however, my mood has improved and I've made up my mind about two things.

'Liv,' I announce as I throw my now less-than-pristine apron into the laundry bin. 'It's a big yes.'

She looks up from the tray of madeleines she was just about to put in the oven. 'What is?'

'Assuming Meg hasn't torn the flat apart from the trauma of being alone, I'd love to do some shifts for you. You were right. It's been good for me, being in here, being busy and chatting to the customers.'

She beams and wraps me in a floury hug. 'I'm so pleased. You looked right at home out there and I'll take all the help I can get, currently. Did you get a chance to think about the other thing?'

'Moving in with you? I did, as a matter of fact. I'll have to check with Meg, of course, but assuming she doesn't object, we'd love to.'

Liv looks like Christmas has come early. 'We are going to have *so* much fun,' she assures me.

I hope she's right. The idea of leaving our flat feels like cutting the final ribbon joining Angus and me, and after nearly ten years together, that's a huge step into the unknown. I shudder as I think about what that means on my journey home. Although the idea of starting again with someone new doesn't appeal in the slightest, I don't want to be single forever either. I giggle as I briefly contemplate putting on weight to see if Liv takes an interest. I love her to bits, but not like that. A thought comes to me: What if she finds 'the one' while I'm living with her? The idea of playing gooseberry until she awkwardly asks me to move out to give them privacy makes my skin prickle uncomfortably.

I hope I haven't just made a massive mistake.

3

'Your parents don't like me,' Darren remarked from the kitchen table as Claire made them cups of tea.

'I think they're just a bit concerned that we're going too fast,' she assured him. 'Moving in with you is a big step, especially when we've only been going out for three months.'

'Do you think we're going too fast?' he asked.

'No. I may "only" be twenty, as Mum said, but I'm old enough to know my own mind, and to know that I love you. What would be the point of waiting?'

'I love you too,' he replied. 'And, for what it's worth, I'm glad you're here. It might be a good idea to see a bit less of your parents for a while though. Let them get used to the idea that you're with me now.'

Claire wasn't sure she liked that plan; she'd always been very close to her mum and dad, but she could see the logic in what he was saying. Maybe seeing less of them would help them to realise that she was grown-up and her own person.

'You're right,' she said as she put the mug down in front of him and squeezed his shoulder affectionately. 'It's you and me now.'

He smiled. 'You and me. I like the sound of that.'

I exhale loudly and rub my eyes. Although this scene is broadly going in the direction I intended, I've just realised that Claire hasn't said anything to Darren about her dream of joining the police, which is kind of central to the plot. I'm scrolling back through the text in frustration, trying to work out where to drop this nugget of information, when a notification pops up on screen to tell me that I have a new email. It's from Ruby, who runs the bookshop that Liv thinks I waste too much time in. To be fair, she's probably right. Ruby is just as passionate about her business as Liv and stocks a wide range of books, including mine. If that wasn't enough, the in-store coffee bar run by her business partner, Jono, serves coffee that's every bit as tasty as Liv's, although I obviously wouldn't ever tell her that. And then there's Samson, the shop cat. Huge, handsome and ginger, he's almost as much of a town celebrity as the Anthony Gormley sculpture on the shore. He has his own chair in the shop, and people have been known to call in just to take selfies with him. It's the kind of place you think you'll just pop into for a minute or two, only to emerge an hour later wondering where the time went. I open the mail to read the text.

> Hi Laura,
>
> Just to let you know I ordered another twenty copies of *Dying to Meet You* by someone called Larry Spalding as I'd sold out, and they arrived this morning. If you get the opportunity to pop in and sign them, I'd be grateful. There might even be a free coffee in it...
>
> Love
>
> Ruby

I smile. Although the number of my books she sells is tiny in the overall scheme of things, Ruby has been a tireless promoter of them ever since I admitted to being the author.

It was the publisher that eventually signed me (after around twenty others had turned me down) who suggested I used a male nom-de-plume. Their view was that the gritty crime novel I had submitted would mainly appeal to a male audience but, where female readers tended not to be bothered by the gender of the writer, men tended to favour books by other men. My agent agreed, so we spent time creating social media profiles for my alter ego, 'Larry', so we could keep my true identity under wraps. I was a little reluctant to begin with, as I'd always wanted to see my name on the cover of a book, but she pointed out that I was hardly the first woman to write as a man. I eventually relented, and that's who I've been as an author ever since.

It's a beautiful day outside, so I decide to follow up on Ruby's email now, while I'm distracted. Meg is on her feet as soon as I push my chair back.

'No,' I tell her firmly. 'You've had a walk today, and I'm going to the bookshop. I'm not taking you, because you and Samson are a bloody nightmare together.'

Sure enough, just the mention of her nemesis is enough to elicit a low growl from Meg. Ruby had initially assured me that bringing Meg into the bookshop on a lead would be fine as Samson was very chilled. Like all dogs, she seems to have chasing cats hard wired into her DNA but, unfortunately for her, Samson isn't like other cats. Not only did he not give her the satisfaction of running away as she strained at the lead to try to get to him, but her barking and carrying on annoyed him to the point where he swiped at her, taking a chunk out of her nose that necessitated a trip to the vet to be checked over. After a couple more attempts with similarly disastrous results, Ruby and I agreed that they probably wouldn't be friends, and I've left Meg at home ever since.

'Goodness, that was quick,' Ruby remarks with a smile as I stroll through the door of her shop a little while later. 'I only emailed you half an hour ago.'

'You caught me at a good moment,' I tell her as Samson studies me with his large, almost luminous eyes before launching into one of those grooming sessions that make it perfectly clear he has no interest in talking to me today.

'Don't be offended,' Ruby explains. 'He's had a busy day with the selfie-takers, so I think he's all peopled out. Do you want a coffee?'

'Love one, thanks.'

Before she has a chance to call the order across to Jono, a baby monitor on the counter bursts into life.

'Someone else obviously wants to see you too.' Ruby laughs as Jono pulls a bottle with a teat out of the fridge and puts it into the microwave to warm before turning his attention to my coffee. 'Hang on, I'll just go and get him.'

She disappears into the back room, emerging a few moments later with a bleary-eyed baby sucking on a bright red dummy.

'Look who's here, Tom,' she coos as the baby fixes his gaze on me. 'It's Auntie Laura, come to sign her latest batch of books.' She turns to me. 'Do you want a cuddle before he gets too wriggly?'

'Of course,' I tell her with a smile, taking Tom off her and planting a kiss on his head. He has that characteristic baby smell – slightly milky with an undercurrent of baby wipe. I notice that Samson has stopped grooming himself and is watching intently from his chair as Jono brings the bottle of milk over, swirling it to ensure the contents are evenly warm.

'Fleabag over there is fascinated by Tom,' he informs me as Tom starts trying to reach for the bottle.

'He's not a fleabag,' Ruby tells him sternly before turning to me. 'Would you like to feed him, as you've got him already?'

'Sure.'

'Take a seat then,' Jono says. 'If you're lucky, he'll hold it himself, although you need to keep an eye on him as he's prone to dropping it, and then Fleabag will be on it like a shot.'

'Listen to you,' Ruby teases him, ignoring the repeated barb as Jono hands me a muslin cloth. 'Surrogate dad of the year.'

Jono smiles. 'It's all good practice for when Robbie and I adopt.'

'I didn't know you were planning to adopt,' I remark as I settle myself in a vacant chair and Jono places my coffee on the table next to it, making sure it's well out of reach of grabbing baby hands. One of the many things I love about this shop is the way the different-sized tables and chairs are dotted about, allowing customers to be social if they wish, but also simply enjoy coffee and a book on their own if they want.

'We're going through the process, but it's a *nightmare*,' he explains, rolling his eyes dramatically. 'I mean, it's no surprise there's a shortage of adoptive parents when they make it so difficult. You'd be forgiven for thinking that our beautiful home has become some kind of meeting place for social workers, the number of them that traipse in and out.' I drape the muslin around Tom's neck. No sooner is the bottle within reach than he grabs it with both hands, beginning to suck greedily as soon as the teat is in his mouth. Ruby and Jono are swiftly distracted by other customers, so I relax and enjoy the warm solidity of Tom's little body against mine as he drinks. When the bottle is finished, I sit him up to burp him, after which he promptly falls back to sleep in my arms.

'You're a natural,' Ruby remarks as she comes to relieve me a little while later. 'I reckon you'll take to it like a duck to water when your time comes.'

I know she means it innocently, but her remark triggers an odd wave of longing inside me, reminding me of the joke Angus made about Meg being a precursor to us having children ourselves. I can see the similarities; like a baby, she needed to be supervised constantly when she was awake, and we got precious little sleep as she howled the place down at night. I remember how we congratulated ourselves on our superb puppy parenting when we realised she hadn't had an accident in the house for over a week. Angus was incredibly patient with her, consistently repeating the training exercises and rewarding her when she got them right. It's not surprising that she adored him; he was the perfect hands-on dad, and I'll admit that I used to entertain regular fantasies of him being just as involved with our children when the time came.

'Sorry, that was crass of me,' Ruby remarks, evidently clocking the expression on my face. 'Still no word, I take it?'

'To be honest, I'm not expecting to hear from him now,' I tell her. 'Time to move on. Liv has invited me to live with her and I've said yes.'

'Really?' She sounds dubious. Although they are perfectly civil to one another when they meet, I'm not sure Ruby and Liv are destined to be friends. In fact, Ruby's husband, Cameron, once confessed to me in an unguarded moment that Ruby found Liv 'a bit much sometimes'. It's not an entirely unfair assessment; Liv can come across as pretty full-on if you're not used to her.

'I think it'll be good for me,' I tell her. 'Everything in the flat reminds me of Angus, so this will be an opportunity to put him behind me once and for all. And, if anyone is going to help me purge his ghost, it's Liv.'

Ruby laughs. 'That's certainly true. I don't imagine she'll put up with any moping, for a start. You're right; she'll probably be good for you. Now, I've got a pile of books in the stock room waiting for Larry's signature when you're ready.'

As I reluctantly hand back a still-sleeping Tom and pick up my coffee to follow her towards the back of the shop, I reflect on our conversation. I know I keep telling myself this, but it really is time to let Angus go, and Ruby is right. Liv may be a force of nature, but that makes her exactly the person I need to help me do it.

4

'You're totally, 100 per cent sure about this?' Liv asks. Meg and I moved in with her yesterday and we're sitting in her kitchen with an open bottle of wine between us while something delicious-smelling cooks in the oven.

'I am,' I tell her.

'OK. Hand me your phone.'

'What are you going to do?'

'Erase Angus from it. I'm going to start by deleting his number and all the text messages between you. Then I'm going to wipe him off all your social media. Have you updated your relationship status?'

'No.'

'Right. I'll do that too. We need the world to know that Laura Spalding is open for business.'

'That doesn't sound right, somehow.'

'You know what I mean. The easiest way to forget the old horse is to jump on a new one, but we'll look at that once I've de-Angused you. Phone, please.'

'I'm not planning to jump on any new horses,' I tell her firmly as I slide the phone across the table.

'You say that now, but give it a bit of time. The good news is that I'm a pro on the apps, so I'll help you put together an absolute knockout profile when the time comes. What's the unlock code?'

'Two-five-oh-eight. It's Angus's birthday.'

'That's the first thing we're going to change then,' she tells me as she prods the screen a few times. 'Right. What do you want your new code to be?'

'Umm, I don't know. Isn't it safer to leave that alone? What if I forget my new code and can't get into my phone?'

'You've got fingerprint ID set up, haven't you?'

'Yes, but it still wants the code sometimes.'

'Fine. I'm going to set it to my birthday. If you forget that, you're in big trouble.'

Fifteen minutes later, all trace of Angus has been wiped from my phone. Liv has unfriended us on Facebook, updated my relationship status to single and unfollowed him elsewhere. She's now brought up my list of contacts and her finger is hovering over his name.

'Don't delete that,' I tell her. 'I might need to contact him to let him know if something happens to Meg. He dotes on her.'

'Hmm.'

'What?'

'He abandoned her as well, didn't he? I'm not sure he has the right to know her business any more than he does yours. What do you think, Meg?'

At the mention of her name, Meg looks up from her basket and thumps her tail a couple of times.

'See? She agrees with me,' Liv states firmly. 'Shall we delete and block the horrid man from Laura's phone, Meg?'

Another tail wag.

'Looks like you're outvoted,' she tells me with a smile as she fiddles with the phone some more. 'Now, what about the pictures?'

'I'd like to keep them. Don't worry, I'm not going to be mooning over him, but he was part of my life for ten years and I'll lose all of that if you get rid of them.'

'Fair enough. We definitely need to change the lock screen one though. Meg, show us your best side.'

Liv advances on the dog, snapping several shots on the phone as she does. 'That one, I think,' she declares after reviewing them. 'Right, here you go. All ready for your new life. Let me know when you're ready and we'll get some dating apps installed.'

'Like I said, I think that will be a while. I've been with Angus for so long that the idea of meeting someone new terrifies me.'

'Oh, you'll be fine. Men are simple creatures and they all broadly work the same way. You just have to treat them like puppies in the bedroom to begin with.'

'I'm sorry?'

She smiles. 'House training.'

'Umm, I'm not expecting them to pee on the carpet, Liv.'

'OK, maybe it's not the best analogy. What was Angus like as a lover, if you don't mind me asking?'

I can feel myself blushing a little. I don't think I'm prudish where sex is concerned, but Liv has sampled so much of the sexual smorgasbord that she always makes me feel a little inadequate when the subject comes up.

'He was all right,' I say carefully. 'Why?'

'All right? Talk about damning with faint praise. I take it the big O wasn't a regular visitor then?'

'Liv, are you seriously asking me about my orgasm history here?'

'Yes,' Liv says robustly. 'This stuff matters. Take a mouthful of wine if you're feeling uncomfortable. I'll go first, if it helps. Trevor may have been a dirty bastard, but at least he knew his way around female anatomy. Do you remember Giles?'

'Umm, vaguely. Was he the one before Sarah?'

'That's him. Utterly clueless. He'd honestly stand more chance of finding a cure for cancer than my clitoris. Women are, unsurprisingly, much better in that department.'

'That makes sense, I guess.'

'So, Angus?'

'He didn't rock my world in the bedroom, if I'm honest. I mean, it was OK. Nice, even. Sometimes it was purely functional, but that's normal, isn't it? To be fair to him, I'm not sure I'm an orgasmic sort of person. Some people just aren't, are they?'

'I've never heard so much nonsense in all my life!' she exclaims crossly. 'There are countless studies out there that show that the female orgasm need be no more elusive than the male one. You just need to be relaxed, understand your body and know how to communicate your needs. Have you read *Don't Hold My Head Down* by Lucy-Anne Holmes?'

'No.'

'OK, that's your first bit of homework. I've got a copy somewhere; I'll dig it out for you. Are you sure you wouldn't like to try dating a woman for a different perspective? I can thoroughly recommend it.'

'Thanks, but no. You might be pretty much in the middle of the sexuality spectrum, but I'm afraid I'm fairly hardwired to fancy men.'

'Fair enough. What about self-pleasure?'

'Liv!'

'What? How are you supposed to be able to tell someone else what floats your boat if you've never put it in the water yourself?'

Even by her standards, this conversation is direct, and I can feel myself blushing furiously. To make matters worse, Liv is obviously enjoying my discomfort as she laughs uproariously.

'Let me get this straight,' she says once she's caught her breath. 'Laura Spalding spends happy hours writing brutal murders where she describes the patterns of arterial spray almost lovingly, but is afraid of her own vagina?'

'I'm not afraid of it! I just don't want to talk to you about it. Can we drop this now?'

This only serves to set her off again.

'Oh, honey,' she breathes eventually. 'Living with you is going to be even more fun than I imagined.'

* * *

'How are you, darling?' my mother's voice asks down the phone a couple of days later. I can't help noticing that it has that tentative 'I want to show I care about you but please don't burst into tears as I'm not sure I know how to handle that' tone which she's used fairly consistently since Angus left. To be fair, I did spend quite a lot of time bursting into tears in the early days, both on the phone and when I visited them, so I can't really blame her.

'OK, actually,' I tell her, making my own voice super-bright to try to reassure her. 'Moving in with Liv was the right choice, I think.'

'And how is Olivia?' Now that she's reassured herself that I'm not about to dissolve into a soggy mess, her tone has shifted to the slight air of disapproval she always has when Liv is mentioned. To be fair to her, I know she also finds Liv 'a bit much', and Liv's ever-shifting sexuality evidently baffles her.

'She's good,' I reply. 'And Meg absolutely adores her.'

'I hope she isn't teaching that dog bad habits,' Mum says sternly. 'Angus worked so hard to bring her up well, and it would be a shame for all of that to be undone.' Mum and Dad have had dogs for as long as I can remember, and they've always been rigorously trained. I glance over at the sofa where Meg is happily curled up next to Liv and thank my lucky stars this isn't a video call.

'She's fine, Mum.'

'And how's work?'

'The book is coming along. I'm doing some shifts in Maison Olivia too, which is getting me out of the house.'

'That's good. I'm sure you could use the money and you know how we worry about you, cooped up alone all day writing that... *stuff*.' It's safe to say that neither of my parents are wild about me writing crime novels for a living. While my mother's problem is mainly to do with the genre ('Why can't you write *nice* stories about *nice* people, Laura?'), my father thinks writing isn't a 'proper' job and I suspect he'd be delighted if I announced I was jacking it in to become a warehouse manager like my brother Michael. They've never asked how much I earn from it, and I've never told them, but they've always laboured under the misapprehension that I make peanuts and Angus was basically bankrolling me. It's frustrating, but I know they love me and just want what they think is best for me, so I generally suck it up like I am today.

'Anyway, the reason for my call,' Mum continues, 'is that we haven't seen you in forever, darling, and we wondered if you'd like to come to lunch on Sunday. Michael will be here with Alison and the children, and I'm sure they'd like to see you too. You can bring Olivia if you like. I'm sure a square meal is the least we can do to thank her for taking you in. It must have been such a worry for you, without Angus there to pay his share of the rent and bills. Oh, hang on a minute, your father is saying something. Here, you talk to her, George.'

'Laura, sweetheart.' Dad's voice is also laced with concern. 'I just wanted to check how things were for you, financially.'

'I'm fine,' I tell him.

'You can always come to me if you need a loan to tide you over. I know how difficult it is for people in your situation to get credit through the normal channels, and I'd hate for you to fall victim to loan sharks or those ghastly payday lenders now that you're fending for yourself.'

'What do you mean, "my situation"?' I ask. This is a new angle from him and, despite knowing his answer is probably going to annoy me, I want to hear it nonetheless.

'You know what I mean, Laura,' he tells me, lowering his voice the way he always does when he thinks he's trying to be tactful. 'People without a *regular income*.'

I sigh. 'I'm not on the breadline, Dad.'

'That's good. Very good.' He knows he's annoyed me and is now trying to compensate. 'But your income is far from certain, and I just don't want you making bad choices if you find yourself in need of a helping hand. Anyway, I'll give you back to your mother. Remember what I've said, won't you?'

By the time I end the call, having agreed that I'll go over there for lunch on Sunday and I'll also consult with Liv to see if she'd like to come, I'm exhausted.

'You look like you've been through the wringer,' Liv remarks, looking up from her laptop as I settle myself on the sofa.

'I do love them, but you'd think I was a penniless waster, the way they go on. Anyway, they've invited us both to lunch on Sunday if you'd like to come.'

'Do you want me to come?'

'It might be nice to have someone there who's on my side.'

'You're a big girl; you can fight your own battles. Why don't you just tell them you're actually as rich as Croesus?'

'Because they think talking about how much you earn is grubby, and the sort of thing that only the *nouveau riche* would do.'

She thinks for a moment. 'To be fair, I don't have a clue how much money my parents have, but that's because I've never really been interested. I'm sure they'd tell me if I asked.'

'Yes, but your parents are very different from mine.'

She laughs. 'That's probably true. I don't think my parents really have any taboo subjects. I remember Mum being absolutely fascinated the first time I started dating a girl. Even though she'd been to an all-girls boarding school, which I know from personal experience are hotbeds of lesbianism, all of that had somehow passed her by. I think she felt she'd missed out and wanted to live it vicariously through me.'

'Weren't you creeped out? I can't imagine ever having a discussion with my mother about something like that. Just the thought of it makes me shudder.'

'That's because you're repressed, and your parents probably are too.'

'No, it's because your family have absolutely none of the boundaries that most of society would consider normal, trust me.'

'Then most of society is missing out. Tell me, how did your parents manage "the talk"?'

'They didn't,' I admit. 'They simply asked whether the school had covered intimate relationships in PHSE. I said yes, and that was the end of it.'

'See, that's tragic,' Liv counters. 'The stuff they tell you at school might help you not to get pregnant, but it doesn't teach you about pleasure. I remember my mum urging me to explore my body, to find out the ways in which it could give me pleasure, both for myself and so I could instruct future lovers on what ticks my boxes. I think she'd have drawn diagrams if I'd let her.'

'Again, not normal. Again, giving me the ick.'

'You might have a point,' she agrees after thinking for a moment. 'Although I think her intentions were good, and I'd certainly want my children to feel free to express their sexuality in the way that they wanted, having your mother practically begging you to masturbate as often as possible is probably unusual.'

'It's very unusual, Liv.'

'I'd still rather that than what you got. Maybe there's a middle way. A friend to guide you on your sexual journey rather than a parent, perhaps.' Her tone is thoughtful, which makes me slightly uneasy.

'Or you could just do what most people do, and figure it out as you go along. Anyway, we've drifted off topic. Are you coming on Sunday?'

'Absolutely.' She grins as she turns her attention back to her laptop and my feeling of unease increases. Liv and my parents are a delicate mix at the best of times, and things could go south quite quickly if she decides to make trouble. Maybe this isn't such a great idea after all.

5

'Are you OK?' Pauline asked as they were clearing up after the lunchtime rush in the Pig & Whistle.

'Yeah, why?' Claire replied.

'You don't seem yourself today. Darren hasn't done anything, has he?'

'He's fine. I've just got a bit of a headache, that's all.'

Claire felt bad about lying to her friend, but she knew Pauline would jump to all sorts of conclusions if she told her about the argument with Darren last night, especially the part where he'd thrown his mug of tea at her. Thankfully, it had missed and shattered against the wall behind her. It wasn't the first time she'd fallen foul of his short temper, but it was the first time he'd actually frightened her. Like the other times he'd lost it, his rage had been over as quickly as it had begun and he'd apologised profusely, explaining that he only got so upset because he loved her so much. Their make-up sex had been typically passionate, but the mug thing had unsettled her and she couldn't stop herself from replaying the incident in her head and wondering what she could have done differently to stop him from getting so angry.

Despite having encouraged her to begin with, Pauline seemed to have taken against Darren more and more as time had gone on. It had started when Claire had stupidly told her that he'd talked her out of her long-term ambition of joining the police; even though she'd explained that Darren was just worried about her being a target for violence, Pauline had seen his behaviour as controlling. Darren, for his part, thought that Pauline was a malign influence and made no bones about the fact he'd like Claire to ditch her. Over the last few months, she'd got very good at filtering what she said to each of them in order to keep the peace, but she felt increasingly like she was walking a tightrope and one wrong remark would set one of them off.

Today is one of those rare days when the words just seem to flow onto the page. I've already written way over a thousand of them as I slowly start to reveal the odious Darren's true nature. It's a delicate balance, as I need Darren to display all the typical behaviours associated with coercive control, progressively isolating Claire from family and friends and taking away her independence, without making her look gullible or weak. I'm not sure I've got it totally right in this scene yet but, as my editor continually tells me, I can always come back to it later. I can practically hear her voice in my head saying, 'You can't edit it if you haven't even written it in the first place.'

When I first moved in, Liv's musical doorbell completely foxed Meg, and she didn't react to it at all for nearly a week. However, the connection is firmly established now, so she's on her feet and barking excitedly before the Big Ben chimes have even finished. I still find it a little odd that someone as posh as Liv should have such a twee doorbell, but she assures me that it's ironic, and she only bought it because her father thinks it's unbearably naff. They might get on pretty well these days, but she still enjoys winding him up.

'Package for Laura Spalding,' the postwoman announces, handing over a cardboard box once I've shut Meg in the kitchen and opened the door. 'I just need to take a picture of you with it as proof of delivery.'

She snaps a photo with her handheld device before thrusting the usual selection of envelopes and leaflets into my hand and disappearing up the path.

'What do you think is in here?' I ask Meg as I place the box on the kitchen table. Now that the excitement of the post arriving is over, she's settled herself back in her basket and is watching me with her soulful eyes. I haven't ordered anything recently, so I turn the box over in my hands, looking for clues, but it's not giving anything away. I check the address in case it's a misdelivery, but it's clearly addressed to me.

I grab the scissors out of the drawer and cut open the lid to reveal a white envelope sitting on top of a mountain of pink tissue paper that's completely obscuring the rest of the contents of the box. Inside the envelope is a printed card.

To Laura,
   A little gift to help you on your journey of self-discovery. I hope you find it satisfying – enjoy!!
   All my love
   Liv xx

'It's something from Auntie Liv,' I tell an uninterested Meg as I start to remove the tissue. 'What do you think it is? It could literally be anything from dietary supplements to a Pilates ball, knowing her.'

None the wiser, I start to remove the tissue but, as Liv's gift finally starts to come into view, I gasp in surprise.

It's not dietary supplements or a Pilates ball.

If only it were. That would be so much easier to deal with than this. What on earth was she thinking? Liv has definitely gone too far this time and, before I know it, I'm grabbing my keys and heading for the door.

* * *

'Oh, hello, Laura,' Bella says as I stride into the pâtisserie a short time later with the box under my arm. 'You're not working today, are you?'

'No. I just needed to have a quick chat with Liv,' I tell her without breaking my stride as I head into the kitchen, closing the door behind me. The conversation I'm about to have is not one I want overheard. Liv is at the counter, whisking some kind of mixture in a bowl.

'Give me a sec, Bella,' she says without looking up. 'This is at a crucial stage.'

'It's not Bella,' I tell her.

'Oh, hello, Laura.' Her voice is irritatingly unperturbed and she still doesn't look up from her whisking. 'I still need a sec. If I don't keep a close eye on this, my *Crème Pâtissière* will turn into scrambled egg, and nobody wants scrambled egg in their pastries. Grab yourself a hair net and I'll be with you as soon as this is done.'

In spite of my irritation, I find myself meekly pulling on a hair net and settling myself on a stool while she carries on with her work. Eventually, she's obviously satisfied as she finally turns her attention to me.

'What's up?' she asks innocently.

'Your present arrived,' I tell her, setting the box on the table and watching her reaction carefully. Annoyingly, there isn't even the slightest hint of shame. If anything, she looks pleased.

'I know. I got a notification on my phone that it had been delivered. What do you think?'

'For starters, I think I'll never be able to look the postwoman in the eye again.'

'Why?' She still doesn't seem bothered.

'Oh, I don't know,' I spit sarcastically. 'Call me old-fashioned, but idle chit-chat becomes a little difficult after she's delivered a box with a sex toy in it.'

'How would she know what was in the box? The packaging is supposed to be discreet. It wasn't damaged, was it?'

'What the hell were you thinking?'

'I was thinking that my friend might need a little help now that she's on her own and, being the kind person that I am, I bought her a gift that she might find useful.'

'A dildo, Liv? Seriously?'

'Technically, it's a vibrator, not a dildo. Dildos are phallus shaped and don't usually vibrate, whereas vibrators—'

'For fuck's sake. I don't care what the technical term for it is. Even you must realise it's not the kind of thing you buy for other people. You'll have to send it back.'

She smiles. 'Nuh-uh. I'm doing you a favour, trust me. There should have been some other things in there too. As well as the vibrator, there should be some lube and toy cleaner. I've thought of everything.'

'Liv, even if I'd said I wanted a vibrator, it's still incredibly weird for you to buy me something so intimate, and have you seen the size of the thing? How on earth am I supposed to fit something that big... Actually, don't answer that.'

'See, this is what I mean. I love you, Laura, but you'll never be able to let go and really enjoy sex until you stop being so repressed about it.'

'I'm not repressed! It's just not...'

'Not what?'

'I'm not comfortable sharing this aspect of my life with you.'

'Sounds repressed to me.'

'Are you seriously telling me you expect me to accept this thing and come bouncing down the stairs to announce what a fabulous wank I've just had?'

This is obviously the funniest thing she's heard all year, if her gales of laughter are anything to go by.

'Oh, Laura,' she breathes eventually. 'I wouldn't mind, you know. I think it's healthy to talk about this stuff.'

'Why am I not surprised? You literally have no boundaries.' I can't stay annoyed with her, however misguided I think her gift is.

'That might be true, but here's the thing,' she says. 'Have you ever considered that there might be a link between Angus leaving and your difficulties with your writing?'

'Sorry, what?'

'I was thinking about it. I've never known you struggle with a book the way you are now, so I asked myself what was different. The main thing is that Angus has gone, obviously, but what effect has that had? Emotionally, it's been very hard on you, but I don't think it's that. I think you're sexually frustrated but don't realise it.'

'How can I be both repressed and frustrated? Oh, and by the way, neither of those things are true.'

'Whatever. The point is that a bit of self-love might unblock you. Studies have shown that the release of feelgood endorphins during orgasm is good for your blood pressure, your mental health and general wellbeing. So, contrary to what your parents would probably have told you if they could get the words out, masturbation doesn't make you go blind. It's actually good for you.'

'How on earth would you even begin to study something like that?'

'I have no idea. Maybe there's a big room full of people all fapping away while they're connected to monitors. The point is it's proper science. So, instead of being all shy and wondering how you're going to talk to the post-woman, you should be saying thank you. And, as far as the size goes, people don't seem to struggle. I did my research and it's a good toy if the reviews are anything to go by.'

'OK, look. I'll admit I'm not exactly experienced when it comes to the world of sex toys because Angus got all peculiar the one time I brought it up, but—'

'Peculiar how?' Liv interrupts.

'I think he was worried I'd end up liking the sex toy more than him.'

'Told you he was insecure.'

'About that, maybe. Anyway, as I said, I'm not an expert in this field, but I can't believe people actually review them, do they? Helen B in Ramsgate gives the Xcite 3000 or whatever it is five stars after it got her off in thirty seconds flat?'

'Incredibly, there are people out there less uptight about sharing their experiences than you seem to be. You can read the reviews yourself if you don't believe me. Did you know that the sex toy market globally is worth billions of pounds a year, and it's estimated that at least 60 per cent of women in the UK own at least one? That's just the ones who'll admit to it, of course, so the real figure is likely to be a lot higher.' She grins. 'Maybe your mum has one.'

'I really don't want that mental image, thank you. Anyway, I suspect they're more of a single person thing, aren't they?'

'Also not true. The vast majority of sex toy consumers are in relationships, apparently.'

'Oh, for goodness' sake. Where are you getting all these statistics from?'

She smiles. 'I told you. I did some research.'

'Of course you did. Anyway, back to Goliath the dildo here.'

'It's a vibrator, as I've already explained, but I like that you've named it. Every sex toy should have a name.'

'Even if I could, umm, *accommodate* it, the idea of trying to use it when you're literally in the room next to me and can probably hear everything is a massive turn-off.'

'You're assuming I'll be listening. Anyway, you have the place to yourself all day most days. Now, do you have any other weird hang-ups you'd like to discuss before I get back to my *Crème Pàtissière*?'

'I'm not repressed or frustrated,' I repeat sulkily.

'How would you describe it then?'

'I'd say I have a healthy, normal attitude to sex.'

'If that's the case then not getting any would definitely cause some frustration. Think of it this way. If we look at your sex life with Angus as a pastry, it would be a jam doughnut. Unfortunately, the jam doughnut has buggered off so, until you find a new supplier, you have a choice.'

'Which is?'

'You could try to style out the doughnut famine, but I think that's making you miserable, probably in danger of getting some kind of wrist injury and affecting your writing.'

'Or?'

'Or you could satisfy your need for sweet treats with the custard doughnuts of Goliath there. Does that make sense?'

The honest answer to her question is no, she's not making any sense at all with her doughnut analogy, but I can see she might have a point generally. Goliath is way too intimidating, but perhaps I should do some research of my own and see if there's something less likely to injure me that I might enjoy.

6

Thankfully, after our discussion in the kitchen of the pâtisserie, Liv seems to have given up trying to micro-manage my sex life. I don't know whether she's accepted that her gift just wasn't for me, or whether she's assuming that I'm spending every hour she's out of the house in some kind of battery-powered state of bliss with Goliath, but I am enjoying her not going on about it any more. We obviously have wildly different attitudes to this subject, but I would argue that mine are fairly normal compared to Liv's, which I think most people would describe as extreme. Goliath is still in the box, which I've shoved under my bed and done my best to forget about, but I have done a bit of online research of my own. After reading the product descriptions with mounting incredulity – who do they get to write this guff? – and looking at the surprisingly frank reviews, another box arrived yesterday. It's also under the bed with Goliath, waiting for the right moment.

'Is there anything you need to tell me about before we get to your parents' house?' Liv asks.

'Such as?' I ask her.

'Oh, you know. The usual. If Great-Aunt Maude has fallen off a ladder and broken both her legs, it's probably not the best idea to ask how her marathon training is coming along.'

'Great-Aunt Maude won't be there.'

'Have you actually got a great-aunt called Maude then?'

'No. That's why she won't be there.'

'Phew. I thought for a moment that I might have forgotten one of your relatives. Are there any other family things I need not to mention?'

'I think you're reasonably safe. Steer clear of the usuals and we'll hopefully get through without any issues.'

'The usuals?'

'Sex, politics and religion.'

She grins. 'Damn, that's my whole set of conversation starters out of the window.'

'Ha ha.'

She smiles. 'I'm looking forward to seeing your brother.'

Liv has never made any bones about the fact that she fancies my brother Michael rotten. Thankfully Debbie, his wife, has either never noticed or doesn't feel threatened by it. I suspect the first, as Debbie has been so totally focused on her children since they were born that I sometimes think Michael could dye his hair green and cover himself with tattoos and she wouldn't notice.

'I've never understood what he sees in dull-as-ditchwater Debbie,' she continues after a moment.

'She's not that bad.'

'Oh, come on. She's hardly the most thrilling person to be around, is she?'

I laugh. 'And you're not biased at all, I suppose.'

'It could be the plotline for your next book,' she says suddenly. 'A married man embarks on a passionate affair with a voluptuous pâtisserie owner, who opens his eyes to how boring his wife is. He's desperate to leave her for the new love of his life, but she's got some kind of hold over him. What could it be?'

'Probably financial,' I suggest, entering into the game. 'Maybe she's got family money and he's reliant on her.'

'Oh, that's good.' Liv is warming to her theme. 'Have you ever considered doing this professionally? Anyway, he's trapped in this loveless marriage but the voluptuous pâtisserie owner—'

'Who doesn't look at all like you, I suppose.'

'Who might look a bit like me,' she admits with a grin. 'Anyway, the pâtissière gives him an ultimatum. Leave his wife or she's off. What's the guy to do?'

'I'm going to hazard a guess that he's going to kill his wife.'

'Bingo. How would he do it though? He's no murderer, so maybe he hires a hitman.'

'Too complicated.'

'Why?'

'One, how's he going to find one? You can't just Google something like that.'

'The dark web. I'm sure there are loads on there.'

'OK. How do you get on the dark web?'

'No idea.'

'Precisely. Most people don't, which is why it's called the dark web. So we're stretching the reader's credibility. However, let's say – just for the sake of argument – that he knows how to do that and finds his hitman. How much do these people charge?'

'Again, no idea.'

'Me neither, but we've got to assume it's going to be several thousand pounds. Given that we've established that the wife holds the purse strings, how's he going to get hold of that kind of money without her finding out?'

'He only needs half the money up front. Isn't that how these things work?'

'With the second half due as soon as the job is done. I don't think hitmen tend to offer payment plans, annoyingly.'

'Yes, but he's got access to her money as soon as she's dead, hasn't he, so that's not a problem.'

'Sorry, but you're stretching the reader's credibility again, Liv. Let's say the hit costs ten grand all in. First of all, we've already established that he's got to find the first five without his wife knowing.'

'Short-term loan. DodgyCash4U dot com or whatever.'

'OK. So he borrows the initial five grand, that's what you're saying.'

'Yup.'

'And when the poor unfortunate woman is dead, he's now got to pay the lender their five grand plus interest, plus the second five to the hitman. Let's say twelve thousand in total.'

'Which he takes out of his wife's estate.'

'That's where your plot falls down. In order for that to work, the whole twelve grand would need to be lying around in a joint account, and that doesn't sound very likely, does it? Anything that's solely in her name, such as savings, investments and so on, would have to go through probate, and the hitman isn't going to wait that long. And even if she were foolish enough to leave that kind of money in a joint account, a big cash withdrawal within days of her demise is going to look suspicious as hell.'

'Bollocks. I think I'll stick to pastries and leave the murdering to you.'

I smile. 'It was a good try. Oh, and Michael's potty about Debbie, so I don't think he's going to leave her for you any time soon.'

'I don't do married men anyway. That doesn't mean I can't appreciate him from afar.'

'Just don't piss Debbie off. Seeing my family is fraught enough without you adding to the tension.'

She grins again. 'I'll be good, promise. Ah, here we are.'

Unsurprisingly, my brother's people carrier is already parked outside the house as Liv swings onto the drive. He and Debbie live just the other side of Ashford, so haven't had nearly as far to come. I do have a key to Mum and Dad's house, but it feels weird just letting myself in having not lived there for years, so I press the doorbell, setting off a frenzy of barking from the other side.

'Yes, Rufus,' I can hear my mother saying firmly. 'You're a good boy for letting me know there's someone at the door but I'm dealing with it, OK? Go in the kitchen. Shoo.'

'Hello, Mum,' I say as she eventually swings the door wide, having successfully banished the dog.

'Laura!' she exclaims as if my visit is a complete surprise to her. 'How lovely to see you.' She doesn't hug me immediately, standing back to appraise me first.

'You look pale,' she observes. 'Are you eating a balanced diet? We were watching a documentary the other night about the obesity crisis. Apparently, all these people are so fat because junk food is much cheaper than eating healthily. You don't look fat, at least. Olivia, darling, welcome. Oh, you shouldn't have!'

Liv hands over a stunning *Tarte aux pommes* that she spent hours yesterday making and, while Mum fusses and acts like she wasn't expecting it at all, I'm certain she was. I'd be amazed if she's even prepared a pudding herself, knowing that there was no way Liv would turn up empty handed.

'I've brought some cream to go with it,' Liv says, handing over a small bag. 'It's from the local dairy that supplies the pâtisserie, so it should be good.'

'You're a darling,' Mum tells her as she ushers us inside. Meg and Rufus, my parents' enormous fox-red Labrador, promptly block the hallway as they embark on an elaborate ritual of bottom-sniffing, making the process of getting through to the sitting room where everyone else is positively hazardous.

'Laura, you made it,' Dad says in the kind of tone that would make you believe we've come from the South Pole rather than a few miles up the road. 'Olivia, lovely to see you as always.'

'All right, Loz?' Michael asks me, punching me on the shoulder. This has been his standard greeting for as long as I can remember, so I'm braced for it.

'I'm fine,' I reply. 'You?'

'Yeah, you know. Debbie's a saint, the kids are a nightmare. Nothing changes.'

'Don't listen to him, he loves his boys to bits,' Debbie scolds as she crosses the room to hug Liv and me. 'I feel like I haven't seen you for ages, Laura. I'm so sorry about Angus, but I gather you've moved in with Olivia now?'

'I'm renting a room in her house, yes,' I say carefully. Communication in my family operates like a game of Chinese whispers. You can feed an accurate piece of information to one person, but the version you get back from someone else is so garbled it's unrecognisable. So, despite making it very clear to Mum what my living arrangements are, it wouldn't surprise me at all if Debbie were to think she ought to be picking out hats for Liv's and my upcoming nuptials.

'Well, as long as you're OK, that's the main thing,' Debbie says soothingly. 'When we heard about the whole Angus situation, Mike's and my immediate reaction was that you should move in with us until you were back on your feet but, on reflection, we thought it might be a bit much for the boys to have to share a room. George is at a sensitive age and needs his own space.'

I glance down at George, who is sprawled on the floor staring at his phone. He doesn't look sensitive to me, but what would I know?

'It's fine,' I tell her. 'Meg and I are very happy with Liv.'

'Oh, goodness,' she says, looking shocked. 'I completely forgot about your dog. Yes, we couldn't have had her at all. Well, I'm glad it's all worked out.'

Debbie's faux concern is starting to grate and I need to get away. I'm pleased to see that, rather than ogling my brother, Liv appears to have roused the supposedly sensitive George from his screen and is chatting with him.

Michael and Dad are deep in discussion about something, so I head for the kitchen on the pretext of giving my mother a hand.

'Are you sure you're all right, darling?' Mum asks as I busy myself washing up the pots and pans she's no longer using. 'Your father and I have been worried about you.'

Uh-oh. Maybe this was a mistake.

'I'm fine,' I tell her, keeping my voice neutral. 'Why?'

'You've been through a lot. The whole Angus thing, moving in with Olivia and so on. I mean, don't get me wrong. Olivia is a charming girl and I know she's your best friend and everything, but I'm not sure she's always good for you.'

'I'm sorry?'

'She's a little... how can I put this... *unconventional*. And I know it shouldn't matter in the modern age, but she's from a very different background. I worry she sees you as a charity case.'

'Hang on. Are you saying that Liv is bad for me because she's a posh bisexual who looks down on me?'

'I wouldn't put it quite as bluntly as that, darling. You're free to be friends with whomever you please, and whether we like them or not. But when that friend is also your landlady and your employer, well...'

I'm flabbergasted but, before I can think of a suitable reply, we're interrupted by Michael.

'Is lunch nearly ready, Mum?' he asks. 'The boys are getting restless.'

'Yes, you can tell them to come to the table if you like. I'm about to start dishing up. Laura, go and tell your father to sort out everyone's drinks, please.'

From the tone of her voice, it's clear that our conversation is over as far as Mum is concerned. She's said her piece and I'm just supposed to accept it, even though she couldn't be more wrong. As I carry the dishes of vegetables from the kitchen to the dining room, I notice Liv is now sitting next to my dad and making a real effort to engage him in conversation. As I think about the times I've been to visit her parents with her, and how welcome they've always made me feel, I realise something that makes me seethe inside. Yes, she may be from a very different background, but it's not Liv or her posh parents that think I'm a charity case. It's my own mother.

7

'That was intense,' Liv remarks once we're safely in the car heading back towards Margate.

'Thanks for going in to bat for me,' I reply.

'Why is your father so completely adamant that you're living on the breadline? It doesn't seem to matter what anyone tells him, he won't listen. I didn't know whether to laugh or cry when I told him you were probably better off than me, and he took that to mean the pâtisserie was about to go out of business.'

'I think it goes back to when I was first starting out. He read this article online that said most authors earn an absolute pittance and sell fewer than three thousand copies of each title. He tried to put me off so many times by trotting out the statistics that I think they've got hard wired in his head.'

'But your last two books were top ten bestsellers! Surely even he must realise that's going to net you more than a few quid.'

I sigh. 'Welcome to my life.'

'And the way your mum kept thanking me for "taking you in" as if you would have been homeless otherwise! I'm sorry, Laura. I know it's not the done thing to be rude about your friends' parents, but honestly.'

'Can I ask you a question?'

'Of course.'

'What do your parents think of me?'

'They love you. Why?'

'I was just curious.'

'No. That's a weird question to come out of the blue, so I'm guessing there's an agenda behind it. Come on, spill.'

I wasn't going to say anything to Liv about the conversation I had with my mother before lunch, but it's been playing on my mind.

'Well,' I begin, unsure how to broach the topic tactfully, before realising this is Liv I'm talking to. 'Your family is much posher than mine, isn't it?'

She glances over at me, her expression suddenly serious. 'What's brought this on?'

'On second thoughts, forget it. You'll think I'm being paranoid.'

To my surprise, her face lights up. 'Oh, I see what this is,' she says with a grin.

'What is it?'

'Fine. It's time to come clean. I haven't said anything before because I didn't want to hurt your feelings, but my parents think you're a terrible chav and can't understand what I see in you.'

I'm horrified. 'Really?'

She laughs. 'I knew it was that! No, of course not, idiot. They absolutely adore you. Nobody cares about how posh anyone is any more, do they?'

'Only someone truly posh would say that.'

That's enough to stop her laughter in its tracks and she looks, if anything, slightly hurt. 'What's that supposed to mean?'

'Nobody has ever looked down on you socially, have they?'

'I'm sure plenty of people have,' she tells me earnestly. 'But it's bollocks, Laura. There are always people who are posher than you or richer than you, just like there are people who are less posh or poorer. Who cares? The only person I can think of who got hung up on stuff like that was my grandmother, and she was a terrible old witch. Did you ever meet her?'

'No.'

'She's dead now, thank goodness. She didn't bat an eyelid when I told her I thought I was a lesbian, but hold your knife the wrong way and she'd positively twitch with disapproval. She'd say, "The Queen won't invite you to tea if you can't eat nicely, Olivia." Mum went for her in the end.'

'Did she?'

'Yes. She pointed out, among a lot of choice words, that none of us were likely to have tea at the palace and, unlike dear Grandmama, the Queen probably wouldn't give a shit how we held our cutlery because she had better things to worry about.'

'I can practically hear your mum's voice saying that.'

'Grandmama used to drive her nuts. I don't think there was a lot of love lost between them, if I'm honest. Anyway, the point is that my parents love you. In fact, I think they might wish you were their daughter rather than me.'

'I'm sure they don't. They're really proud of what you've achieved with the pâtisserie.'

'Yes, but I think we can both agree that they're probably less proud of the journey I took to get there, and they only know the edited highlights. It would probably kill them if they knew it all.'

'I sometimes wish my parents knew less about me. Everything they know seems to disappoint them.'

'They're proud of you too.'

'You think? They have a bloody funny way of showing it. I mean, even when you tried to convince them that I was making a reasonable living, they couldn't be pleased. What was it Dad said? "You're only ever as good as your last book, Laura. Everyone might hate the next one, and then what, hmm?"'

Liv rolls her eyes in exasperation. 'If your next book is total shit, then your publishers should spot that straight away and get you to fix it. That's literally their job, isn't it?'

'Unfortunately, he's kind of right though. Every writer lives in fear that their next book will be the one that flops, triggering the doomsday spiral.'

'Dare I ask what the doomsday spiral is?'

'The publisher drops you, quickly followed by your agent when they can't get any other publishers to come within a mile of you. Having enjoyed seeing piles of your bestsellers on the tables at the front of bookstores, you become "special order only" and the only place you stand a chance of stumbling across one of your books in the wild is in a charity shop, which is where you go to buy your clothes now the royalties have dried up.'

'Wow. You don't think like that, do you?'

'Often. You'd need to have a personality disorder not to.'

She ponders for a moment. 'I guess it's not that different from the recurring dream I have where I give everyone food poisoning and the council shuts me down.'

We travel for a while in silence, each contemplating our own doomsday scenario. My mood, already low after lunch with my family, is sinking further.

'I suspect Mum blames me for Angus leaving too,' I mutter morosely. 'It wouldn't surprise me if she thought he probably buckled under the pressure of having to support me financially.'

'Oh, no.' This is obviously enough to rouse her from her own dark thoughts. 'We're not playing that game. Angus left because he's an arse. Nothing to do with you.'

We lapse back into silence for several miles, each lost in our own thoughts again, before she speaks.

'How's Goliath?'

Shit. I hoped we'd closed this topic.

'Yeah, I'm still not sure it's for me,' I tell her carefully.

She frowns but says nothing. Great, now I've upset her, but what was I supposed to do? Tell her it rocked my world just to make her happy? I'm a little irritated myself now, if I'm honest. I didn't ask her to buy me a sex toy and, no matter what she thinks, I still firmly believe that it's not the kind of thing you buy for other people.

* * *

When we get back, I feed Meg and try to settle down to some writing. I'm at a crucial stage; Pauline has been fierce with Claire about Darren's controlling behaviour, with the result that they're no longer speaking to each other, much to Darren's delight. But it's finally sown a seed of doubt in Claire's mind, because she's realised that Darren has found reasons to take charge of pretty much everything, even her finances. She wants to believe that Darren has her best interests at heart, but she's uncomfortable that she's basically totally reliant on him. The stage is set for a tense conversation which is going to start the sequence of events that lead to the climax of the first half of the book.

Normally, I have no problem focusing on the story at points like this. I know where I need the conversations to go and my fingers usually fly across the keyboard because I can pretty much hear the dialogue in my head.

However, I'm distracted after my conversation with Liv in the car, and my mind is once more circling around all the possible things that could have caused Angus to leave. The truth is that our sex life was the one disappointing aspect of our relationship, from my perspective. The first couple of times were quite good, if I remember correctly, but he turned out to be a lazy lover who didn't take much interest in whether I was having a good time or not. My suggestion to add a vibrator to the mix was intended to wake him up to my frustration, but he completely freaked and said the only way he'd even contemplate such a thing would be if he basically kept it under lock and key so he could ensure I wasn't using it behind his back. I rather lost interest after that and, as time went on, sex with him became increasingly mundane and infrequent, to the point that I started to think I just wasn't a very sexual person after all.

What if Liv is right though, and my writing is suffering because I'm actually frustrated? I glance down at the boxes under the bed. I'd rather have done this while I was alone in the house, but my curiosity is piqued now and Liv is downstairs so won't hear anything as long as I'm discreet. I bend down to pull out the boxes, opening them and pushing the tissue aside. Goliath is definitely staying where it is, but I transfer the lube and toy cleaner from Liv's box into the drawer in my bedside cabinet before turning my attention to the box I ordered. Inside, there's a blister pack containing a much more subtle bullet vibrator, and a pink box with the words 'LadyBliss 2' on it in a swirly font, which is a clitoral stimulator that had such rave reviews (it really did get one reviewer off in thirty seconds) I had to order it to see what the fuss was about. I lift it out and turn the box over to read the writing on the back.

We've taken everything you said you loved about the original LadyBliss and added extra. You said you wanted more settings, so we've given you more. From the gentlest whisper to the most powerful pulsation we've ever featured on a stimulator, the LadyBliss 2 delivers. In addition, the LadyBliss 2 is fully waterproof for bathtime fun, and recharges swiftly thanks to the supplied USB lead. The new Silent Night mode ensures total discretion, allowing you to enjoy LadyBliss 2 in more locations than ever before.

This is exactly the same copy as I saw on the website, and I snort with laughter at the phrase 'waterproof for bathtime fun'. Dear God. My idea of the perfect bath is some candles and relaxing bath salts, not grappling with 'the most powerful pulsation we've ever featured'. Is pulsation even a word? I set the box down and pick up the blister pack with the vibrator inside. It's much less intimidating than the ridiculous thing Liv bought. In fact, at first glance, it could be a lipstick; it's a similar size and is covered in a sleek, shiny material. I turn the package over to see if the description of this one is also as ridiculous as the website.

There's a reason the Joy Unlimited Silver Bullet vibrator has won so many awards, and it has nothing to do with werewolves. With no fewer than 14 powerful modes, there's something here for everyone. Use the tip for maximum stimulation, or lay it lengthwise to spread the sensation over a wider area, the choice is yours. The Silver Bullet is waterproof and quick to charge, so it's ready for any adventure.

Adventure? From the way they're describing it, you'd think it was as indispensable in the wilderness as, say, a compass. And the waterproof thing again, presumably for more 'bathtime fun'. It looks less complicated than the LadyBliss, however, and my eye is drawn to a QR code at the bottom. The text above urges me to 'scan here for hints and tips'. I could probably use some of those, I admit to myself as I follow the link. The website is surprisingly informative, and I learn that some people find using it directly is a bit much, so it suggests trying it through clothes or underwear to begin with. There are also some diagrams that show different ways to use it. After studying the site for a while, I feel sufficiently reassured to take the next step. I glance across to the dog basket, where Meg is fast asleep. I'd be happier if she wasn't in here at all, but she'll only stand outside the door and whine if I wake her up and throw her out, so I decide to leave her. She's not going to know what I'm doing, after all.

It takes a while to wrestle the vibrator out of the blister pack but, when I do, the first surprise is how heavy it is. It might pass for a lipstick visually, but it would give the game away as soon as someone picked it up. I set it down on the desk next to my bed, unbutton my jeans and lie down, trying to conjure up some sexy images as I reach for the vibrator and press the button to turn it on. When it comes to life, I nearly drop it in shock. Why is it so loud? It sounds like an angry hornet has somehow got into my room, and I'm sure Liv must be able to hear it even though she's downstairs.

I press the button again to turn it off, but it doesn't work. Instead, the intensity of the buzzing goes up several notches. I keep pressing, but it seems all I'm doing is cycling it through its various modes. How the hell do I turn it off? It's now doing a convincing impression of a motorbike going up through the gears. It's no good, I'm going to have to consult the website again. I put the still buzzing vibrator down on my desk as I reach for my phone. Big mistake. The whole desk seems to act as some kind of sounding board, to the point that people in the street must now be able to hear it. Not only that, but it's woken Meg up and she's staring at it intently. Thankfully, the din is short lived as it rolls off onto the carpet almost straight away but, no sooner has it landed than Meg is on top of it, grabbing it in her mouth.

'Drop it, Meg,' I tell her sternly as I advance on her, but she's evidently decided this is a new and tremendous game, making sure she moves just out of reach every time I try to grab it. It's still making an unholy noise as it rattles against her teeth, but I'm now more worried about her swallowing it. If I have to take her to the vet because she's swallowed a 'waterproof for bathtime fun' sex toy that would probably still be buzzing in her stomach, that's going to result in the most humiliating conversation it's possible to have. Maybe a piece of cheese, her favourite treat, will persuade her to give it up. I'm paralysed with indecision though. If I leave her here on her own while I fetch the cheese, she could do herself a mischief. But there's no way she's going to let me near enough to grab her collar and take her with me.

In the end, it seems the only option is to imprison Meg up here while I fetch the cheese. She's watching me carefully, wagging her tail as I button up my jeans and make my way over to the door. I start to open it so I can creep out, but that's obviously the moment she's been waiting for as she shoots through the gap with an alacrity I didn't know she had, evidently keen to put as much distance between us as possible. I thunder down the stairs after her, only to find her in the sitting room, where Liv is sitting on the sofa with a cup of tea and a macaron, staring at her curiously.

'What's this then?' Liv says to her, offering her a piece of macaron and gently prising the vibrator out of her mouth. 'What are you doing with Mummy's toy, eh? It's not for dogs.' She looks up at me. 'Goliath seems to have shrunk in the wash,' she observes drily.

'I wasn't, umm...' I begin, feeling my face flushing scarlet as she presses the button and holds it in, finally turning the bloody thing off.

'Hey, no judgement from me,' she tells me with a smile. 'I'm just glad you're taking care of yourself. Maybe shut the dog out next time though, eh? Some things are best done alone. Oh, and definitely give it a good clean before you use it again.'

She holds it out and I take it gingerly, between the tips of my fingers, before fleeing to my room. I could literally die with embarrassment.

8

'Oh, God. Look what you made me do!' Darren yelled in panic as Claire gingerly touched the wound on the back of her head where the blood was pouring from. She was surprised more than shocked at this point. Technically, Darren hadn't hit her, although he'd pushed her roughly enough that she'd lost her balance and hit her head on the side of the kitchen worktop on the way down. This was a new low, though, but she was too confused and upset to process it right now.

'You need to take me to hospital,' she murmured. 'I think I'm going to have to have stitches.'

Darren looked horrified. 'What will you tell them? You'll say you slipped, yeah?'

She didn't have the energy to fight with him any more. 'Yeah.'

'How's it gooiinnng?' my agent Tamara's voice trills. 'Are you going to send me some sample chapters to whet the publisher's appetite?'

This is the phone call I've been dreading. Although there are parts of the book I'm reasonably happy with, it's still not going very well and I'm a long way behind schedule. I need to try to deflect her until I hopefully get back on track.

'No, Tamara,' I tell her firmly. 'You ask this every time and I say no every time because there's no point sending sample chapters if I'm only going to change them when I come to read the finished manuscript through.'

'They're champing at the bit, darling. You need to give them something.'

'You've got the synopsis, haven't you?'

'Yes, and they absolutely *love* it, but they want more.'

I don't believe her for a minute. She knows as well as I do that the publisher has already contracted for this book, and they're probably up to their ears with their other authors right now. This is just her way of pressurising me into showing her where I've got to, because she doesn't trust me to hit the deadline. Even though I've never missed one yet, I share her nervousness this time. The new chapters are proceeding at a snail's pace, and I'm wasting lots of time going over and over passages I've already written, wondering if they're shit, or the whole concept of the book is fundamentally flawed. It sounded like a good idea when I was pitching it to Tamara, and she was certainly enthusiastic, but now I'm not so sure. Maybe I can use that to buy a bit of time.

'The thing is,' I begin carefully, 'now that I'm actually writing it, I can't help wondering if the whole dual timeline thing is going to work.'

'Nonsense! It's a brilliant concept, as I told you when you pitched the book to me.'

'Don't you think the reader might feel like it's two books glued together?'

'No. It's definitely got two distinct parts, but they're so closely linked that it just wouldn't work as two books. What if we did that, and someone read the second part first? They wouldn't have a clue what was going on. No. Stick with the original plan, darling. It's genius, and I know your writing will fizz just as it always does.'

'I'm just at that stage where I doubt everything,' I tell her with a sigh.

'Hmm.' She doesn't sound pleased. 'It sounds to me like you've lost your way a bit. Have you?'

I should have known she'd see through me. The doomsday spiral has now started to play in my head and I can practically hear her telling me the publisher has lost faith in the project, I need to pay back the advance, and she's also dropping me. To my surprise, her response is almost sympathetic when she continues.

'I'm going to take your silence as a yes,' she says gently. 'Look, I know you've been through a lot lately, with the breakup of your relationship, moving house and everything. Maybe you should think about getting away. A change of scenery might be just the thing. There are some great-sounding retreats coming up. I can send you details if you like.'

This is another well-worn topic of hers. She's a big believer in writers' retreats and seems to think that every writing problem can be fixed by going on one. To be honest, being stuck with a load of other writers sounds like my version of hell and I've always shut her down. It's not that I don't like other writers; the ones I've met have all been fine. It's just that I have visions of everyone sitting round in a circle at the end of the day, discussing what they've written and giving each other 'helpful critique'. If anything is going to worsen my writer's block, it's 'helpful critique'.

'I'm fine, thank you,' I say. 'I just need to fall back in love with the story, that's all.'

'And what better place to do that than the South of France or Tuscany, darling? There's also a retreat coming up in Wales, but who'd want to go there when you could be soaking up the sun and culture with a glass or two of vino while you chat all things authorly with your fellow writers? I'll send you through the details. Promise me you'll have a look at least? I really think this would be good for you.'

'Fine.' I like Tamara, and we generally work well together, but I have to admit that her obsession with retreats does wind me up. Hopefully, letting her send me the details of these ones will get her off my back for a while and, by the time she follows up, I'll be able to tell her that I don't need it because I'm back on track.

'I'm home!' Liv shouts from the bottom of the stairs an hour or so later. This is something she's started doing ever since vibrator-gate. I think she does it to alert me in case I'm in the middle of a passionate moment with the Silver Bullet but, although I followed the instructions on the website, both it and the LadyBliss have been about as successful as Angus in the 'rocking Laura's world' department. To be fair, I suspect the problem may be less to do with them and more to do with ten years' worth of bad sex making it difficult to conjure up the right level of enthusiasm but, after a few disappointing attempts, I consigned them back to their box under the bed.

'Hello, Meggie. Did you miss your Auntie Liv?' she's saying to an ecstatic Meg as I come out onto the landing to greet her.

'Honestly, I sometimes wonder whether that dog loves you more than me,' I say, feigning irritation.

'Of course she does,' Liv coos. 'You and Laura are both much happier living with Auntie Liv, aren't you?'

She's got a point. She's not perfect – which of us is? – but living with her is definitely a lot better than being on my own, and I'm grateful for my shifts in the pâtisserie too.

'Your lovers were in again today, so Bella tells me,' Liv says as I follow her into the kitchen, where she flicks on the kettle without even breaking her stride. 'Tea?'

'Yes, please. How were they?'

'Looking very happy, according to Bella. She wondered out loud if they were having sex yet, but then the image of "old people doing it", to use her phraseology, gave her the ick. I think she's a little bit obsessed with them. Do you think I should have a word? I don't want her being intrusive and putting them off.'

'I'm sure she's very discreet,' I assure her. 'It's just Bella's thing – psycho-analysing the customers. It's harmless and keeps her entertained. Actually, it keeps me entertained too. I might use some of her backstories in future books.'

'And how is the book coming?' Liv asks as she gets two mugs and a teapot out of the cupboard. 'Any better?'

'Not really. I had my agent hassling me about it on the phone earlier. She wants me to go on a writers' retreat because she thinks it might help.'

'Sounds sensible. Are you going to go?'

'I'd rather drill holes in my head, and what would I do with Meg?'

'I could look after her.'

'You're at work all day.'

'I'm sure there must be dog sitters and people who can come and spend time with her while I'm not here.'

'There probably are, but she was so upset when Angus left, and I don't want her thinking I've abandoned her too. Anyway, it's academic as I don't want to go.'

'Why not?'

'It just sounds cliquey and rarefied. Every time I think about it, all I can see is sniffy authors looking down on each other and being generally insufferable.'

'Is that what they're like then?'

'I don't know. It's just what I've imagined. Some haughty so-and-so telling me my writing is nothing more than commercial doggerel.'

'Umm, sorry. But your commercial doggerel, as you put it, is probably outselling their weighty tomes by thousands to one. If anyone should be looking down on anyone, it's you on them.'

'I'm not sure, Liv. Do you remember exams at school?'

She laughs. 'I hardly took any, remember?'

'Good point. OK, when normal people, who aren't you, take exams, there's this moment at the end where everyone checks in with everyone else. "What did you put for question three?", that kind of thing.'

'What's this got to do with writing retreats?'

'I'm getting to that. The point is, I hated that moment, because all it did was make you second-guess yourself. You'd put the answer as twelve, for example, and you'd find out everyone else had written down fourteen. Then you'd spend the rest of the day riddled with self-doubt.'

'Still not seeing the connection.'

'It's the same thing, don't you see? People ask you what you've written today, and you tell them all about how your serial killer has chopped up their latest victim, only for them to rip into you and tell you all the anatomical reasons why that wouldn't work.'

'That sounds pretty unlikely, unless they were either in the medical profession or a fellow crime writer. Anyway, I'm sure a bit of online research would clear that up, and better to be corrected during the writing process than having some smug reader leave a shitty review because you've got something wrong. That always winds you up.'

'No, it doesn't.'

'It so does. What was the last one you got? Someone had the arse because they thought a fall from a second-floor window wouldn't cause the type of injuries you'd written. You obsessed over it for days, looking up stuff online and poring over your medical textbooks.'

'I was sure they were wrong. I just needed to make certain. Anyway, we're getting off the point. I'm not going on retreat.'

'Has she sent you the details?'

'Yes, but I haven't looked, because *I'm not going*.'

'Can I see? I've always wondered what goes on on a writers' retreat. Oddly, nobody seems to run retreats for pâtissiers. I know, I've looked.'

'Maybe there's a missed business opportunity for you there.'

'Where would I get the time? I'm flat out as it is.' She pours water into the teapot, swirling it round to warm it before emptying it out and spooning in the tea leaves. 'That's why I want to see yours, so I can live vicariously through you.'

'I'll go and get my laptop. Hang on.'

It only takes me a minute to fetch it from upstairs but, by the time I return, she's already placed two chocolate éclairs on plates.

'They were left over,' she explains when she sees my raised eyebrows. 'It seemed a shame to waste them. We've got a couple of minutes before the tea is ready, so let's have a gander.'

I click the links that Tamara has sent me, loading each one onto a new browser tab, before handing the laptop over to an eager Liv.

'Don't get tea or éclair on it,' I warn her. 'That thing is expensive and doesn't react well to liquids or baked goods.'

'Relax, I'm being careful. OK, so number one is in Tuscany. Looks like a nice place, and all your meals are provided. They even give you wine with dinner.'

'Not being funny, but I eat and drink pretty well here.'

'Of course you do. I'm a fabulous chef, among my many other talents.'

'Modesty being chief among them,' I say with a laugh.

'Ha. Modesty is overrated in my opinion. If you're good at something, be honest about it. First rule of marketing. How successful do you think my business would be if my advertising was modest? Come to Maison Olivia, where you'll get a tolerable macaron and hopefully leave without being poisoned? No. Come to Maison Olivia, because it's the best bloody pâtisserie in East Kent. Anyway, brilliant chef as I am, I still think eating genuine Italian food in Italy would be worth the trip on its own.'

'Mm-hm. What about the writing retreat bit?'

'Let me see. It says there are a number of places for writing, including their very own library, tables and chairs in the garden, or your room if you prefer. That's OK, isn't it? Sitting under an olive tree, typing away. Sounds blissful if you ask me. There's also a retreat leader on hand to give guidance and feedback, and each day starts with a session on story arcs, character journeys and keeping the reader engaged, whatever those things mean.'

'See, that's what I'm talking about. If there's anything guaranteed to send me down a rabbit hole into analysis paralysis, it's someone telling me how to write a story arc or questioning my character journey. Having confidence in your writing is difficult enough without someone standing over your shoulder and telling you you're doing it all wrong.'

'OK. We'll rule this one out. The next one is in Croatia. Oh, hang on. Same problem with the daily sessions, although they've upped the ante by saying the person running the daily sessions is a leading industry professional.'

'That's even worse.'

'This one looks interesting. South of France – nice – and no daily sessions. There's a mentor if you want one, but other than that it looks like you're left to your own devices. They also lay on trips to local markets and other activities to give you breaks if you want to recharge. Again, all your meals are provided, including dinner with wine and a bar with an honesty box. Fuck it, Laura. If you don't go, I'll pretend to be you and go instead. Have a look.'

She pushes the laptop over to me and focuses on pouring out the tea. She's right; it does look nice. The house is large and decorated in a very French style, although the website states that the owners are English. There are artistic shots of delicious-looking plates of food in the dining room, the well-stocked bar, the bedrooms and gardens. The text makes it clear that the owners are aware that writers are a diverse bunch, so you can be as social or antisocial as you want. The only time you all have to be together is for meals.

'What do you think?' Liv asks.

'I'm still not sure.'

'Why don't we let fate decide?'

'What have you got in mind?'

'It seems to me that you have two fundamental blocks where this retreat is concerned. One is the fact that you're convinced you're going to hate it. But, as we've already agreed, you won't know that until you try it, so we'll mark that one as resolved. The second is Meg.'

'Yes.'

'So, I'm going to challenge you to investigate doggy daycare options. If they're all terrible, then you stay. But if you find one you like, that's the universe clearing a path for you and you have to go.'

'I don't know, Liv.'

'Look, she's not going to feel totally abandoned. Apart from the fact that, love her as I do, her emotions just aren't that complex, I'm still going to be here for her in the evenings so she'll have continuity. Just do a bit of research, will you?'

I sigh. 'Fine. I won't find anywhere though, I'm certain of that.'

9

Claire stared at the bedroom ceiling as she ran through the checklists in her head. Although she couldn't see it in the darkness, she was acutely aware of the crack that ran from the tatty light fitting to the corner of the room. How many hours had she spent lying here, tracing its contours while planning her escape from Darren? She glanced across at him, his rhythmic snoring the only sound in their otherwise silent house. She'd never known she was capable of such hatred until these last few months.

Of course, the shove in the kitchen had just been the beginning. Since then, the violence had escalated and, although he'd been pitifully apologetic afterwards each time, buying her flowers and showering her with gifts, the gaps between outbursts were getting shorter and she needed to get away before he did something really serious to her. The problem was that he controlled virtually every part of her life now; even her passport was locked away in a filing cabinet 'for safe keeping'. Still, he didn't know about the shoebox at the back of the wardrobe where she was slowly starting to build her getaway kit. Any cash tips from work went straight in there, along with the replacement passport she'd ordered because she'd 'lost' the original and the card for the secret bank account she'd set up. She just had a few more things to get, and then she'd be ready.

Thankfully, the threat of having to go on retreat appears to have unblocked me a little. The book has started to flow slightly better and I'm making good progress towards the climax of the first half. It's always tricky, this bit. You want to accelerate and get on to the next part of the story, but you know that the reader wants to savour the journey without feeling rushed. I'm reviewing the last couple of chapters, checking the pace, when my phone rings.

'Hi, is that Laura?' a female voice asks when I answer.

'Yes.'

'This is Donna, from Donna's Doggy Daycare. You left me a voicemail message this morning. How can I help?'

I glance down at Meg, curled up asleep in her basket. If I'm ambivalent about the idea of going on retreat, that's nothing compared to the guilt I feel about potentially dumping Meg on strangers while I'm away. Liv has been very firm with me and I do understand that I can't let Meg dictate my whole life but, as I've pointed out several times, she is a living being and I am responsible for her welfare. I've looked at all sorts of options for her while I'm away and, up until now, I haven't liked any of them. There are plenty of dog walkers who will call in once or twice a day to take her out, but she's used to being around people for most of the time and I worry she'll be lonely.

'I'm thinking of going away for a couple of weeks,' I explain to Donna. 'I've not left my dog before and I usually work from home, so she's used to being around people all day.'

'Of course she is,' Donna says robustly. 'And you worry about her being on her own for long periods.'

'Yes.'

'I'm sure we can help. When would you be going?'

I give her the dates.

'Yes, we could definitely squeeze her in. So, there are several options, depending on what you think would suit her best. She could either come to us as a boarder and stay for the duration of your trip, or she could come as a day-doggy.'

'I was thinking probably the day-dog option. I think she'd prefer to be here overnight.'

'I assume that there would be someone in the house at night-time to look after her?'

'My flatmate Liv, yes.'

'Perfect. So, with the day-doggy option, you have another choice. Either your flatmate could drop her off here before work and collect her afterwards or, for a small extra fee, we could collect her and bring her home.'

'And what happens during the day?'

'We have a number of activities for the dogs, depending on what they like. They're encouraged to socialise with each other and we walk them in pairs. There are areas for play where we provide stimulating toys, as well as rest areas for them if they want some downtime. There are always humans on hand to supervise and also reassure where necessary. If you want to come and have a look, that's something we definitely encourage. What's your dog's name?'

'Meg.'

'Bring Meg along too. We offer a free taster session so you can see how she fits in and we can check there aren't any red flags from our side.'

I hadn't considered that there might be an issue on their side. 'What kind of red flags?' I ask.

'I'll be honest with you,' Donna says. 'Doggy Daycare isn't for everyone. How is Meg around other dogs?'

'She's generally fine. She likes a sniff and then moves on.'

'Probably not an issue then. Some dogs are very anxious and can get aggressive around others. We tend not to accept those ones, not because we can't handle them, but because it upsets the general atmosphere. We like happy dogs here.'

I'm finding Donna very reassuring and, by the time we disconnect the call a while later, I've agreed to visit with Meg in a couple of days.

'I think I may have found a solution to the Meg problem,' I tell Liv as we're sipping a cup of tea later that afternoon. Thankfully there are no treats from the pâtisserie today; I haven't dared weigh myself lately but I can definitely feel the effects of her baking in the tightness of my trousers.

'Oh, yes?' She's only half listening, as she's flicking through one of the trade magazines she loves at the same time.

'Someone called Donna. She runs a daycare centre for dogs, a bit like a crèche. She sounded really nice, so we're going to have a look in a couple of days. Want to come?'

'It'll have to be an afternoon. Flat out in the mornings,' she says listlessly.

'I thought of that. I booked us in for four o'clock on Friday.'

'That could work. I'll ask Bella to lock up.' She finally moves her gaze from the trade magazine to glance down at Meg's head on her lap. 'Auntie Liv needs to make sure naughty Mummy isn't sending you to some horrible hellhole, doesn't she? We don't want you all traumatised.'

'It's not a hellhole. It sounds really nice, actually. They'll even pick her up and drop her off if we want them to.'

'Hmm. That's probably so we can't see the pound she's going to spend all day locked up in. Have you thought of that? It's like boarding school all over again. When you're looking around, it's all sunshine, roses and "of course your child's welfare is our top priority". Then, no sooner have your parents turned out of the driveway than it turns into a Victorian workhouse.' She turns to the dog again. 'Don't worry, Meggie. Auntie Liv has plenty of experience and can smell out a rotten boarding school from a mile away.'

'Liv!'

'What?'

'This was your idea, remember? You're not being helpful right now. Plus, I'm pretty sure you said your schools weren't that bad.'

'You're right. They were fine, actually. Sorry, I didn't mean to guilt trip you.'

'Is everything OK?'

'Yes, fine. I think I'm just having one of my existential crisis days. Nothing to worry about.'

'Do you want to share?'

'It's not very interesting. I'm sure you have days where you wonder whether your life is going in the right direction, don't you?'

'What's brought that on?'

'Dad was asking me the other day if I had any expansion plans for the business. He thinks I lack ambition, that I should be looking to centralise production in a commercial kitchen somewhere and open multiple outlets. I can see his point, but it's not really where I want to go. I love my little pâtisserie, and I love Margate. Does it make me a bad person for that to be enough? Should I want more?'

'Your dad is always going to be looking for the next thing, Liv. It's the way his mind works.'

'I know, but he was basically saying I'm vulnerable because my business is too small. What if one of the big players moves in next door?'

'And what if they don't? You've got a great business with a loyal customer base. People travel to come to you. Did Bella tell you we had a couple in the other day who'd read the reviews online and come all the way from Tonbridge to sample your *Tarte au citron*?'

Her face brightens. 'Really?'

'Really. So yes, you could expand the business if you wanted to, but there's risk in that as well, isn't there? If you became more corporate, people might not love you so much. It's the personal touch, your passion for what you do, that makes you special.'

She looks like a weight has dropped from her shoulders. 'Thanks, Laura. I needed to hear that. I know Dad means well, but—'

'He doesn't understand your business like you do. Remember that.'

'You're right. So, tell me more about this doggy daycare then.'

* * *

'It's nice, isn't it?' I say to Liv as we load Meg into her car a couple of days later at the end of our test visit to Donna's Doggy Daycare. 'Meg certainly seemed to like it.'

'Donna was really good with her, and I like the way she introduced her to the other dogs gradually. I think she'd have freaked if she'd been confronted by that German Shepherd off the bat.'

'He was a bit bouncy, wasn't he?' I agree. 'I was worried he was going to squash her at one point, but they seemed to settle down well together in the end.'

'You know what this means, don't you?' Liv says with a grin. 'The universe has spoken and you're going to France.'

I sigh, knowing I'm defeated. 'Are you sure you're going to be all right being in charge of her?'

'Oh, I'm going to feel horribly guilty dropping her off here in the mornings. But it'll probably be good practice for abandoning my own children at school when the time comes.'

Liv doesn't talk about children generally, so I'm intrigued.

'Would you send your children to boarding school, having been through it yourself?' I ask.

She grins. 'That would depend entirely on how annoying they were. Anyway, I'll use Meg as practice to see if I'm tough enough to do it.'

'Except she won't be boarding, and you know she'll be having a lovely time all day. If you prefer, I can get them to collect her so you don't have to feel bad about leaving her.'

'And have her eyes following me as I leave the house? That would be even worse. No. What did you think of Donna?'

'She seemed nice. She certainly knows a lot about dogs.'

'And what about the partner, Kate?'

'What about her?'

'Business partner, or do you think they're a couple?'

I smile. I couldn't help noticing that Liv was very attentive towards Donna. I suspect she may have taken a bit of a shine to her.

'Business partner only,' I reassure her.

'Based on?'

'Wedding ring, picture on Kate's desk of her with a man I'd hazard a guess is her husband and two adorable children.'

'You're so observant.'

'I've had training from Bella.'

'What about Donna? Any evidence of family there?'

She's definitely interested.

'You like her, don't you?' I ask.

'What kind of question is that?'

'You were bordering on flirtatious.'

'No, I wasn't. I was just listening carefully to what she said,' Liv bristles, making me smile. She's so transparent when she gets a crush on someone. 'I didn't want to miss a single detail which might affect my darling Meggie, did I?'

'You're such a model dog mother,' I tell her with a laugh. 'Promise me one thing though.'

'What?'

'Actually, two things. One, don't give Meg so many treats while I'm away that she gets fat.'

'Deal. What's the second?'

'Don't frighten Donna off. At least, not until I get back.'

'Why would I frighten her off?'

'You get a bit... predatory... sometimes, when you like someone.'

'I do not! Anyway, this is all in your head.'

'Mm-hm? I know you, Liv. I can recognise the signals, and you were giving off all of them. You were even flicking your hair at one point. Total cliché.'

'It was getting in my eyes. You read too much into things.'

'OK. So tell me, hand on heart, that you don't fancy her at all. I mean, I can't see why you would. She's pretty, curvy, fairly no-nonsense about life. Oh, wait a minute. Those are all things you're really into, now I come to think about it.'

'You're funny. You should think about writing some of this stuff down. Fine. I may have noticed her. But that doesn't mean anything.'

'I'm just saying be subtle. The last thing I need is for poor Meg to be expelled from doggy daycare because you're sexually harassing the owner.'

'I'm not going to sexually harass anyone, thank you. I might ask a few probing questions now and then, but that's all.'

I laugh. 'Now I don't know who to feel more sorry for. Meg, for going to daycare, you for having to leave her there, or Donna for having to put up with your inquisitions.'

'Pah. Go off and do your writerly thing and stop worrying about us. We'll be just fine, won't we, Meg?'

I glance across at her. She might be trying to play this cool, but it's a long time since I've seen her so instantly and strongly attracted to someone. I just hope, for her sake, that Donna doesn't give her the brush-off. However, I've got a bigger problem. I now have no excuse not to go on this bloody retreat.

10

'Are you all right? You look a little lost, if you don't mind me saying.' The voice is male and, when I turn to look at him, I'm confronted by a man that I'd guess is probably a couple of years older than me. His blue eyes are bright behind his frameless glasses and his mop of light brown hair is unruly without being unkempt.

'I am a bit confused,' I admit. 'The last time I flew, there were check-in desks, but I can't see any.'

He smiles, revealing even, white teeth. 'Welcome to the cut-throat world of budget airlines. You have to do everything yourself. Have you got your boarding pass?'

I show him my passport, which has my boarding pass tucked inside.

'Great. Let me show you what you have to do. I'm Finn, by the way.'

'Laura,' I tell him.

He leads me over to the baggage drop terminal and shows me how to scan my boarding pass, print off my luggage labels and attach them to my bags.

'Oh, you're on the same flight as me,' he remarks as he repeats the process with his own boarding pass. 'Business or pleasure?'

'Pleasure,' I tell him. I suppose the truth is somewhere between the two but, if I tell him the truth about going on a writing retreat, that might lead to loads of questions. It sounds silly, but I always feel like a bit of a fraud telling strangers that I'm a writer. 'What about you?'

'A bit of both,' he replies. 'I'm working on a project from tomorrow, but I'm taking the opportunity to meet up with a friend who lives in Toulouse first. Right, all we need to do now is feed our bags into that machine over there, and we can go through security.'

'Really?'

'Yup. If the dark magic is working, they should find their way onto the right plane.'

'And if it isn't?'

He grins. 'Then you'll probably never see your suitcases again. There isn't anything valuable in them, I hope?'

'No, just clothes. All the important things are in here.' I tap my cabin bag.

'Great. Shall we?'

Although I'm grateful for Finn's help, it does present me with a dilemma, which is how to detach myself from him without seeming rude. He looks like the kind of nice guy who would happily shepherd me all the way to the gate, given half a chance, but I'm not sure I've got the reserves to make small talk with a stranger for nearly two hours.

'Thank you so much for your help,' I say to him as the bags disappear on a conveyor. 'I'm just going to pop to the loo before security. I'll see you on the other side, yeah?'

I don't need the loo at all, but thankfully he appears to take the hint.

'No problem,' he says with a smile. 'Enjoy your trip.'

I watch with relief as he turns away before heading in the direction of the ladies'. As soon as he's out of sight, I plonk myself on a bench and wait five minutes before following him. I can practically hear Liv laughing at my social awkwardness, but I'm starting to wonder for the umpteenth time whether this is a horrible mistake. If I can't do two hours with a single stranger, how the hell am I going to manage a group of them for two whole weeks?

* * *

The first thing that strikes me as I step out of the airport building in Toulouse is the brightness. Despite it still technically being summer, the last couple of weeks in Margate have been unseasonably cold and damp, and I can practically feel my skin soaking up the sunshine as I hunt through my bag for my sunglasses. It has felt odd, travelling alone after so many years of always having Angus by my side, but I'm pretty proud of how well it's gone so far. I did see Finn again at the gate, but he didn't try to engage with me beyond a friendly wave, thankfully, and our seats on the plane were nowhere near each other. He was right at the front so, by the time the people in my row disembarked, he was long gone.

All that's left now is to find the kiosk the man at the car hire desk told me should be out here somewhere, pick up some keys and navigate my way to the retreat house, where a richly deserved glass of cold white wine will hopefully be waiting for me. I can practically taste it on my tongue as I push my trolley over the hot concrete. I will confess to being a little nervous about the whole hire car thing. I haven't driven for a while, and this will all be on the wrong side of the road, but Liv and I agreed that I needed a means of escape in case the retreat proved to be awful, so I swallowed my nerves and booked one. Liv was typically gung-ho about it, pointing out that people hire cars abroad all the time without incident, so it couldn't possibly be that hard.

By the time I reach the outskirts of Saint-Antonin-Noble-Val, I can't decide which is more important, the glass of wine or ringing Liv to tell her that, actually, it is that hard. Just getting out of the airport was fraught, as the navigation app kept telling me to switch lanes just as someone was zooming up the side of me, or gleefully informing me I needed to perform a U-turn as soon as possible when there clearly wasn't anywhere suitable. When I finally made it out onto the main road, the tiny Fiat was buffeted all over the place by huge lorries and my knuckles were soon raw from repeated attempts to change gear with the door handle. The roads did get quieter once I was off the autoroute, but they brought their own challenges, with people pulling out of side roads seemingly without looking and overtaking me on what felt like blind bends. Thankfully, the directions provided by the retreat hosts are very clear and I only make a couple of wrong turns before turning down the track that promises to lead me to L'Ancien Presbytère, my home for the next two weeks.

'Oh, wow,' I breathe as the house comes into view. I've seen it in the photos, obviously, but they don't do it justice at all. The tall, arched front door is flanked on either side by lavender bushes, and the exposed stonework positively glows in the late afternoon sunlight. Each dark window is framed by bright blue shutters, hinting at coolness and shade within. The gardens are enclosed by another stone wall and the fields beyond are a riot of sunflowers. As I climb out of the car, all I can hear is the buzz of bees in the lavender and the ripple of water from the fountain in the middle of the courtyard I've parked in.

'You must be Laura. Welcome to L'Ancien Presbytère,' an English voice says to me as I begin to wrestle my luggage out of the boot. I look up to see a man who doesn't look that much older than me. He's deeply tanned, with sandy-coloured hair and a full beard. 'I'm Hugh, and I'm delighted to meet you. My wife, Cara, would be here to greet you as well but she's just sorting out an issue with one of the guest bedrooms. Ants are a constant problem at this time of year and, much as we warn guests not to leave food lying around, they don't always listen. Let me take those.'

He lifts my heavy bags with such ease that you'd think I'd filled them with tissue paper, and strides towards the front door. The coolness as I step into the hallway is welcome after the hot journey, although it takes my eyes a moment to adjust to the comparative darkness.

'Most of the other guests have arrived already. The final one will be joining us tomorrow,' Hugh tells me as I follow him towards the staircase. 'We've put afternoon tea and pastries out on the terrace, but you might prefer something stronger. How was your drive?'

'Interesting,' I admit. 'When I booked it, I thought having a hire car would be fun because I could go out and explore, but now I'm not so sure.'

'Most of our guests use the shuttle service we offer,' he admits. 'But this is a beautiful part of France for touring round, so some do prefer to drive themselves so they can explore at their own pace rather than be tied to our excursions. I'd definitely recommend a trip to Cordes-sur-Ciel while you're here if you get time. It's a terrible tourist trap, but still worth seeing. Bruniquel is also a very pretty medieval village. This is you.'

He opens a door and stands aside to let me go through. The room is large, with a wrought-iron double bedframe against the far wall. There is also a wardrobe, chest of drawers and substantial dressing table. The colours in the rugs covering the bare floorboards complement the bedspread perfectly, lifting the ambience without making it garish. The windows, under one of which sits a wide desk, look out over the gardens, which are a riot of blooms.

'This is gorgeous,' I tell him.

'I'm glad you like it. The place was pretty run down when Cara and I bought it five years ago, but I like to think we've brought it up to date sympathetically. It's been quite a project, but so much more rewarding than the daily grind of living and working in London.'

'What did you do?'

'I was a stockbroker and Cara was a chef in a high-end restaurant. We were doing well financially, but we realised we just weren't having any sort of a life. So, much to the horror of our friends and family, we chucked it all in and moved here. Best decision we ever made. Cara looks after the food side of things for our guests and I do the garden and boring maintenance stuff.'

'Including dealing with ants,' I observe with a smile as the sound of the hoover in the distance shuts off.

'We share the ants,' he agrees. 'Don't worry, we haven't hoovered them up. It would be pretty pointless as they'd just march straight back out again. She's just making sure there aren't any crumbs to tempt them and then we'll spray peppermint oil around the room. Ants hate peppermint oil.'

'And are all your retreats for writers?' I ask.

'Goodness, no. We do all sorts of different ones. Writers are generally the easiest because they just need somewhere to work and meet together. Cara does cookery courses sometimes, and they're very popular, but we usually need a week off afterwards to get over them as they're pretty intense. We also do wellness retreats, art retreats and so on.'

'And you run all these yourselves?'

He laughs. 'No. We don't have the first idea about writing, art or any of that stuff. We just provide the venue and an expert. Thinking of which, I'll introduce you to Tess later. She's the mentor for this retreat.'

'I wasn't planning on using a mentor,' I tell him.

'That's fine, but she's there if you want her. She's lovely, actually. She's a freelance editor now, but she's worked for quite a few of the big publishing companies and knows the industry like the back of her hand.'

Our conversation is interrupted by the arrival of a slender, dark-haired woman wearing a white T-shirt and dungaree shorts.

'Ants banished,' she says to Hugh, evidently not having noticed me. 'I've also reminded bloody Gina about not taking food to her room. Honestly, you'd think she'd know, the number of times she's been here.'

'This is Laura,' Hugh tells her, obviously trying to cut her off, although I'm rather enjoying the rant. 'Laura, this is my wife, Cara.'

'I'm so sorry,' she says with a blush as she turns to me. 'I didn't know you'd arrived already. How was your journey?'

It quickly becomes apparent that, minor indiscretion aside, Cara is absolutely lovely. Her eyes sparkle with pride as she shows me round the rest of the house, which is just as beautiful as my room.

'What we've tried to achieve here is to give you all the mod cons, but in a traditional setting,' she tells me as she leads me out onto a terrace where three women appear to be in the middle of enjoying afternoon tea. 'Ladies, this is Laura, who's just arrived. I'm sure you'll make her welcome. Gina, Suzie and Grace are regulars of ours,' she explains to me before turning back to them. 'How many years have you been coming now?'

'This is our third year,' the oldest one says with a sniff. 'We come twice a year, so it's actually our sixth visit though. Laura, is it?'

'That's right.'

'And are you a writer, Laura?' There's something in her tone that I can't quite pin down, but it's definitely not friendly.

'I am, yes.'

'And what do you write?' All three ladies are staring at me now, and I feel a little bit like I'm being interviewed.

'Crime fiction,' I tell them. This is obviously the wrong answer, as I swear I see the chief interrogator's lip curl a little.

'I see,' she says after a pregnant pause. 'I'm afraid I don't get the attraction of that type of thing. It seems' – she pauses dramatically as if searching for the right word – 'a little *sordid*, if you don't mind me saying.'

'Gina's just signed a deal with a *publisher*,' one of the other women explains in a tone that implies that such an honour confers instant deity.

'Oh, congratulations,' I say to her. 'What's the book?'

'It's a Tudor saga,' the other woman says once more. '*Such* a tall order to bring that world to life but, if anyone can do it justice, it's you, Gina.'

'Thank you, Suzie, but I don't think a writer of Laura's calibre would appreciate my oeuvre,' Gina says haughtily. I may only have met her a few minutes ago, but I've already decided that I really don't like her. She's literally epitomising everything I said I didn't like about the idea of writing retreats, and I'm not at all sure about her two sycophants either. Thankfully, before the conversation can get any more stilted, we're joined by two other women.

'Tea and pastries!' the shorter one exclaims excitedly, advancing on the table where everything has been laid out. 'Would you like something, Tess?'

'Just a cup of tea, thank you, Lynette. One thing I've learned from running retreats at Hugh and Cara's is to pace myself. The first time I came, I swear I went home a stone heavier.'

'Fair enough,' Lynette replies. 'What about you ladies, can I offer you a top up while I'm at the table?'

'No, *thank you*,' Gina huffs. From the look on her face, you'd think Lynette had just offered to stab her in the eye, and my curiosity is piqued. I may not like Gina, but I can see that's nothing compared to the hatred that Gina feels for Lynette. Before I get an opportunity to probe any further, however, Tess approaches me.

'I don't believe we've met,' she says. 'I'm Tess, the retreat coordinator.'

'Laura,' I tell her, shaking her proffered hand.

'Laura writes *crime*,' Gina adds, sounding as if I were something she'd stepped in.

'Really? I love a good crime story,' Tess tells me. 'I've edited a number of crime writers in my time. It's such a complex art, isn't it? The constant misdirection so the reader is surprised by the outcome. Very clever. Did Hugh and Cara explain how I work? Basically, I'm here if you want to chat anything through at any time, although it's a good idea to give me a synopsis of your story beforehand so I have some chance of understanding what you're talking about. If you'd rather just crack on by yourself though, that's absolutely fine.'

'Tess is brilliant,' Lynette enthuses as she brings her a cup of tea. 'I've just spent half an hour with her and she's worked miracles on my blowjob.'

My eye is instantly drawn back to Gina, who looks like she might be about to have a seizure. Lynette, on the other hand, is smiling mischievously and I notice that even Tess is struggling not to laugh. I may not like Gina, but I suspect that Lynette and I might get on very well indeed. Maybe this retreat won't be so awful after all.

11

'I should perhaps explain that Lynette writes spicy romance,' Tess tells me with a smile, once the three of us are ensconced at a table out of earshot of Gina and her acolytes. 'Much as I'd like to claim the credit for transforming her sex life, we were actually discussing a scene in her latest novel.'

'I hope I didn't startle you,' Lynette adds. 'I don't know what it is, but there's something about those three that just makes me want to shout words like blowjob. One day, I reckon I'm going to find the right sexual trigger word, and Gina's just going to melt, like the Wicked Witch of the West in *The Wizard of Oz*.'

Tess laughs softly. 'You're very bad, Lynette.'

'Oh, you know I don't mean her any harm really,' Lynette clarifies. 'Well, maybe a little bit, but you have to admit that she is spectacularly irritating.'

'You're certainly very different,' Tess replies before turning to me. 'Tell me more about you, Laura. Are you published?'

'Under a pen name, yes,' I tell her carefully.

'And are you going to tell me who you write as?'

This is the question I've been dreading. I'm not ashamed of Larry Spalding, whatever Gina and her ilk might think of my writing. But flying under the radar is like a safety net; it sounds stupid, but it kind of allows me to distance myself from him if it all crashes and burns. So, admitting that I'm actually Larry feels as uncomfortable as stepping out onto a spotlit stage completely naked. Also, while I think Tess would probably understand my desire for anonymity and be discreet, I don't know Lynette at all, and I don't want her blabbing my identity to everyone.

'Do you mind if I don't, just yet?' I say to Tess eventually.

Tess studies me for a moment. 'Interesting,' she observes.

'Oh, I'm not sure it is,' I counter, but she's still looking at me slightly strangely.

'It definitely is. You see, I've been in this industry for a long time, and I know most of the mainstream British crime writers. Hell, I've probably edited over half of them at one time or another. So, either you're not mainstream, in which case why conceal your pen name because it probably won't mean anything to me, or you are mainstream but nobody knows who you really are. There's only one mainstream British crime writer I can think of like that, and that's Larry Spalding.'

Shit.

'Are you Larry Spalding?' Lynette asks, eyes wide.

'Look, please don't say anything to the others,' I stammer eventually.

To my surprise, Lynette bursts out laughing. 'Oh, your secret's safe with me,' she tells me when she's got herself vaguely back under control. 'But that is just the funniest fucking thing ever.'

'Why?' Whatever I'd been expecting her to say, it wasn't that.

'Because Gina...' is as far as she gets before she loses control of herself again. I glance across the garden, worried that her outburst might attract the attention of Gina and her friends, but they appear to be engaged in a debate of their own, thankfully.

'Oh, shit. I think I may have wet myself a little bit,' Lynette breathes eventually. 'Totally worth it though. Laura, you've made my day. Actually, you've made my retreat and we've still got two weeks to go.'

'Are you going to explain what's so funny?' I ask her. I'm not offended, at least I don't think I am. But I'm definitely not used to people reacting to me revealing who I am in quite this way.

'OK.' Lynette leans forward and tries to look serious, before breaking off into another fit of giggles. 'Sorry, Laura. Tess. You tell her.'

'Oh, no,' Tess says firmly. 'This is not my story to tell.'

'Fine.' Lynette makes another concerted attempt to compose herself. 'What do you know about Gina?'

'Not much,' I admit. 'She's written a Tudor saga, according to Suzie. She thinks crime fiction is sordid and obviously doesn't think much of spicy romance either, if her reaction to you is anything to go by. Oh, and she's just signed with a publisher.'

Lynette's mouth drops open. 'Did she say that?'

'No. Suzie did. Why?'

Lynette grins. 'Oh, Gina. You naughty, naughty girl,' she murmurs.

I must look as baffled as Tess, so Lynette continues.

'OK,' she says. 'Gina's magnum opus is a book called *The Lion and the Snake*. She's been hawking it around publishers and agents for the last two years, with no success. The only people surprised by this are her, Suzie and Grace, who believe it's the pinnacle of twenty-first century highbrow fiction because that's what she's told them. There's just one, tiny problem standing between her, a publishing deal worth millions and the inevitability of the Booker Prize landing in her lap.'

'Which is?'

'Gina is very secretive about it, but I managed to get a glimpse of the manuscript once, when she left it out by mistake. *The Lion and the Snake* is basically one hundred and fifty thousand words of totally impenetrable bollocks.'

'You're being a bit harsh, Lynette,' Tess chides her. 'I've seen the synopsis and there are some strong themes in it.'

'If you can find them under the mountain of hyperbole and clunky metaphors,' Lynette says defiantly. 'Anyway, the point is that this pile of literary manure is the pinnacle of human achievement, according to Gina. I've even known her to refer to herself in the third person when she talks about it, that's how self-important she is.'

'But she's sold it to a publisher,' I repeat.

'No. That's what's so funny. Well, it's one of the things that are so funny. Have you heard of a publisher called Florianus?'

'No.'

'You wouldn't have, but that's who's publishing Gina's book. Now, who do you think the directors of Florianus are, hm? I'll tell you. Only one John and Gina Atkinson. So, she hasn't sold anything to anyone. What she's done is forced her poor, long-suffering husband to help her set up her own imprint to publish her book.'

'There's nothing wrong with that,' Tess says. 'Lots of successful authors are self-published. I work with quite a few of them.'

'Of course there's nothing wrong with being self-published. It's what I am, after all. But telling people you've signed with a publisher when it's actually your own company is a little misleading, isn't it? God, I bet Suzie and Grace absolutely lapped that up. And then, for the icing on the cake, there's you, Laura.'

'What about me?'

'I saw how she was being with you, all hoity-toity. If she only knew who you really were. God, I'd pay good money to be a fly on the wall for that.'

'Laura's asked us to keep her identity confidential,' Tess reminds her.

'I know that. But the irony is going to keep me laughing all fortnight. A real, live, bestselling author right under Gina's nose, only that nose is too far up her arse to spot it. Sorry. That's probably a mangled metaphor, but you know what I mean. Right, I'd better go and assess the damage all this hilarity has caused. I love my children to bits, but they haven't half fucked up my plumbing.'

'There isn't much love lost there, I take it,' I say to Tess as Lynette heads for the house.

She smiles softly. 'Not a lot, no. But the funny thing is that I don't think they'd actually survive without each other. Did you notice anything about the two of them?'

'Apart from the fact that they hate each other, no.'

'Hm. Maybe that's not my story to tell either. Let me put it this way. They absolutely hate each other's guts, but there's also a strong bond between them. How easy would it be for them to book retreats at different times, for example? But no. Every year they rock up on the same ones, regular as clockwork. Gina makes no bones about the fact that she thinks what Lynette writes is basically porn and, as you'll have noticed, Lynette isn't much more polite about Gina's stuff. So what does that tell you?'

'I don't know.'

'OK, well, as I said, it's not my story to tell, so I'll have to leave you to work it out yourself.'

'I'm supposed to be here to concentrate on my book, not whatever's going on between my fellow guests.'

'Yes, but you know what they say about all work and no play, don't you?

Plus, it's good for your detective skills. Now, I'd better go and talk to the others for a bit. I'll see you at dinner.'

* * *

'I've been thinking about you. How is it?' Liv asks when I call her that evening. I've helped myself to a glass of wine from the bar and I'm sitting on a lounger, enjoying the cool of the evening. I'm not sure what's for dinner, but if the smells coming from the kitchen are anything to go by, it's going to be delicious.

'Interesting,' I tell her.

'Interesting good or interesting bad?'

'A bit of both. The house is amazing, even better than I'd hoped, and Hugh and Cara are lovely.'

'What about the other writers?' she says impatiently.

'Yeah, a mixed bunch. It's probably too early to tell, although there's one who's definitely taken against me.' I fill her in on my conversation with Gina.

'She sounds vile. Did you tell her you're a bestselling author?'

'No. I'm keeping that under my hat, although the retreat leader rumbled me pretty much straight away.'

'I thought you were steering clear of the mentor. Analysis paralysis and all that.'

'Yeah, but she came to find me at teatime and we ended up having a bit of a chat. She's nice, actually.'

'OK, so you've got a snotty author and a nice mentor. Who else?'

'The snotty author has a snotty entourage, but I don't know anything about them yet. We've got one person still to arrive, apparently, and then there's Lynette, who writes spicy romance. She's very funny, but there's something about her and Gina. They hate each other, but still come on every retreat together. What's that about?'

'Ex-lovers, perhaps?'

'I don't know.'

'Hm. Maybe one stole the other's boyfriend. Oh, hang on. Someone wants to see you. Meggie, who's Auntie Liv talking to?'

She turns the camera and, for a few moments, I'm treated to a close-up of Meg's nose as she sniffs the phone, evidently trying to work out if it's edible. As soon as she realises it isn't, she wanders off and jumps up on the sofa.

'Donna says she settled really well today,' Liv tells me. 'There's a cocker spaniel called Bubbles that she's apparently formed a friendship with, and they went on a long walk together.'

'Every inch the proud dog-parent,' I say with a laugh. 'How was it, dropping her off?'

'I felt surprisingly guilty and tearful, but she trotted in quite happily without so much as a backward glance.'

I laugh. 'You could be describing your child's first day at school, you know that?'

'I just wanted you to know that I'm taking good care of your baby, that's all.'

'Thank you. And how was Donna today?'

'Chatty, but I can't work out whether that's because she wanted to reassure me about leaving Meg with her, or whether she's just friendly, or whether there's something potentially more.'

'Remember what I said about not frightening her off.'

'Relax. I know what I'm doing. Tell me more about the retreat. I want all the details.'

By the time I've filled her in on everything including the traumatic car journey, which she found predictably hilarious, darkness has fallen and Cara is calling us to dinner.

'For your starter tonight, I've made a *Soupe au Pistou*,' she tells us as she sets bowls of steaming broth in front of us. 'It's a traditional dish in the South of France and you'll actually find markets selling the ingredients pre-mixed at this time of year. *Bon Appetit!*'

After my experiences this afternoon, I've been vaguely dreading the whole group coming together to eat but, to my relief, hostilities seemed to be paused as everyone tucks in. I note with vague amusement that Gina offers the basket of warm crusty bread to Lynette without either of them resorting to name-calling. Tess's words are rattling around in my head though, and I can't help studying their interactions, looking for clues. They're so different in every possible way that I can't see them having the same taste in men, which blows Liv's theory out of the water, so what is the connection between them?

12

Even though the bed is every inch as comfortable as it looked, I'm awake early the next morning. I do make a couple of half-hearted attempts to get back to sleep before giving it up as a bad job and heading for the shower. The sun is already high in the sky when I step outside, but the air is still cool and fresh, so I decide to walk in the direction of Saint-Antonin-Noble-Val to build up an appetite for breakfast. If last night's dinner was anything to go by, I'm going to be extremely well fed while I'm here, so I need to pace myself.

I'm trying to concentrate on the upcoming plot points of my story as I walk, but I'm sidetracked by the beauty of the scenery around me. The town, when I reach it, is still pretty much shuttered and deserted. A few shopkeepers are setting up ready for the day ahead, and I exchange a cheery *Bonjour* with them as I pass. When I reach the river, I stand on the bridge just watching the water slide beneath me for a while. I did see most of this yesterday, but I was busy fighting with the satnav and the directions, so I didn't get the opportunity to appreciate it. It really is lovely here. Hugh and Cara couldn't have chosen a better location if they'd tried. I pull out my phone and take a few pictures to send to Liv before turning back towards the house and breakfast. However, I've only travelled a couple of yards before I hear a car pulling up alongside me.

'*Excusez-moi, mademoiselle. Habitez-vous ici?*' a male voice says. It's vaguely familiar, but I can't quite place it. It's only when I turn to address him that the penny drops along with my mood.

'Hello, Finn. What are you doing here?' I ask suspiciously. It would be just my luck to discover that the man who was so helpful at the airport is actually some kind of stalker.

'Hi, Laura. What a surprise! I'm actually looking for a place called L'Ancien Presbytère. You haven't come across it, have you?'

I study him for a moment while part of my brain frantically tries to remember if I mentioned where I was staying during our brief conversation at the airport. If he's followed me, then that's creepy as hell and his intentions can't be good. I glance around furtively, trying not to raise his suspicions while scanning to see if there's anyone who would come to my aid if I shouted. The other part of my brain is trying to remember what 'help!' is in French. *Au secours*, I think.

I'm sure I didn't tell him where I was staying.

'How did you find me?' I ask.

'Sorry?' He looks genuinely confused. 'I wasn't looking for you. As I said, I'm booked into a place called L'Ancien Presbytère, which is somewhere round here. I think this is the fourth time I've driven over this bridge so far this morning and, pretty though this town is, I'd like to get to my destination before I die of old age. So I stopped the first person I saw to ask for directions, and that happened to be you.' His face falls. 'You didn't think…'

Oh, God. He looks absolutely crestfallen now as the reason for my questions has evidently dawned on him.

'You've got to admit, it is a hell of a coincidence that you should pitch up here,' I say.

'Shit. I haven't followed you, I swear. I didn't even know you were going to be here. I'm doing a two-week retreat here, that's all.'

'At L'Ancien Presbytère.'

'Yes.'

'What sort of retreat?' He seems increasingly legitimate, but I can't help testing him further. If he gets this wrong, I'm out of here.

'It's a writers' retreat,' he tells me. 'Why?'

'Oh, no reason,' I tell him. 'It's just that I'm staying at L'Ancien Presbytère as well, and the chances of that being a coincidence are infinitesimally small, wouldn't you agree?'

'So you know where it is then?' His face has lit up with hope.

'I do.'

'This is probably a stupid question, given what you evidently think of me, but you wouldn't be able to show me, would you? I'd be eternally grateful.'

A memory is stirring of Hugh telling me that there was one more guest to arrive in our party. Yes, it is a hell of a coincidence that it should be Finn, but everything he's said so far has checked out. Normally, I'd run a mile before getting into a car with a strange man who, up until a few seconds ago, I suspected was stalking me. I take a moment to study him. It sounds silly, but his blue eyes have exactly the same imploring look that Meg uses when she wants something, and I can feel myself softening. His slender physique and soft-looking hands also add to the impression that he's not a threat. Nevertheless, I'm cautious as I open the door and slip into the passenger seat.

'I should warn you that I'm trained in martial arts,' I tell him as he pulls away. 'Take the next left.'

'Noted,' he replies with a smile. 'Although I really am only after directions, I promise. I take it you're a writer then.'

'Yes,' I admit.

'What do you write?'

'Crime.'

There's a brief kerfuffle as he swings onto the wrong side of the road after making the turn, to the consternation of a van driver coming the other way, but thankfully he manages to swerve out of the way just in time.

'What about you? What do you write?' I ask him as we leave the town behind us.

'Ah. Confession time,' he replies as he attempts my trick of changing gear with the door handle. 'I'm not strictly a writer. I, umm, devise TV shows.'

'Take the next turning on the right. What kind of TV shows?'

'Game shows, quizzes, that kind of thing. Have you ever seen *Cash in the Theatre*?'

'I can't say I have, no.'

'OK. I only mention it because it's one of my more successful shows. It goes out at three o'clock every weekday.'

'I'm not a daytime TV person, I'm afraid. What's it about?'

'It's loosely based on the board game *Operation*, do you know that?'

'Is that the one where players have to remove various objects from a body using tweezers?'

'That's it. If they touch anything other than the thing they're supposed to be removing, a buzzer sounds and they forfeit their turn. At the end of the game, the person who has successfully removed the most objects wins.'

'I used to play it with my brother. We always ended up fighting and I think we lost most of the objects in the end. I'm not sure how you'd make a TV show out of it though.'

'There's a bit of a formula, at least there is to mine. The first thing you need for a successful show is something the audience can engage with. I agree, just watching two people trying to retrieve objects without setting off a buzzer isn't very immersive. So you need to add another element, and the easiest one is some form of quiz. Audiences love a quiz. You also need elimination, and some kind of jeopardy in the final.'

'I'm intrigued. Go on.'

'In the show, the contestants have to start by answering questions across a number of categories to amass as many points as they can. We start with ten people, and lose the two with the lowest number of points at the end of each round until there are just two finalists left. That's your elimination stage.'

'Yup, got that.'

'The finalists then go head-to-head in a general knowledge round to decide who will get to go into the operating room. Then we add the jeopardy, by converting the highest scorer's points into seconds of time. They're against the clock in the operating theatre to fix as many things on the "body" as they can. The more things they fix without setting off the buzzer, the more money they can win.'

'That sounds straightforward enough.'

'Yes. You don't want it so complicated that the audience loses interest. We also add an extra layer by allocating different cash sums to different operations depending on how hard they are to do. So, a gallstone is worth five thousand pounds, because you have to remove a number of other organs to get to it and put them back in the right place afterwards, all without setting off the buzzer. An ingrown toenail, on the other hand, is only worth a hundred. So the contestant has to decide how best to use the time they have available.'

'Turn right there,' I tell him, pointing out the track that leads to L'Ancien Presbytère. 'What's the biggest prize?'

'The slipped disc,' he tells me. 'One hundred thousand pounds.'

'That doesn't sound very hard.'

'It isn't, if you go from the back. But you can only get to it from the front on our patient, so you have to remove pretty much all the other internal organs first, and we've made it particularly hard to get out without setting off the buzzer. The show's been going out for five years and we've only had three contestants manage it.'

'Hm. And this is on every day of the week, you say?'

'Yes. It's very popular.'

'So why a writers' retreat?' I ask as he pulls up outside the house.

'I'm working on a new show that I want to pitch, but I'm a bit stuck,' he tells me as he switches off the engine and we climb out. 'I thought this might be a good place to un-stick myself. I'm sorry. I've been prattling on and I haven't asked you anything.'

'Don't worry about it,' I tell him as Hugh throws open the door and comes to greet him. 'I'm sure there will be plenty of time. I'll see you around, yeah?'

'Absolutely. And thank you so much for showing me the way. I don't think I'd ever have found it by myself.'

* * *

'Everyone, this is Finn, the final member of our little group,' Hugh announces as we're congregating for breakfast. Cara has excelled herself again; as well as the croissants and pains au chocolat you'd expect to find at a French breakfast table, there is a selection of cold meats and cheeses, as well as eggs in various forms, fruit juices and a selection of teas. Cara herself is deftly operating a coffee machine that looks very similar to the one I've been using at Maison Olivia.

All conversation ceases immediately as everyone turns to study the newcomer. I note with amusement that Gina's eyes are as wide as saucers, although her mouth is set in its customary downward curve of disapproval. Suzie and Grace are looking unsure, evidently waiting for Gina to tell them what their reaction to Finn should be, and Lynette is eyeing him up in a similar manner to a lion assessing its prey.

'Bloody hell, he's going to be a bit of a distraction,' she murmurs when I sit down next to her. 'If I were twenty years younger, I'd be all over him.'

'Really?' I ask, studying Finn once more. He's chatting to Cara while she makes him a coffee so is hopefully oblivious to our scrutiny.

'You don't think he's utterly gorgeous?'

'He's OK. I mean, he's no Henry Cavill, but he's not Shrek either.'

'The Superman guy?'

'That's the one.'

'Bit old for you, isn't he?'

'Says the woman eyeing up a man half her age!' I retort.

'Fair point. I wonder what he writes?' Lynette continues after a brief pause. 'Cosy crime?'

'He's not a writer,' I tell her. 'He makes TV game shows.'

'Really? How do you know that?'

'I bumped into him in the town this morning. He was lost so I showed him the way to the house. We chatted.'

She smiles mischievously. 'Gina isn't happy about him at all, which pleases me immensely.'

'She doesn't know anything about him.'

'That doesn't matter. The fact that he's a man will already have ruffled her feathers. We've never had a man on these retreats before, and it's going to change the dynamic. Look at the way she's sizing him up.'

'You were sizing him up yourself just now,' I remind her.

'Yes, but in an entirely different way. I was, and still am, enjoying a bit of eye candy. She's trying to work out if he's a threat. When she finds out he's a non-writer on a writers' retreat, it will probably blow her mind.'

'Does it matter? We're all here for the same reason, aren't we? He's just after inspiration for a TV show rather than a book.'

'It doesn't matter to normal people like you and me. But Gina is already off kilter because of you, and now she's got another complete unknown to deal with. She doesn't like things she can't control.'

'I wouldn't say she controlled you. You seem to take pleasure in winding her up.'

'Yes, but I'm still a known quantity.'

'Tess said that there's a connection between you, but it wasn't her role to tell me what it is.'

She smiles. 'There is. Have you worked it out?'

She obviously thinks this is a big mystery and is clearly dying to tell me. I can't say that I haven't really given it more than a couple of passing thoughts, so I simply shake my head instead.

Her smile broadens. 'Would it help if I told you that we've known each other since I was born?'

I stare at her, and then at Gina. Apart from their eyes, which I'll admit are the same colour, there is no resemblance between them that I can spot.

'You're sisters?' I ask. OK, I have to admit that this is a bigger reveal than I'd given credit to.

'Yes. She's six years older than me and, boy, did she like to remind me of that fact when we were little. I think she still would, if she thought I gave a crap. I did ask our mother once whether she was sure one of us wasn't a changeling, because we couldn't be more different in every conceivable way.'

'You're both writers,' I point out.

'A fact that irritates her every day. She can't bear the fact that I'm a reasonably successful author with eight books out, while her first is still in the doldrums.'

'Does it have to be a competition? It's not as if you write in the same genre.'

'If you want to understand one thing about Gina, it's that *everything* is a competition and she's a sore loser. That's her Achilles' heel. If she could just chill the hell out, she might actually be someone worth talking to. As it is, well...'

'You hate her and she hates you.'

Lynette grins. 'It's more of a love/hate thing. She hates me because I'm more successful than her and, after years of her telling me how much better and more important she is than me because she's the older child, I love rubbing her face in it.'

I flick my gaze across to Gina, who is deep in conversation with Suzie and Grace. From the way she keeps looking at Finn, who is still chatting with Cara, it's not hard to work out what they're talking about. I'm not naïve enough to buy Lynette's version of events wholesale – I'm sure Gina has her own story about the feud between the two of them – but it's become clear to me that Lynette's friendliness is a thin veneer over a desperate desire to have an ally. It's a shame, because I do like her, but I'm not here to embroil myself in her family dynamics. Who knew that a writers' retreat would be so complicated to navigate? Let's hope Finn doesn't turn out to be some long-lost cousin from a branch of the family they both loathe. I think I might have to go home early if that happens.

13

'I'm in the kitchen,' Darren called as soon as Claire closed the front door behind her. 'Would you mind very much doing me a favour and joining me?'

The tone of his voice was enough to tell her that something was seriously wrong, and her hands shook as she hung her coat on the rack.

'Sure,' she called back, hating the way her voice wobbled with nerves. 'What's up?'

'It's probably best if I show you.'

She wracked her brains, trying to think what on earth she could have done to annoy him this time. The slightest thing could set him off these days; last week he'd completely lost his shit because she'd put the mustard back on the 'wrong' shelf in the fridge. She winced as she touched the bruise on her hip, where she'd banged it against the counter when he'd shoved her. He didn't even bother to apologise after his outbursts any more, and they were ramping up both in intensity and frequency. She was genuinely scared he was going to seriously injure her or kill her if she didn't get away soon. Thankfully, everything was now in place. Darren was going to be away overnight at a work conference next week, which would give her two clear days to move her stuff out.

Darren was sitting at the table when she walked into the kitchen. He was ominously still, and her heart went into her mouth when she saw the shoebox in front of him. How the bloody hell had he found her secret hiding place? And, more importantly, what could she tell him to stop him ruining everything?

'Would you like a cup of tea?' she asked, trying frantically to buy enough time to concoct a plausible story.

'Yes, why not?' He smiled at her, but there was no warmth in it. It was the smile of a predator playing with its prey. Fuck. What was she going to do? Her hands were shaking so badly as she filled the kettle that it took all her concentration not to spill water everywhere.

'I found this at the back of the wardrobe,' Darren told her, taking the lid off the box once she'd switched on the kettle and summoned the courage to turn and face him. He started methodically taking the items out, laying them carefully on the table like trophies. 'Let's see what we've got, shall we? A passport in your name, a surprising amount of money, some bank statements for an account that's also in your name, and a debit card. Now, I'm no detective, but it looks awfully like you were planning on going somewhere.'

I've managed to find a quiet, shady corner of the garden well away from everyone else and, for the first time in ages, I'm definitely in the zone. I've been writing for two hours solid and, now that I've reached the climax of the first part of the novel, my fingers have almost taken on a life of their own as they dance across the keyboard. However, I've been doing this job for long enough to know that I need to take regular breaks if I don't want to end up with painful stiffness in my neck and shoulders, and the alarm on my phone is telling me that I need to get up and move. The temptation to ignore it is huge; I've spent chapter after chapter carefully laying my breadcrumb trail, and this is a really inconvenient place to stop.

'That's why you have an alarm, Laura,' I tell myself firmly as I close the lid of my laptop and force myself to stand, moving my head from side to side, stretching my arms and twisting my torso to loosen the muscles. I breathe deeply, enjoying the mixture of floral scents in the air. I glance at my watch. Eleven o'clock. I think I've earned a cup of coffee and maybe one of Cara's delicious pastries.

This really is a stunning garden. Hugh and Cara have obviously put a lot of thought into both the layout and the planting. As well as the table I've been sitting at, there are a number of other semi-private spots set up with benches, tables and chairs. The area where I've been working is surrounded by riotously colourful flower beds, but even the herb and vegetable gardens that I'm walking through now have a functional beauty to them. Finn obviously likes it here, as I spot him on a bench ahead of me. He's leaning back, with his eyes closed beneath his wide-brimmed hat and his long legs stretched out in front of him, almost blocking the path. The crunch of the gravel beneath my feet evidently alerts him to my presence, as he sits up with a start when I approach.

'Hi, Laura,' he says with a smile. 'How's it going?'

'Good, thanks,' I reply. 'I was just going to get a cup of coffee. Would you like me to bring you one?'

He heaves himself to his feet. 'Do you mind if I come with you? I'm not stalking you, I promise. There's something I wanted to ask you, actually.'

'Oh, yes?'

He falls into step beside me and lowers his voice. 'Is it me, or is there a seriously fucked-up dynamic at play here?'

'What do you mean?'

'I may be imagining it, but there seemed to be an atmosphere at breakfast. The three women who were sitting together at the end of the table kept staring at me like I was some kind of monster, and the one you were talking to cornered me outside my room earlier and started babbling all this stuff about how excited she was to have a man in the group, as if she'd never come across one before.'

'Lynette is pretty full-on,' I agree.

'That's one way of putting it. I'm starting to wonder if you and I are the only normal people here.'

'Tess is OK, and the jury's still out about you, stalker.'

Thankfully he takes my remark in the spirit intended and smiles.

'I will find a way to convince you that I'm not, but I agree about Tess. She came to introduce herself to me earlier and we had a good chat. She was lovely, but we agreed that she probably wouldn't be able to help me with my new show format. There's definitely something going on between the Double-Doubles and the hippy, though.'

'Who?'

'Sorry, I have a habit of nicknaming people in my head. The three women reminded me of Macbeth's witches.'

'"Double, double, toil and trouble",' I quote with a smile.

'"Fire burn and cauldron bubble",' he replies, grinning.

'Have I got a nickname?'

'No,' he says so firmly that I'm sure he's lying.

'Come on. What is it?'

'Promise you won't be offended?'

'Absolutely not. If it's offensive, I reserve the right to take as much umbrage as I can.'

'It's not offensive.' He's blushing now, I notice.

'Just spit it out, Finn.'

'Don't read anything into it. I only gave it to you because it alliterates with your name and it relates to the way we met.'

'Finn!'

'Fine. It's Luggage Laura, OK?'

'Luggage Laura?' I repeat slowly.

'Yes, because we met over your luggage.'

'I think there are more complimentary alliterations you could have picked. Lovely Laura, perhaps, or even Luscious Laura?'

'I think they would have been inappropriate, and would only have served to make you more certain that I was stalking you.'

'Lickable Laura – now that would have been inappropriate and definitely stalkerish,' I tell him, before realising what I've just said and blushing a little myself. 'Sorry. I didn't mean anything by that. I was just getting carried away with the alliteration thing.'

'Maybe I should rename you Alliteration Laura,' he says with a smile, thankfully defusing the rather awkward atmosphere that was between us.

'I'll take Luggage Laura,' I say as we start to help ourselves from the coffee jug that has been laid out. 'I've been called much worse, and at least I'm not one of the witches.'

'You won't say anything to them, will you?' he asks, his expression suddenly serious. 'Things here are weird enough as it is.'

'Your secret is safe with me,' I assure him.

* * *

'How's the game show coming?' I ask once we're settled at the table with our drinks and a couple of pastries so delicious that they give Liv's a run for their money – not that I'd ever tell her that. The tantalising aromas coming from the kitchen indicate that Cara is evidently in the middle of preparing lunch, and I'm keen to keep the conversation going, if only to disguise the sound of my stomach growling in anticipation and to reassure him that I'm no longer suspicious of him. I may have teased him about his assertion that he and I were the only normal people here, but there's quite a lot of truth in it. I could do with an ally and he's surprisingly easy to talk to.

'Slow,' he admits.

I smile. 'I'm no expert, but I imagine that it goes faster if you're actually awake.'

'What do you mean by that?'

'You were dozing earlier, weren't you?'

'I wasn't! I was just thinking with my eyes closed, that's all.'

'Dozing,' I repeat.

'It was a late night and a very early start this morning.'

'What have you got so far?' I ask. 'Or is it secret?'

'That depends. Are you going to steal my idea and pitch it to the TV networks?'

'I wasn't planning to, no. But sometimes it helps to have a sounding board.'

'OK. Do you remember me telling you about the essential ingredients of a game show earlier?'

I cast my mind back to our car journey. 'Umm, it has to engage the audience, involve elimination and an element of jeopardy.'

'Very good. So my idea, as far as I have it, is a kind of valuation game. The working title is *The Auction Room*, which we'll have to change because it's too close to an existing show called *The Bidding Room*, but that's the least of my problems right now. The contestants get shown a number of items that have recently sold at auction, and they have to guess how much they went for.'

'OK, but how do they get points? I assume there are points involved.'

'There are, but it's related to the jeopardy element. As they go through the game, the price of the items they have to value increases. So, let's assume the objects in round one all went for ten pounds or less. It might be a hundred, but the principle is the same. Their opening prize pot is therefore a tenner.'

Let's say item one went for five pounds. If they guess correctly, they get the prize, but every pound they're off comes out of the pot.'

'I don't follow.'

'Let me give you an example. The item went for a fiver, but you guess seven pounds. That's two pounds out. So you only win eight pounds instead of ten.'

'I get it. Not exactly white knuckle though, is it?'

'Not to begin with, no. But remember, we're looking more at elimination in the early stages of the game. We'll start ramping up the potential prize pot in the head-to-head and the final.'

'It sounds like you've got the formula pretty much nailed. What's the problem?'

'Exactly that.' He sighs. 'At the moment, it's purely formulaic. Apart from the auction room thing, it's pretty much a carbon copy of every other daytime quiz show. I need an edge, and that's what I'm missing.'

'Perhaps you should ask the Double-Doubles to give you an inspiration spell,' I quip.

'I think not,' he replies with a laugh. 'They'd probably suggest introducing a sudden death round where the contestants actually die suddenly.'

'That would certainly give you an edge,' I tell him through my own laughter. 'You might struggle to recruit contestants though.'

'Do you know, the worst thing is that I'm not totally sure I would? You'd be amazed what risks people are prepared to take to get their five minutes of fame, particularly if they think there's gold at the end of the rainbow. However, there are one or two ethical issues with it, and I can't see it getting past the safeguarding teams, somehow.'

'I'm sure you'll come up with something,' I encourage him. 'You just need more of that magical eyes-closed thinking time.'

'I hope so. Actually, can I ask something while you're here?'

'Sure.'

'Would you mind very much sitting next to me at lunchtime?'

'Why?'

'Because you're the only person here, apart from Tess, who doesn't seem to have some sort of hidden agenda. I feel comfortable around you, which isn't something I can say about the others.'

'Are you seriously proposing that I act as some sort of human shield between you and the Double-Doubles?' I ask.

He does at least have the grace to look bashful. 'That's not quite how I would have put it, but yes, kind of.'

'Don't worry,' I tell him. 'I'll protect you from the scary witches. Although I should warn you that Lynette thinks Gina will implode when she finds out you're not a "proper" writer. Apparently, she takes this stuff very seriously.'

He looks completely nonplussed, and I realise he has no idea who I'm talking about.

'The hippy told me that the head of the Double-Doubles will implode,' I clarify.

His face clears. 'Ah, right. Well, we don't want that. Do you think I should come up with a cover story?'

'Honestly? I'd leave her to it,' I say, surprising myself with the firmness in my voice. 'She may think she's queen bee on this retreat, but I don't see why the rest of us should pander to her.'

'Wow. Don't sit on the fence, will you?'

'I mean it. I'm here to get inspiration and work. If the rest of them want to waste their time stabbing each other in the back and generally playing power politics, that's up to them. I've got a book to finish.'

He grins. 'It could be the plot of your next book. A body is found stabbed in the back on a writers' retreat. Everyone has a reason for wanting Gina dead, but who killed her?'

'It has potential,' I agree.

I'm smiling as I make my way back to my little corner of the garden. Finn is easy to talk to, and if being his human shield keeps me out of the family rift that is Lynette and Gina, so much the better.

He might have a point about the book too.

14

'Now, I realise that can't be true,' Darren continued in his ominously saccharine tone. 'I mean, where would you go? Who would even want you? But you've been keeping secrets from me, Claire, and that's a problem. You know how I feel about secrets.'

'Let me make your tea,' she said, turning back to the kettle as it clicked off. Her mind was such a maelstrom, working feverishly to come up with a plausible lie, that she barely registered the telltale scrape of his chair on the kitchen floor as he got up. Before she knew what was happening, he was on her, grabbing a fistful of her hair and yanking her head back so hard it felt like her neck would snap.

'What were you planning – *argh, fuck*!'

He released her as quickly as he'd seized her, and she was momentarily confused until she saw the kettle in her hand. She'd just gripped the handle when he'd attacked, and she'd obviously brought her arm up in a protective reflex, hitting him in the head with it and spraying him with boiling water in the process.

'*I can't see! What have you done?*' he bellowed, clutching at his face as he staggered in the direction of the sink, reaching blindly for the tap.

What happened next was a blur. As Darren bent over the sink, Claire felt almost detached from her arm as it brought the kettle down hard on his head. She was oblivious to the pain of the water scalding her hand and wrist as she dropped the kettle in the sink and reached towards the knife block. She felt as if she were an observer, even though it was clearly her hand plunging the knife into his neck. He tried to fight her off, but she seemed to have been imbued with almost superhuman strength as she stabbed him again and again, only stopping when the knife was so slick with his blood that she was unable to grip it properly.

It seemed like an age before Darren's lifeless body slumped to the floor, even though it couldn't have been more than a minute or two. All Claire could hear was her ragged breathing. Dropping the knife, she sank down until she was curled up in a kind of squatting foetal position as her gulps of air turned into full-on sobs.

What the hell had she just done?

'Lunch, everyone!' Cara's voice calls across the garden as I try to picture the scene in my head. This is one of those tricky moments where I need to get the descriptions completely accurate, because there's nothing readers like more than pointing out an inconsistency to prove how clever they are, and they can be forensic in their quest to find something wrong. Everything matters, from the relative height of attacker and victim, to whether the attacker is left or right-handed. I once received a lengthy diatribe on Larry's Instagram page from a reader who explained in huge detail how the murder as I'd described it was physically impossible.

Finn is waiting for me on his bench and gets to his feet as I approach.

'I owe you an apology,' he says as he falls into step next to me.

'Really? Why?'

'I've been a terrible conversationalist. I've only talked about me so far, so I want to put that right over lunch. Why crime?'

I consider the question for a moment. 'I think it's important to write in a genre that you're passionate about,' I tell him. 'The very first crime novel I read was *The Surgeon* by Tess Gerritsen, and it gripped me from the start. I binge read all of hers before moving on to Stephen King, Patricia Cornwell – you get the picture. It never even occurred to me that I'd write anything else.'

'It's hard though, isn't it? Lots of research.'

'Yes, but that's one of the things I love, getting deep into the detail.'

'How do you research something like that?'

'Well, as I said, the first part is reading lots of other books in the same genre. But I've also got books on human anatomy, police procedure, and it's amazing what you can find online.'

'Good point. I'm surprised your browsing history hasn't fired up a red flag somewhere. Tell me about your book.'

'What do you want to know?'

'What's happening, where's it going, all that stuff.'

I smile. 'You might steal my idea and sell it to a publisher.'

'Unlikely. You've got insurance because I already told you about my idea for the show. Let's agree to stay in our own swim lanes and I'm sure we'll be fine.'

'OK, so I'm about halfway through and my main character, Claire, has just killed her coercively controlling and abusive boyfriend, Darren,' I tell him.

'How?'

'She stabbed him in the neck with a kitchen knife.'

'Nice. Hang on, though. Does the reader know it's her who killed him?'

'Yes.'

'I thought the whole point of these types of books was that you didn't know who the killer was until the last moment. Haven't you kind of given that away?'

'That's one option, and I've written a few like that, but it's by no means the only trope in the genre.'

'Really?'

'Yes, "whodunnit", which is what you're talking about, is a fairly common trope. But you can also have stories where the murderer is known but their motive is unclear until the end, for example.'

'A "whydunnit".'

'Exactly. So, in this book, I'm playing with a few tropes. The first half of the book focuses on the abusive relationship between Darren and Claire.'

'Sounds grim. Do people want to read that kind of thing?'

'People are inherently voyeuristic. It's why we all crane our necks when we pass a car crash, even though we know we shouldn't. So yes, even though it's grim, as you put it, there's a market.'

'Right, so you've got your abusive relationship and then she kills him. I might be being dim here, but isn't there still meant to be an element of suspense?'

'Absolutely. So, what the reader will know when they buy the book is that it contains at least one murder that will have repercussions years later. What they *don't* know until the scene I've just written is whether Darren is going to kill her or the other way around. I've been very careful to lay breadcrumbs along the way, hopefully pointing the finger towards Darren killing Claire in an attack that goes too far.'

'So it's a surprise when she turns out to be the killer instead. I like it.'

'Thank you.'

It's no surprise, however, to find that Gina and her acolytes are already ensconced at the head of the table when we arrive. Tess is sitting next to Suzie, so I take the place opposite her and motion Finn to sit next to me so I'm a barrier between him and Grace. I'm just congratulating myself on my tactics when I realise that I've left a massive open goal, as the only place for Lynette to sit is now opposite Finn. What I'm unprepared for, however, is that she doesn't look happy about it either when she joins us a minute or two later. She's almost scowling with displeasure, but it's only when I see the delighted expression on Gina's face that I realise I've played a double fault because I've also denied Lynette direct access to needle her sister and her cronies.

'I've got a choice of starter for you today,' Cara tells us as she places jugs of iced water and carafes of wine on the table. 'I've made a vegetarian version of *soupe à l'oignon gratinée à l'ancienne*, which is a traditional French onion soup with a crouton and a layer of grated Gruyère cheese on the top, or, for the meat lovers, a kind of pork terrine called *Civier Bressan*, which is very popular throughout France. It goes by a variety of names and many regions claim credit for inventing it but I stick with the traditional one, which is that it originates from Bourg-en-Bresse.'

'Ooh, they both sound delicious,' Grace coos next to me. 'What are you going to have, Gina?'

'What does it matter what she has, Grace?' Lynette snaps grumpily. 'You've got a brain of your own, haven't you? Why not bring it out of retirement and choose what you'd actually like, rather than mindlessly following her all the time.'

'Someone got out of bed the wrong side this morning,' Gina observes smugly before turning to an indignantly pink Grace. 'But you know how I love all things French. "*Quand en France, fais comme les Français*", as I always say. I'll have the terrine, please, Cara.'

'I think I'll have that too,' Grace says, causing Lynette to snort derisively.

'And me,' Suzie adds.

'Soup for me, please,' Tess says. 'I'm a vegetarian.'

'Yes, I'll have the soup as well,' Finn says, hastily putting down his phone as Cara glances at him.

'Terrine,' Lynette practically barks, staring at Gina as if willing her to question her choice.

'I'll have the terrine as well,' I say. I'm sure Cara's onion soup is delicious, but it's something that Liv makes regularly, and I can't see myself enjoying it without the richness of the beef stock to underpin it.

'So,' Finn says to me once Cara has disappeared to deal with our orders. 'Claire stabs him in the neck. That sounds messy.'

'Oh, it is,' I reply. 'If you hit the carotid arteries, you're looking at literal fountains of blood and the victim will likely bleed out within a minute or two. That's the tricky bit I've got to navigate now.'

'How so?'

'First of all, I have to consider the angle of attack. She's right-handed and standing behind him when she stabs him, so we're looking at the right carotid artery. All the initial bleeding will therefore be to the right-hand side of them.'

'Yup, that seems straightforward enough.'

'Now you need to think about what happens. He's bending over the sink when she hits him with the kettle, because he's trying to get to the cold water to splash it on his face. The force of that blow is going to stun him for a moment, so he's still there when she stabs him for the first time. The initial spurt will therefore be low level, probably across the worktop. However, what's the first thing he's going to do when he feels her plunge the knife in? He's going to straighten up and probably turn around, so now you're looking at an arc of arterial spray across the wall. Also, she's now going to be stabbing him on the left of his neck.'

'Must you?' Gina interrupts crossly. 'I know this kind of thing is absolutely fascinating to people like you, but it's hardly suitable for the dinner table. Perhaps someone else would like to contribute a more tasteful snippet of their morning's work?'

'I've been struggling with something that I'd appreciate the group's help with, actually,' Lynette says quickly.

Gina's face is a mask of suspicion, but she evidently realises she's fallen into a trap of her own making and has no option but to try to style it out.

'Really?' she says smoothly. 'I'm sure we'd all love to help. What's the problem?'

'I'm struggling with synonyms for an erect penis,' Lynette announces triumphantly, causing Gina to flinch. 'I've used all the usual ones – cock, shaft and so on. Throbbing member is a possibility, but that just sounds a bit like an angry bank manager at a golf club. Any ideas?'

'For God's sake!' Gina exclaims, clearly trying to cut her off, but the damage is done. Lynette is beaming with delight. 'There must be someone around this table who is writing something we can discuss in a civilised manner. Finn, tell us about you.'

'I'd prefer to keep my project under wraps for the time being,' Finn says tactfully, impressing me with his ability to dodge Gina's question.

Thankfully, the conversation pauses as Cara and Hugh bring out the starters. The terrine is not quite what I was expecting; it's basically small pieces of meat and vegetables in a kind of jelly and doesn't look particularly appetising, but I can almost hear Liv's voice in my ear telling me not to judge it without tasting it first.

'How is it?' Finn asks as I take a mouthful.

'It's OK, actually. More flavour than I was expecting.'

'Interesting. Gina, Suzie and Grace are obviously enjoying it too.'

I follow his gaze and have to stifle a laugh as Gina takes a big mouthful, closing her eyes and sighing as she chews. You'd think she was tasting a fine wine rather than a slightly unusual pâté.

'This is fabulous,' she says when Cara emerges from the kitchen a moment or two later. 'You must give me the recipe.'

'I'm happy to do that, but I have to warn you that it is a bit of a faff to make and you might struggle to find some of the ingredients in England.'

'Oh, I'm sure there isn't anything here that the chap in our charming local delicatessen can't source,' Gina says dismissively. 'If he can get the ingredients for an Ottolenghi recipe, I'm sure he won't struggle with a rustic French dish like this.'

'Fair enough,' Cara replies. 'There aren't any set quantities, but basically you start by boiling the head of a pig or wild boar and a couple of trotters for three hours or so.'

'I'm sorry,' Suzie interrupts, looking horrified. 'Are you saying there's a pig's *head* in this?'

'Absolutely. All the meaty parts of the terrine come from the head, especially the cheeks and tongue, but there's also some from the ears and snout. The jelly is made from the stock the head was boiled in, and then you simply add vegetables and aromatics. It's not actually hard, it just takes a long time.'

'That's *disgusting!*' Grace cries, shoving her plate away from her so hard that it almost falls off the other side of the table. Suzie looks like she might be about to cry and Gina has raised her napkin to her lips, not-so-subtly ejecting the terrine from her mouth into it.

'*Quand en France...*' Lynette says triumphantly, earning herself a filthy look from Gina.

'I do think,' Gina says, evidently trying to rescue the situation, 'that it would be wise in future to warn us, Cara, before serving foods that might be more *challenging* to a British palate. We're all adventurers on life's journey and I'm as open minded as the next person, but sometimes we might need to dip a toe into the waters of a country's more *barbaric* practices before jumping in completely, if that makes sense.'

'I'm sorry, but I can't let that go unchallenged,' Finn tells her. 'I'll confess that I had the soup because I googled the terrine before making my choice and realised it wouldn't be for me. Correct me if I'm wrong here, Cara, but isn't it basically the same as brawn, which is as British as they come?'

'There are a few minor differences, but the basic ingredients are the same,' Cara agrees. 'I'm sorry you didn't like it, Gina, and I'll certainly provide trigger warnings in future if you think they might help. Simply make a list of things you're not keen on. Did you like it, Laura?'

'It's actually really nice, even if the texture is a little unusual. My best friend Liv would approve, too. She's a big fan of nose-to-tail eating, not wasting any part of an animal, so I'm sure she's come across it in her travels.'

I glance up the table towards Gina, who is no longer looking even vaguely smug any more. I know I said I wasn't going to enter into the politics between her and Lynette, but she's being so insufferable that I can't resist. Unfortunately for Finn, he's also put himself firmly in her crosshairs after challenging her so openly, so I suspect she'll be looking for any excuse to bring him down, whether I'm acting as a human shield or not.

At least it's not dull, I suppose.

15

'Cup of tea?' I ask Finn some time later. Once again, I've been so firmly in the zone, making sure every detail of my murder scene is correct, that I've had to rely on my phone alarm to make me get to my feet and move. Finn is still on his bench, but does at least have his eyes open and a notebook in his hand.

'We might need to wait a little while,' he tells me. 'Gina's on the terrace with Tess and it didn't sound like it was going particularly well earlier.'

'Hm. Well, if she doesn't want to air her dirty linen in public, then there are plenty of more private places they could have their meeting. I don't see why I should be denied a cup of tea simply because she's there. Coming?'

Finn gets to his feet. 'Sure. Why not?'

As we approach the terrace, I can hear what he means. Although I can't make out the individual words, I can hear Gina's voice sounding a bit agitated, interrupted occasionally by Tess's more measured tones.

'All I'm saying,' Tess is telling her as we come into earshot, 'is that some-times less is more. Look at that sentence there. Read it out loud to me.'

'"The dewy fragrance of the early-morning air eagerly snaked its way into Donald's hungrily appreciative nostrils, stimulating his olfactory nerves and causing the synapses in his brain to fire like a fusillade of canons as they conjured up vivid images in his mind's eye of other dawns breaking when he'd raced across these downs as a youngster, his hair flying in the breeze as boy and horse cantered together in perfect synchronicity." What's wrong with that?'

'Nothing, except you've basically taken a four-line sentence to say that Donald breathed deeply, and the scent of the air reminded him of early-morning rides when he was a teenager. It's a little over-described, don't you see?'

'Yes, but this is *art*, Tess, not the kind of drivel that people like Laura write. I'm appealing to a highbrow audience, who expect more than just humdrum prose with a few bloodstains thrown in.'

OK, so this is awkward. They're still oblivious to our presence, and part of me contemplates retreating to prevent an embarrassing scene, but I would actually like a cup of tea and there's no way of getting one without alerting them. In the end I clear my throat, making them both start.

'How long have you two been standing there, eavesdropping?' Gina accuses as soon as she regains her composure, evidently deciding that attack is the best form of defence. *Quelle surprise.*

'That doesn't matter,' I tell her coolly. 'If you didn't want to be overheard, you should have found somewhere private for your chat. Finn and I are only after a cup of tea, and then we'll be out of your way.'

'I suppose you think you're better than me, don't you,' she continues, evidently spoiling for a fight. 'I know your little secret, you know.'

'What secret would that be?'

'That you're the supposedly great Larry Spalding.' My face obviously betrays me as she continues in a triumphant tone. 'Oh, come on. You didn't seriously think Lynette was going to keep something like that to herself for long, did you? She's leakier than a colander, that one. So, what's someone like you doing here, that's what I want to know. Come to spend time with the little people, to remind yourself how fabulous you are while you spew out the next instalment in your production line of gore?'

I'm gobsmacked. Not only by her hostility, but the fact that she genuinely seems to believe that's the way I think.

'Of course not!' I exclaim. 'If I've given you that impression then all I can say is that I'm sorry. As far as I'm concerned, we're both here for the same thing, which is to write something our audience will enjoy.'

She stares at me for a moment in silence. 'Then why not be honest with us from the start, hm? Why conceal your identity if you didn't think we'd all be fawning over you if we knew who you really were?'

'Because I'm not in the habit of broadcasting who I am. Look, Gina. I'm not sure what your problem with me is, or why you seem to have taken so violently against me, but I really am just here to write, the same as you.'

She sniffs. 'I'll tell you why I have a problem with you. You lied about who you were. That doesn't sit well with me.'

'I didn't lie, I just—'

'Failed to tell the truth,' she cuts me off. 'Same thing. Well, if you're the kind of person who can happily deceive others and sleep at night, then good luck to you. You'll forgive me if I don't wish to associate with you though.'

She gets to her feet and starts to stalk towards the garden, before her eyes fall on Finn and she stops in her tracks.

'And what about you?' she spits at him. 'Are you secretly a bestselling author too?'

'Hey, leave me out of this,' Finn says, holding up his hands.

'Why? You're being just as evasive as Laura here. All that stuff at lunch about "I'd prefer to keep my project under wraps". I'll unmask you, be certain of that.'

We all stare after her as she sweeps regally down the path, and an uncomfortable silence descends.

'Well,' I say eventually. 'That was…'

'Intense,' Finn offers when I run out of steam.

'She's not normally like that,' Tess says. 'I think she's just feeling the heat at the moment.'

'Oh, really?' I retort. 'She's normally sweetness and light, is she?'

'I wouldn't go that far, no. But I think the reality of publishing her book, and other people actually reading it, is making her jittery.'

'That wasn't jittery. That was mean.'

'Yes, fair enough. She wasn't at her best, that's for sure. But try to see things from her perspective for a moment.'

I sigh. 'Which is?'

'This book means everything to her. She's been working on it for years, telling everyone who'll listen what a masterpiece it is. But, until now, nobody apart from her and the people she's submitted it to have actually read any of it.'

'But Suzie and Grace must have done. The way they were talking about it...'

'They haven't, trust me. Gina is, to put it kindly, quite a forceful personality, so if she tells you something is good, your natural inclination is to believe her. Suzie and Grace are in awe of her, and that's part of the problem. Suddenly, she's worrying whether her magnificent statue actually has feet of clay, and she's insecure. Lynette doesn't help, of course, but I suspect having you walk up and hear what you did is going to have sent her spiralling inside. She doesn't take criticism well at the best of times, but criticism in front of someone like you is just humiliating.'

'Tell me,' Finn asks before I have a chance to respond, 'is her whole book like that?'

Tess smiles enigmatically. 'I couldn't possibly comment. What I will say is that the basic story and structure is good. She's done her research too but, like any draft, it needs refinement. That's what editing is for. Do you know what the real tragedy here is?'

Finn shakes his head.

'That if she and Lynette could get over themselves and work together, they'd have a winning formula. Who doesn't love a Tudor romp, eh?'

I'm up early again the next morning. I didn't get any work done after Finn's and my chat with Tess, as my mind was busy replaying the conversation with both her and Gina. My initial outrage at Lynette's indiscretion and the things Gina said has faded a little and, although I'm still not particularly sympathetic to either of them, I do understand where Tess was coming from. By the time dinner came around last night, I'd semi-resolved to try to build some bridges with Gina at least, but it had quickly become apparent that the timing wasn't right. Finn's summary of the atmosphere between the two sisters as 'colder than a nuclear winter' was pretty much bang on, and we ate in a tetchy silence that was only broken by the occasional request for someone to pass something. Even Cara's amazing cooking and the carafes of wine that Hugh had topped up as soon as they were half-empty had failed to lighten the mood, and everyone had retired to their rooms as soon as the meal was over.

However, today is a new day and I've decided to walk into Saint-Antonin-

Noble-Val again before breakfast, taking my notebook so I can write down any ideas as they occur to me. I'm reasonably confident that my murder scene is as it should be, so now I need to start thinking in detail about the next part of the story. Gina, Lynette and the weird dynamics are quickly pushed to one side as I allow myself to become immersed in Claire's predicament. It therefore takes me a moment to realise that I'm not alone as I step into the early-morning sunshine.

'Oh, hello,' Finn says, straightening up from tying the laces on his walking boots. 'I thought I'd be the only one up at this time. I'd forgotten you were an early bird too.'

'I'm not, usually,' I tell him. 'There's just something about this place that makes me not want to waste an hour of the day. I thought I'd walk into town again to build up an appetite for breakfast.'

He smiles. 'That was my plan too. I don't want to crowd you though. Would you prefer it if I went the other way?'

I study him for a moment. Part of me would prefer to be on my own, but he's easy company and I don't want to seem rude. One enemy is more than enough to be going along with, thank you.

'No,' I tell him. 'Unless you'd rather be alone?'

'I think, given the atmosphere last night, us sane ones should stick together,' he says, smiling again as he pulls a pair of sunglasses out of his pocket and puts them on. 'Shall we?'

Although we don't speak for the first part of the journey, having Finn striding along beside me is surprisingly comfortable.

'Tell me more about you,' I say after a while.

'Oh, no,' he replies, and I can practically feel his eyes twinkling with amusement behind his dark glasses. 'I'm still trying to make up ground for talking so much about myself yesterday. Your turn.'

'I'm not very interesting. I live in Margate with my best friend and my dog. You already know I'm a writer. Your go.'

'Uh-uh. Why Margate? What sort of dog? How old?'

'You're not going to let this go, are you?'

'Nope. In my experience, the people who think they're fascinating are usually monumentally dull and vice versa. I'm therefore betting you're much more interesting than you let on.'

'Fine.'

I don't know whether it's because he's determined to make up for his perceived selfishness yesterday, but Finn turns out to be an attentive listener and, by the time we reach the outskirts of the town, I've told him all about the implosion of Angus's and my relationship, shown him far too many pictures of Meg and given him the lowdown on Liv.

'She sounds nearly as frightening as Gina,' he observes as we reach the bridge and pause to look out over the water.

'She's a force of nature but, unlike Gina and the Double-Doubles, she has a heart of gold. She's been my rock since Angus left.'

'Everyone should have a best friend like that,' he says wistfully, and I sense this might be my opening.

'Don't you?' I ask.

'I did. Or at least I thought I did.' He takes off the sunglasses and I can see the sadness in his eyes.

'Do you want to tell me what happened?'

He sighs. 'Adam and I have been friends since primary school and we've always had each other's backs. We both moved to London after university so it seemed entirely natural that we'd share a flat, and it was a lot of fun, to begin with, anyway. We had the typical bachelor lifestyle, you know?'

'Umm, not having ever been a bachelor, I can't say I do.'

'Work hard all week, play even harder at the weekend. I don't think I'd be boasting if I said we used to have the best parties.'

'Sounds fun.'

'It was. Things did calm down a bit as we got older and, after a while, Adam started going out with Holly, and I met Roisin. The parties stopped and were replaced by the four of us enjoying long Sunday brunches and walks in the park instead.'

'Still sounds pretty good.'

'It was, until Adam and Holly split up. Suddenly, he resented me spending time with Roisin. He wanted to resurrect the party lifestyle and got pissed off with me because that wasn't what I wanted any more. He blamed Roisin, of course, and started being really snappy with her too.'

'He was jealous of your relationship.'

'That's the weird thing. I'm not actually sure he was. What he wanted was us to split up so he and I could go back to the old days.'

'That's not how the world works.'

'I know that, but Adam didn't seem to. Anyway, he made it some kind of personal quest to break us up, by fair means or foul. In the end it turned out to be foul.'

'What did he do?'

'He slept with Roisin.'

16

'I don't understand. He hated her, right? She didn't like him either. How does that even work?'

Finn gazes into the river. 'I've lost count of the number of times I've asked myself that very question.'

'How did you find out?'

'He engineered it so I'd walk in on them.'

'Bastard. What happened?'

'Oh, he was clever. It's a move I like to call the "reverse Iago". You could probably use it in one of your books, although I'll want a share of the royalties.'

'Iago as in the *Othello* character?'

'That's it. So, in the play, Iago fills Othello's head with doubts about whether his wife, Desdemona, is being unfaithful to him. That's what Adam did to Roisin. I found out later that he'd been engineering ways to bump into her when I wasn't around, and he'd use the opportunities to suggest I'd been closer to Holly than he'd been comfortable with. He even insinuated that he and Holly had split up because there was something going on between her and me. Anyway, Roisin didn't believe him to begin with, but Adam is a good salesperson and knows how to spin a yarn, so it wasn't long before the doubts began to creep in.'

'And she didn't talk to you about this?'

'No, but what could I have said anyway? We'd all got on really well when it was the four of us and the best way to sell a lie is to lace it with a known truth. So he used the fact that Holly and I had been friendly towards each other to imply that there was more, and over time she came to believe it. From there, all you apparently need is some alcohol to lower inhibitions, a suggestion of revenge sex to settle the score and bingo.'

'Bloody hell.'

'Yes. Of course, Roisin realised that he'd played her the moment I walked in and caught them, but it was too late. The damage was done.'

'What did you do?'

'Roisin was distraught, but I'll never forget the look of satisfaction on Adam's face. I moved out the next day and haven't spoken to him since.'

'And Roisin?'

'We tried to patch it up, but it proved to be too big a thing for us to get over. We split up a few weeks later. Last I heard, she'd moved back to Ireland.'

'I'm sorry.'

He smiles ruefully and points at the river. 'It's literally water under the bridge, isn't it.'

'And now?' I ask.

'Now, I live on my own in a fairly crappy one-bed flat in Mile End, which I'll lose if I don't come up with a decent idea for this game show. Shall we think about heading back?'

Without thinking, I reach out and wrap him in hug.

'What was that for?' he asks when I let him go. I'm relieved to see his expression is curious rather than offended.

'I don't know,' I tell him honestly. 'I just felt you needed it.'

'I'm not sure I'm the only one,' he says as his arms come up to draw me back in. This is a much longer hug and, after a while, I become aware that we're no longer alone on the bridge. An elderly woman is making her way towards us.

'Finn,' I murmur. 'I think that woman is watching us.'

'So she is,' he replies as he releases me before waving to her and calling, 'Bonjour, Madame! C'est un matin tres beau, n'est-ce pas?'

The old woman smiles as she comes closer. 'C'est une belle matinée pour être jeune et amoureux, oui!'

'What did she say?' I ask.

'I'm not sure, but amour is love, isn't it. She obviously thinks we're a couple.'

Unfortunately, neither of us have sufficient grasp of the language to interpret the stream of French that comes from the old woman when she reaches us, but the expression on her face and the way she presses our hands tightly together while exhorting us to do something or other is enough to confirm our suspicions. Unable to say anything to correct her, we resort to embarrassed nodding and smiling and let her get on with it until, with a final squeeze of our hands and an earnest plea to '*aimer férocement pour toujours, comme Bertrand et moi*', she releases us and continues on her way.

'That was interesting,' Finn says as we start to make our way back towards the bank. He hasn't let go of my hand, but I'm surprised to find I'm enjoying the sensation, so decide not to mention it.

'I think we made her day,' I agree.

* * *

'Tell me more about your book,' Finn says a few minutes later. 'Claire has murdered Darren. There's arterial spray all up the walls and a hell of a mess. Now what? I'm guessing the police don't pitch up and arrest her, because that wouldn't give you much of a storyline.'

'You're right,' I agree. 'Initially, she's numb and in shock, of course, horrified by what she's done. But then self-preservation kicks in and she does what a lot of young women faced with a seemingly impossible situation would do.'

'Which is?'

'She calls her dad.'

Finn's expression is inscrutable behind his sunglasses, but he's making no move to release my hand as we walk.

'Aren't they estranged? I mean, if Darren has been coercively controlling her, he'll have cut her off from her family early on, won't he?'

'Yes, but what father is going to resist a call from a daughter in distress?'

'Fair point. So he comes round on his white charger.'

'Something like that. But he's out of his depth too. We've got a kitchen that resembles an abattoir and a dead body to dispose of.'

'I guess you can clear up the blood with enough bleach, but I can see the body is a problem. Is there a garden they can bury it in?'

'There is, but the risk of being spotted by the neighbours is too great.'

'Put him in a body bag, bundle him into the boot of the car and dump him somewhere?'

'Again, there's a risk the neighbours will see. Plus, if the body bag leaks in the car, that's DNA evidence tying Claire and her dad to the crime. And that's before you factor in the risk of someone finding the body later.'

'Bloody hell, this is hard. Remind me never to kill anyone. What's the solution then?'

I smile nervously. I hope he doesn't shoot this idea down in flames as it's central to the second half of the story at the moment. 'I was thinking that he never leaves the house.'

'Go on.'

'Claire's dad is a builder by trade and notices that the fireplace in the sitting room has alcoves either side. So they wrap him up securely, put him in one of the alcoves and brick them up. Bit of plaster and redecoration and you'd never know it wasn't original.'

He considers for a moment and I'm aware that I'm chewing my lip, waiting for him to reveal his verdict.

'Can I ask a couple of questions?' he says eventually.

'Of course.'

'Presumably the dad would have to bring building materials into the house. Wouldn't the neighbours see that?'

'Yes, but they wouldn't find it suspicious. They'd just think Darren was having some work done.'

'OK. Question two: Wouldn't the body start to smell after a bit?'

'It would, but if you wrapped it securely and sealed the cavity properly, you wouldn't be able to smell it from the rest of the house.'

Finn grimaces. 'Do you know, I'm starting to wonder if evil Gina has a point. Your mind must be a truly macabre place to come up with something like that.'

'Oh, it's not completely original. I saw something similar on a true crime documentary and decided to adapt it.'

'I've just thought of another question. What about the missing person aspect?'

'Yes, that's got to be done carefully. Darren's a loner, so we don't have friends as such to worry about, but he will be missed at work, and there needs to be some sort of plausible explanation for his disappearance that points the finger away from her.'

'She's going to be the prime suspect though, because they lived together.'

'Yes, but remember the coercive control. The neighbours will have seen her coming and going, but she won't have been allowed to socialise with them. Also, there's no way he'd have allowed her name to appear on any official documents to do with the house, because of a further twist I'm planning to throw in right at the end.'

'So people would know he had a girlfriend, but nothing about her.'

'Exactly. All she needs is time to construct a plausible story.'

'OK, so I guess she could call his work and say he's sick.'

'Not call, because we don't want to risk anyone recording her voice. So she'll email from his work laptop, pretending to be him.'

'How does she have the password? There's no way he'd have let her know what it was.'

'I'm working on that. Then she's going to clear all of her stuff out, making sure the neighbours see her leaving with it. And finally a forged suicide note saying he can't carry on after his girlfriend left so everything's tied up in a neat bow.'

He thinks for a moment. 'What about the body though? Wouldn't there be a body if he'd committed suicide?'

'Good point.' I think for a while. 'How about this? At some point after she's very publicly left, Claire and her dad sneak back to the house in the middle of the night to set the scene. Dad dresses up in some of Darren's clothes and puts on a cap so his face can't be seen when he passes any CCTV cameras. He then drives Darren's car to a remote car park at the coast and leaves it there. The working assumption would be that he'd drowned himself.'

'That would work. But it means she gets away with it.'

'She does.'

'Is that allowed?'

'Everything's allowed, but remember that this is just the first half of the book.'

'So something will happen in the second half.'

'It will.'

'Are you going to tell me?'

'Not yet. I've got the broad-brush strokes of it, but not the detail.'

We lapse into a comfortable silence for a little while, before Finn unexpectedly laughs.

'What?' I ask.

'I was just thinking. There I am, wrestling with a concept for a daytime TV show and thinking how difficult it is, but it's a walk in the park compared to the tangled web you're having to weave. Do you have one of those collages stuck to your wall at home, by any chance?'

'What collages?'

'You know. There are pictures of suspects, maps, news articles and stuff, and then random bits of string going from one to the other, usually with a big red question mark somewhere.'

I smile. 'You've been watching too much TV, and no. I think Liv would chuck me out if I started doing stuff like that.'

He chuckles again. 'Yes, from what you've told me about her, she probably would.'

We fall back into silence as we cover the final part of the journey but, when we reach the end of the track that leads to L'Ancien Presbytère, Finn pauses, turning to face me.

'I'm a little nervous about what we're going to find down there,' he admits, letting go of my hand and removing his sunglasses. 'But I wanted to say thank you for this morning. It's been a welcome break from the shitfest.'

As I look back at him, the sunlight catches his blue eyes, making them sparkle. For a moment, everything outside the two of us seems to fade into insignificance, and I briefly wonder whether to hug him again. The truth is that I've enjoyed this walk much more than I expected to, and it's not just because it's given me a respite from the deeply unpleasant atmosphere in the house. The long hug on the bridge, followed by the simple act of walking along, hand in hand with Finn, has relaxed me in a way that I never could have expected. There's no tension across my shoulders or any of the other usual places. I feel languid, as if I've just had a long massage. The conversation, on the other hand, has sharpened and focused my mind, and I can feel ideas fizzing in my brain, eager to find their way onto the page later today.

'I think it's me who should be thanking you,' I tell him honestly. 'This has been really good for me.'

'Same time tomorrow?' he asks.

'On one condition.'

'Which is?'

'Tomorrow we brainstorm your show.'

'It's a deal.'

17

'I wonder if you'd like to do something different tomorrow?' Finn asks as we return from our now regular morning walk a few days later.

'What did you have in mind?'

'We're at the halfway point of the retreat and, while I may not have found the thing that's going to sell this show, sitting in the garden going over the same options while the Double-Doubles give me death stares every time they pass is not proving very fruitful. You seem to be making good progress, so I wondered whether a day out might be fun.'

I stop walking to look at him. I've come to really value these early-morning strolls together. We generally alternate between trying to come up with something that's going to make his auction show stand out, and me explaining what's going on in my story. Thankfully, Gina seems far too busy fighting with Tess over her edits to bother with Finn and me beyond the odd pointed remark, which naturally means Suzie and Grace are broadly ignoring us as well. Even Lynette seems to have lost interest; I wasn't best pleased with her for 'outing' me to the others, and I think she picked up on that and realised I wasn't going to be her playmate any more.

All of this means that Finn and I have formed a kind of bubble away from the others. We walk before breakfast, sit together at the bottom end of the table for mealtimes, and meet up regularly through the day for tea and coffee breaks. I've found that I'm enjoying both the routine and his company. He may not be Henry Cavill, but his personality more than makes up for that. I've come to love the way his eyes light up and his speech quickens when he's excited about something, usually because he's had an idea that might dig me out of a plot hole. His enthusiasm is genuinely infectious, but he's also a really good listener and sounding board. I've already decided to include him in the acknowledgements for this book, but I still wish I could return the favour by helping him unlock the USP for his show. Unfortunately, although I am devoting some time to it, I'm hampered by the fact that I know very little about auctions and even less about daytime TV.

'A day out,' I repeat, shielding my eyes from the sun with my hand as I look up at him.

'Yes. I could do with a fresh perspective, and I thought different scenery might help.'

I smile. 'And what's in it for me? What's my motivation in this scene, as the actors say?'

'A day off to reward yourself for working so hard and making such good progress?'

It is a tempting idea. My shady spot in the garden of L'Ancien Presbytère is lovely, but it would be a shame to spend all my time there without getting out and seeing some of the surrounding countryside, particularly as I went to all the expense of hiring a car.

'Did you have somewhere specific in mind?' I ask him.

'Yes. It's just a suggestion, obviously, but I was doing some online research yesterday and there's an aquapark about half an hour's drive away.' He grins. 'Although, given my woeful sense of direction, it'll probably take us around three hours to get there.'

'An aquapark? Isn't that all flume slides and screaming children?'

'No. This is a natural one. So there's a lake you can swim in if you like, but there are also rowing boats, pedaloes and picnic tables set up around the shore. I talked to Cara yesterday and she's quite happy to put a hamper together for our lunch if we want her to.'

This is enough to seal the deal. Cara's food has definitely been one of the high points of the retreat, so I'm sure whatever she would put together would be rather more spectacular than the slightly sweaty ham and cheese sandwiches we used to have on picnics as children.

'Sure,' I tell him as we start to make our way down the drive. 'Why not? I might even bring my swimming costume. There's just one thing though.'

'What?'

'Would it be better if I drove?'

He laughs. 'Knock yourself out.'

* * *

'This was a superb idea,' I say to Finn as we set up a kind of base camp at one of the picnic tables in the park the next morning. Although I say so myself, the drive over was considerably less alarming than the brief journey I endured with Finn behind the wheel on the day he arrived. Something seems to have clicked in my brain so, not only did I stay on the right side of the road all the way, but there were no attempts to change gear with the wrong hand either. The only downside was that I was concentrating so hard that I didn't get to enjoy the view, which Finn kept telling me was spectacular.

The park itself is just as he described. I don't know whether the lake is natural or man-made, but it blends perfectly into its surroundings. The area around it is mainly neatly mown grass, with mature trees providing shade for the picnic tables. We're early enough that it's not particularly busy yet, but there are already a few people in the water and a couple of boats out in the middle of the lake.

'Do you think our stuff will be all right here?' Finn asks as he carefully places the cool box that Cara has packed for us out of the sun. She's also given us swimming towels and special aqua shoes to stop us hurting our feet in case the bottom of the lake turns out to be rocky.

'Yeah,' I tell him as I slip off my shoes, enjoying the sensation of the cool grass underfoot. 'Lots of the other tables have stuff by them, see?'

He glances around and seems reassured. 'OK,' he says. 'So what I thought was maybe we should take a boat out before it gets too hot, and then we can swim to cool down later if we need to.'

'You've really put a lot of planning into this, haven't you?'

'A little,' he admits. 'It's been nice, actually. Something other than my non-existent show to think about, for a change. I had this image in my mind of you relaxing in the back of the boat with a glass of champagne while I rowed you.'

'Very *Brideshead Revisited*,' I say with a laugh. 'Although I probably should have brought a parasol rather than a sun hat to complete the look. A slim volume of poetry would help as well.'

'Good point. Do you like poetry then?'

'No. On second thoughts, it would look like a poetry book but actually be a thriller inside.'

'What about me?'

'Oh, you'd be dressed in linen trousers rather than those shorts, and a long-sleeved shirt with the sleeves rolled up.' To my surprise, an image of Finn dressed exactly like that forms in my mind, and it's far from unpleasant.

'Damn. See, this is what happens when you try to arrange things for authors,' he quips.

'What's that supposed to mean?'

'You've taken my vague idea, instantly coloured in all the detail and the final picture is completely different from the original. Now I feel like a total failure. I mean, what kind of man forgets a parasol and his linen trousers on a trip like this?' He slaps his forehead. 'Shit. I've just realised I've forgotten my full-body woollen bathing costume as well. We're doomed.'

'Are you having a nice time?' I ask him.

He grins. 'I am, actually. Now, despite my abject failures, shall we go and see a man about a boat?'

There's a short queue at the boat hire kiosk, and I'm intrigued by the different ability levels of the other customers as they set off. Some are obviously experienced rowers, pulling away confidently from the jetty and gliding smoothly out towards the middle of the lake, but others are finding it more of a struggle, and one unfortunate guy has veered straight into the bank and appears to be stuck. One of the kiosk staff is shouting instructions to him, but he's either unable to hear or doesn't speak French, as not much seems to be happening.

I turn to Finn. 'Can I ask you a question?'

'Of course.'

'Is your rowing better than that?'

He blushes slightly. 'Umm. It's not something I have much experience in,' he admits. 'But I'm sure I can work it out.'

'Let's take a pedalo.'

'What? I thought we were doing the full 1920s experience.'

'I don't want to rain on your parade, but I'm not sure being repeatedly rammed into the bank and shouted at by irate Frenchmen is really going to conjure up the right vibe. At least we have a vague chance of going in the right direction with a pedalo.'

He sighs. 'You're right. OK, pedalo it is.'

Any final hope of recreating a scene Evelyn Waugh would have been proud of is dashed by the bright orange lifejackets we're given before we're allowed anywhere near the water.

'*Vous devez aller a droite et rester loin des nageurs,*' the attendant tells us firmly as he helps us onto the pedalo.

'*Oui, Monsieur. Merci,*' Finn replies as he lets go of the rope and we start to drift away from the jetty.

'Any idea what he said?' Finn asks as we start to turn the pedals.

'I think we need to keep right and keep away from the *nageurs*, whatever they are?'

'Aren't they clouds?'

'That doesn't make sense though. How would we keep away from the clouds?'

'Snow?'

'No, that's *neige*. Got it. They're swimmers.'

'That makes more sense. How did you figure it out?'

I smile. 'There's a sign over there that says *Nageurs interdit au-delà de ce point*, and there's a picture of a swimmer with a line through. Pretty big clue, wouldn't you say?'

* * *

'So, I did have an idea about your show last night, but it's probably no good,' I tell him some time later. We returned the pedalo once the heat started to build and we're now sitting at our table in the shade with the remnants of Cara's picnic around us, although the word 'picnic' doesn't do any justice to the banquet that we found inside the cool box. As well as the cold meats, pâté and cheese that you'd expect to go with the obligatory baguette, there was a selection of salads, a bottle of white wine that we haven't opened, and some pastries for pudding that wouldn't have looked out of place at Maison Olivia.

'Go on. Any ideas at all are more than welcome.'

'As I said, I'm no auction expert, but Liv is a sucker for *Antiques Roadshow* on TV. We watch it every week when it's on, and it occurred to me that it meets one of your criteria for a game show.'

'I'm not with you.'

'OK, so people bring their stuff to the experts, hoping against hope that the tatty teapot or whatever that they've inherited from Great-Aunt Mildred actually turns out to be worth millions.'

'I'm not sure all of them think like that.'

'Of course they do. You can see it in their eyes on the rare occasion that their junk does actually turn out to be worth something. They say things like "Oh, I could never part with it. It's my only connection to Great-Aunt Mildred", but you can practically hear them thinking, "Yes! I'm totally flogging this at the first opportunity."'

'I'll have to take your word for it. How does this tie in to my show?'

'Have a ringer in each round. So, there was one week when someone brought this really tatty watch to be valued. I mean, the thing looked like it was barely worth a tenner, but it turned out to be some really rare Rolex that was actually worth tens of thousands. So, you include something like that in every round, with some kind of reward or penalty depending on whether the contestants correctly identify it.'

He thinks for a while, tilting his head back and closing his eyes. 'I like it. No, actually, that's genius,' he says with a smile. 'Although I might adapt it slightly, as I think it could be difficult to find something that could do that in every round.'

'What are you thinking?'

'Have one ringer item per episode, like a joker in the pack. The contestants know it will appear at some point, but it could be in any round. If they guess it correctly, it doubles their prize fund, providing they make it to the final round.'

'Potentially expensive.'

'Oh, prize money is the least of the producer's worries on a show like this. The audience will love it too.'

'What about the jeopardy aspect?'

He thinks a little more. 'Firstly, we don't reveal whether any of them have correctly identified the rogue item until the very end. That introduces tension because even the winner won't know in the final round if their fund is going to be doubled or not. Furthermore, if they choose an item that turns out not to be the joker in the pack or don't choose one at all, their prize fund is halved. We could also reveal the item to the audience at home at the start, instructing them to look away if they don't want to know what it is. I'll say it again, Laura. You're a bloody genius. That's absolutely brilliant!'

Before I know what's happening, he's taken my head in his hands and planted a full-on smacker of a kiss on my lips.

'Oh, shit,' he exclaims, suddenly realising what he's done and turning crimson with embarrassment. 'I'm so sorry, I got caught up in the moment.'

'It's fine,' I tell him, eager to defuse the sudden tension in the air. 'I'm just glad I could help.'

What I'm not going to tell Finn is that it's rather more than fine. It's a long time since anyone has kissed me as uncomplicatedly and joyously as that, and I liked it. I liked it a lot.

18

'Are you sure you're OK?' I ask Finn. Although the afternoon has been enjoyable, it hasn't been as relaxed as the morning was. We swam in the lake, which turned out not to be rocky on the bottom after all, and then lay on our towels, letting the afternoon sun bake us dry. On the surface, Finn has been just the same as he always is, but I know him well enough by now to pick up that something is bugging him. We're in the car on the way back to L'Ancien Presbytère but, instead of talking about the view, his show or my book, like he normally would, Finn is uncharacteristically quiet.

'Fine,' he says flatly. 'Just, you know, thinking.'

'Do you want to share? Is it something to do with your show?'

'No.' He sighs deeply. 'Look, can we talk about what happened earlier?'

So that's what this is about. 'Do you mean when you kissed me?'

'Yes. I know you said it was fine, but it wasn't, was it. I really like you, Laura, and I love spending time with you, and I'm just worried this thing is going to hang in the air and ruin the rest of our retreat.'

'Why would it do that? It's a kiss, Finn. It's not like you groped me or anything.' I risk a glance away from the road down at his hands, clenched tightly in his lap. He's got nice hands. They may be soft, but I bet they'd feel incredible against my skin. I do generally go for more manly men, but gnarly hands are a bit of a turn-off. I'm horrified to find that the thought of Finn putting his hands on me is actually rather nice, and hurriedly switch my attention back to the road.

'I know, but I crossed a line. I really am sorry, Laura. I'm not that kind of man, honestly. I don't know what came over me. It was a moment of madness, that's all I can say... *What are you doing?*'

I've swerved off the road onto the verge, braking hard and causing the Fiat to skid a little, kicking up a cloud of dust as we come to a stop.

'For God's sake,' I growl as I take his face in my hands and lean towards him, planting an equally, if not slightly more, full-on kiss on his lips.

'Right,' I tell him firmly once I've released him. 'That's one all. Better now?'

'What was that for?' he asks as I put the car back into gear and ease out onto the road.

'I don't know. To say thank you for all your help with my plotting. To stop you torturing yourself. Because I wanted to. Any of those do?'

'You *wanted* to,' he repeats in a slightly stunned voice.

'Yes. It doesn't have to mean anything. I'm not expecting you to propose, just because I kissed you. But if it stops you beating yourself up and brings you back out of yourself, then that's a good thing. Let me ask you this. When you kissed me, were you coming on to me, or was it just a physical expression of the joy you felt at unlocking the secret of your show?'

He laughs and, to my relief, it's a genuine one that seems to come from the core of him, rather than the more superficial laughs I've had so far this afternoon.

'Oh, Laura,' he breathes. 'I'd never dare come on to you.'

'What? Why not? I'm not that revolting, am I?'

He obviously realises his mistake, as his expression turns serious. 'Quite the reverse. You're so far out of my league that I probably wouldn't have dared speak to you that first morning if I hadn't been desperate.'

I don't think anyone has ever described me as out of their league before and, although I know he means it as a compliment, it's caught me completely by surprise. I'm most honestly described as 'incredibly average'. There's a scene in one of my favourite books by Jane Austen where the Morland family are described rather scathingly as having 'heads and arms and legs enough for the number', and that's what I would say about myself. I'm not hideous, but I'm certainly never going to be scouted to be a model.

'I think you need to reassess your league,' I tell him with a smile.

He says nothing, but I'm aware of him staring at me. 'What?' I ask eventually.

'You're either delusional and genuinely have no idea how attractive you are, or you're fishing for compliments,' he says. 'I'm just trying to work out which it is.'

'And you patently need glasses,' I retort. 'Now, stop staring at me. You're putting me off my driving.'

Although he does as instructed, and returns his gaze to looking out of the windscreen, the atmosphere in here has clearly shifted again. He's no longer miserable, which is a good thing, but my mind is a whirlwind. Finn is, on paper at least, not at all the kind of man I would normally go for, so why has him telling me he finds me attractive got me all stirred up? Today has been a weird day: First there was the way the whole mental image of him when we were talking about the rowing boat made me feel, then him kissing me, me kissing him back, and the strangely erotic thoughts that I had when I was looking at his hands just now. To be fair, Angus wasn't my normal type either, and we lasted ten years despite his hands being nowhere near as nice as Finn's. Oh, get a grip, for goodness' sake, Laura. This is a moment of madness, probably caused by spending too much time in the sun. Stop reading more into it than there is.

I'm relieved when we pull up outside L'Ancien Presbytère. The majority of the journey after Finn's revelation was silent, which is most unlike us, but we've both been lost in our thoughts. I did try to get inside Finn's head a couple of times, but he wasn't having it. I suspect he's concerned that he's over-stepped the mark again, but there's nothing I can do to reassure him if he's not prepared to talk about it. For my part, I've been trying to mentally reset our relationship in my mind. I realised very early on that I'd like to stay friends with Finn after the retreat ends, but I've never even considered the possibility of anything more than that before today. Should I? Is he? One thing is for certain. I need to talk to Liv as soon as I've showered off the sunscreen and changed into fresh clothes.

* * *

'You're a mind reader,' I say into the handset. I barely had time to wrap my hair and body in towels before my phone rang. A glance at the caller ID told me it was Liv. 'I was just going to call you.'

'Really? Why?'

'I need your advice on something.'

'Sounds interesting. Go on.'

'So, you know Finn, who I told you about?'

'The TV guy you're pally with, yes.'

'I'm wondering if perhaps it's more than pally.' I tell her about everything that happened today and she listens so quietly that I have to check the screen hasn't frozen a couple of times.

'Hmm,' is all she says when I finish.

'That's not very helpful, Liv!' I exclaim. 'I was hoping for a bit more than that.'

'OK, let me summarise. This guy arrives at your retreat. You don't fancy him physically, but he turns out to be a nice guy and you enjoy his company.'

'Yes.'

'That's got friendzone written all over it. But now, after a couple of PG-rated kisses and him telling you that you're attractive, you're all hot under the collar.'

'I think "hot under the collar" might be overstating it.'

'Did you take shrunk-in-the-wash Goliath with you on this retreat?'

'What's that got to do with anything?'

'I'm just wondering if you're pent up, sexually, and that's clouding your judgement. What stage of your cycle are you at?'

'I'm not pent up and I'm not mid-cycle either. He's not physically *un*attractive, I just tend to go for men who are rather more well-built than him. It's his personality that I like most.'

'And his hands.' She laughs. 'To be fair, Angus was hardly a beefcake, was he? Maybe you're secretly attracted to scrawny men, but just haven't had the lady-balls to admit it to yourself yet.'

'Finn isn't scrawny, he's just not especially muscly either.'

'There's more to men than their muscles. At least, the good ones. Let's look at this from another perspective. You could hold out for Mr Beefcake, but what is that going to get you beyond an admittedly attractive physique? In my opinion, beefcakes tend to come with a raft of unnatural habits, like gyms and protein shakes. What's wrong with a walk or run in the fresh air and proper food? I may be generalising here, but I suspect a lot of them rely on their muscles to disguise the fact that they're actually monumentally dull, personality wise. It's very rare to find someone who's the complete package.'

'Henry Cavill is the complete package,' I counter. 'When he smiles, it does things to me.'

'He's also over ten years older than you, with a partner and baby in tow.'

'If any of my books ever get made into films, I'm going to demand they cast him in a leading role,' I tell her, undeterred.

'And that's your prerogative. But you'll never get any further than admiring him from afar. Let's return to planet Earth for a moment, shall we? Leave the geriatric gym addicts alone.'

'He's not geriatric, and what makes you think he's a gym addict?'

'You don't get a physique like that without putting in the effort. I bet he spends all day in the there, drinking protein shakes and working out. Anyway, Finn. How did you feel when he kissed you?'

'Surprised, mainly.'

'So not disgusted or revolted. You didn't want to brush your teeth immediately or slap him?'

'It was just a normal kiss, Liv. There wasn't any tongue.'

'I know that, but even normal kisses can be revolting. There was this guy I thought I was attracted to once, but as soon as he kissed me for the first time, I knew nothing was going to happen. He had fishy breath, like cat food. I nearly threw up in his face. It doesn't sound like Finn was like that.'

'No. There was nothing wrong with it at all.'

'And then you kissed him back.'

'Yes, but only to stop him beating himself up. I thought it would help him see that I wasn't offended.'

'Interesting approach. And how was that one?'

'It was nice.'

'Nice? That's all you've got?'

'Yes. It was a couple of seconds, maximum, Liv. We're not talking snogging here.'

'OK, but these two very normal, apparently nice kisses have sent you into a spin. What does that tell you?'

'I don't know! That's why I'm asking you.'

'I think it's pretty simple. Finn's basically admitted that he's into you, so I think the choice is yours. Either you dismiss what happened today and go back to not fancying him—'

'But how do I do that without ruining our friendship?' I interrupt. 'I do like him, Liv.'

'Or,' she continues as if I hadn't spoken, 'you jump his bones and see where it goes.'

'I think we're a long way from bone jumping. What would you do?'

'Oh, I'd jump his bones. It's one of Liv's lessons for life.'

'Dare I ask?'

'It's much easier to live with the regret of something you did than something you failed to do.'

I grin in spite of myself. 'You're like Descartes and Confucius all rolled into one. Anyway, enough about me. How are things with you? Any progress on the Donna situation?'

Now it's Liv's turn to smile. 'There might be. We're going out for a drink tomorrow.'

'Ooh. How do you feel about that?'

'Well, she said yes when I asked her. That's got to be a good sign, I reckon. She absolutely adores Meg, by the way.'

'So she should. But have you got anything in common with her besides your mutual love for my fabulous dog?'

'That's what I intend to find out. Don't you worry about me, honey. I know exactly how to play this. You focus on you and whatever this thing with Finn might or might not be. I'll catch up with you soon, yeah?'

As we end the call, I think about what she's said. The thing with Liv is that she makes perfect sense when you're talking to her, but it's only afterwards that you start to realise the massive holes in her seemingly impenetrable logic.

Oh, God. I'm no further forward at all, and I still don't have the faintest idea what to do.

19

DI Harrison was tired and, to top it all, she could feel the beginnings of a migraine coming on. Her desk was right next to the window, which combined with the inadequate heating and ventilation of the police station to ensure that she consistently froze in winter and boiled in summer. Today was typical; the hot sun had blasted her relentlessly from the moment she'd arrived this morning, and was undoubtedly a contributing factor to the pain building in her head.

'Have you got a minute, Ma'am?' She looked up as DS Rogers spoke. Unlike her, he looked crisp and comfortable in his shirtsleeves and tie. Maybe she should pull rank and get him to swap desks with her. The problem was that the window desk was seen by everyone as the best one because it came with a view, even if said view was only over the car park, and her complaints about the temperature had fallen on totally deaf ears. On the one occasion that the sun was so strong she'd closed the blind, there was such an outcry from the other occupants of the office that she'd been forced to open it again.

'Sure, what's up?'

'We've had a call from uniform. There's a crime scene they'd like us to go and look at.'

So much for her plan to slip away early and spend the rest of the day in the cool darkness of her bedroom, with a box of paracetamol and a jug of iced water. She rummaged in her desk drawer for the box that she kept in there, only to find an empty blister pack inside. Great.

'Fine,' she sighed as she got to her feet. 'Let's go. You're driving though, OK?'

Although I'm trying hard to concentrate and the words are coming, after a fashion, my mind is firmly on the situation with Finn. We walked into Saint-Antonin-Noble-Val as usual this morning and, on the face of things at least, everything seemed normal. We chatted about both his show and the next part of my story. But something was off. An elephant has crept into the room and it seems neither of us quite know what to do with it. The moments of exuberance yesterday have passed and, although I certainly want to talk about what happened, I'm still processing how I feel about him and my conversation with Liv. He also doesn't seem in any rush to talk about anything other than our usual subjects, so I don't have a clue what's going on in his head either.

I try to immerse myself back into the story, but I'm disturbed by the ringing of my phone. I'm surprised to see it's Liv, and my heart misses a beat. Something must be wrong for her to be calling during the day when she'd normally be at work, and my instant thought is that it's to do with Meg.

'Hi, Liv, what's up?' I ask, trying to keep my voice light.

'Sorry to call you, but I've got a bit of a situation here,' she says, her voice tense.

'Is Meg all right?'

'She's fine. It's, umm, Angus.'

'Angus?'

'He's here.'

'What's he doing there?'

'I'm looking for you, what do you think?' The voice and accent are familiar, but I'm surprised by the anger that surges through me on hearing him and his critical tone.

'Why?' I ask.

'Because I came back to find someone else in our flat, my dog missing, you nowhere to be found and I couldn't help wondering what the hell was going on. I tried to call you but it kept saying number unobtainable.'

'I've moved out of the flat, Angus.'

'Where's all my stuff?'

'Storage. Pay me the back rent on the unit and I'll happily give you the key so you can go and get it.'

'And Meg?'

'Doggy daycare.'

'So you just dumped her on some stranger?' He sounds outraged. 'Tell me where she is and I'll go and get her.'

'No, Angus, you won't,' I tell him firmly. 'What are you doing? Why aren't you on the cruise ship?'

'It's a break between voyages. I thought I'd come home, but it seems you've decided to cut me completely out of your life. Where the hell are you, anyway?'

'France. On a writing retreat.'

'What? But you always said you'd rather drill holes in your head than go on one of those.'

'Yes, well, I changed my mind.'

'It seems like you've changed your mind on a lot of things since I've been gone.'

'Don't try to play the wounded innocent here, Angus. You were the one that walked out. I'm just trying to make the best of my life, OK?'

'But Meg—'

'Meg is absolutely fine. Liv's taking good care of her and she's enjoying the daycare. I'm not having you pitching up out of the blue and unsettling her, do you understand? Liv, are you still there?'

'Yes,' Liv's voice says. 'Kind of hard not to be, given that Angus is in my kitchen.'

'Whatever you do, don't let him anywhere near Meg, OK? She's just starting to get used to life without him, and I'm not having him waltz back into her life only to waltz out again and set her back.'

'Understood.'

'You can't do that,' Angus says, sounding mutinous. 'She's my dog just as much as she is yours.'

'No, she isn't. You walked out on both of us, and with that you forfeited any rights you think you have. I mean it, Angus. You're to stay away from her.'

'So that's it, is it? Just like that, you've moved on.'

'Can you hear yourself?' I ask in disbelief. '*You* left, Angus. What did you expect me to do?'

'I just thought the ten years we had together might have meant a bit more to you than they did. Evidently, I was wrong.'

'You're fucking unbelievable, you know that?' My temper has finally deserted me. 'You made it abundantly clear that we were over when you buggered off. And now you come back and dare to challenge me because I've moved on with my life? Fuck off, Angus. Leave me alone, leave Liv alone and, above all, leave Meg alone. You're not welcome, do you understand?'

'And where am I supposed to go, exactly? That flat was my home too.'

'I honestly don't give a shit. Like I said, you can collect your stuff from storage whenever you like, once you pay the back rent on it, and then you can fuck off back to Glasgow for all I care.'

'Wow. You really hate me, don't you?' His voice has lost its petulant tone and he just sounds sad all of a sudden.

'Do you blame me?'

He sighs. 'I guess not. For what it's worth, I'm sorry, Laura.'

'It's a bit late for that, Angus.'

'Well, good luck with everything, yeah? Give my love to Meg when you see her.'

In spite of myself, I can't help wishing him luck as well before we end the call, but I'm fuming as I put the handset back on the table. Did he honestly think he'd come back after all this time and find me waiting for him? What an arrogant prick. After a couple of minutes, I grab the handset again and call Liv back.

'Has he gone?' I ask her when the call connects.

'Yup. He looked like he'd had the stuffing knocked out of him.'

'Serves him right. I can't believe he did that, and I'm so sorry you got caught up in it.'

'Oh, don't worry about me. Drama like this is like water off a duck's back.'

'Don't let him anywhere near Meg, OK? I meant what I said. She'll be so excited if she sees him, and then it will break her heart all over again when he goes.'

'Laura, I love her, but once again I think you're giving her more complex emotions than she actually has.'

'Remember how she moped when he first went?'

'OK, fine. I'll call Donna and make sure she doesn't let anyone other than me collect or see Meg. I don't think she would, but if it puts your mind at rest.'

'It does. Thanks, Liv. And good luck for tonight. Keep me posted.'

'I will. What about you? What have you decided about the enigmatic Finn?'

I sigh. 'I don't know. He doesn't seem to want to talk about it, and I haven't found a way to broach the subject either.'

She laughs softly. 'It seems you're quite the siren lately with all these men fighting over you.'

'They're hardly fighting, Liv. I still can't believe Angus thought he was just going to pick up where he left off.'

'Yes, I admit that was odd.'

'And Finn? I have no idea what he's thinking.'

'You need to talk to him. Don't let this fester. Do it now.'

'I don't know what to say though, Liv. I've realised he's an attractive man and we've shared a couple of, as you put it, PG-rated kisses. That doesn't mean we have a future.'

'You definitely won't have a future if you don't talk to him. What's the worst that can happen?'

'Another disaster?'

'Look. Angus is behaving like a tit, we can both agree on that. But don't write off an entire ten years as a disaster just because it ended. Shit happens, Laura. People you thought were going to stay together for life unexpectedly divorce after years of marriage. It doesn't mean the marriage was a disaster, just that it's run its course. Maybe you and Finn have a future and maybe you don't. But remember Liv's life lesson.'

'It's always better to regret something you've done than something you haven't,' I parrot.

'Exactly. Now, go and talk to him, OK? I've got to get back to work. Love you.'

'Love you too.'

When she ends the call, I sit for a while just staring into space. It's easy for Liv to say 'just talk to him', but the risk of getting it wrong and just making things incredibly awkward is huge and, quite apart from the fact that I really enjoy Finn's company, I don't want to lose my only ally here.

Once more, I try to get my head back into the story, but it's no good. The conversation with Angus has thoroughly unsettled me, and I'm not going to get any work done until I've decompressed from that, at least. And then there's the conversation I know I need to have with Finn. Liv may like to trot out her little sayings, but do I really have the courage to tell Finn how I feel, especially when I'm not completely sure myself? I think the last time I actually took the reins and told a boy I liked him was in secondary school. I shudder as I cast my mind back. I was so sure he was as into me as I was him, but he just looked really embarrassed and tried to let me down gently. Ugh. There's no way I could go through that again.

But then, what if Liv is right? There was all that stuff in the car where he said I was out of his league and had no idea how attractive I was. That must mean he's attracted to me, mustn't it? I try to picture myself in a relationship with him, and it's actually not that hard. I mean, I can't imagine what having sex with him would be like, but that's mainly because the idea of having sex with anyone new fills me with anxiety. Shit. Maybe Liv is right and I am repressed.

I sigh. Whatever happens, I need to know how he feels. Even if he can't find the words and I have to kiss the truth out of him, I will. Actually, I could do that. Liv may think we're strictly PG, but I enjoyed both of our kisses yesterday. With renewed energy, I get to my feet to go to find him.

To my surprise, Finn's not in his usual spot on the bench in the vegetable garden, so I continue round, checking the other places where tables and chairs have been laid out. Suzie and Grace are in their usual places and shoot me their customary hostile gazes as I pass. I still have no idea what either of them are writing, but their absolute loyalty to Gina means that I'm unlikely to break any ice with either of them while she persists in her hatred of me. However, the next sight I come across does cause me to break my stride. Gina and Lynette are sitting on a bench in the sunlight, apparently engaged in a deep conversation. From their facial expressions, it's not hostile either. Curiosity gets the better of me and I decide to approach.

'Hi,' I say as they look up. 'I don't suppose either of you have seen Finn, have you?'

'I haven't, I'm sorry.' Gina's voice is as unexpected as her expression. There's no animosity in it at all.

'OK, thanks,' I tell her. 'It's nice to see you two seemingly getting along,' I add.

'I'm helping Gina with a scene in her book,' Lynette tells me.

The surprise must show on my face as Gina smiles. 'There's, umm, a liaison,' she explains. 'Tess felt strongly that it could be improved with some input from Lynette and, much as I hate to admit it, she has been extremely useful.'

'The only thing we're struggling with is the terminology. How would the Tudors describe an erection? It's not something I've ever had to think about before.'

'Tumescence?' I offer.

Lynette smiles. 'Nice. The sex itself is fairly straightforward, I think.'

'I agree,' Gina says to her. 'They weren't really into foreplay and he's pretty pent up, so I think a few thrusts and it would all be over.'

'Disappointing for her,' Lynette observes.

'Yes, but there's another place that Tess thought I could perhaps insert a slightly more romantic encounter. If you're interested, we could look at that once we've sorted this bit.'

'Of course. I'd be delighted.'

'I'll leave you to it,' I tell them.

'We'll tell Finn you're looking for him if we see him,' Lynette calls after me.

Today just keeps bringing the surprises, I think as I head for the house. Of all the things I never thought I'd see, Lynette and Gina being civil and working together pretty much tops the list. I don't know how Tess managed to persuade her, but if it's going to thaw the frost between the two of them, that can only be a good thing.

Finn isn't in the library either, so I head for his room, knocking tentatively on the door.

'Who is it?' he calls.

'Me. Can I come in?'

'Sure.'

I open the door, only to find yet another surprise. Finn is sitting at his desk, with a laptop in front of him and papers strewn everywhere. On the bed, his case is open and half-packed.

'What's going on?' I ask.

'I spoke to my agent earlier,' he tells me, his face alive with excitement. 'He's got me a pitching slot.'

'That's brilliant. Congratulations!'

'Yeah. The only problem is it's tomorrow, and I have to have everything ready by then.'

'Tomorrow?' I repeat.

'Yeah. I'm booked on a late flight out of Toulouse tonight. There's just so much to be done, but if there's one thing I've learned about working with TV companies, you don't mess them about. If they offer you a pitching slot, you grab it with both hands.'

'Oh, right.' I'm unable to keep the disappointment out of my voice. 'I was going to suggest a coffee break, but I'll leave you to it.'

'Sorry, Laura.'

Well, I guess that solves that, I think to myself as I go back down the stairs towards the garden. There's no point in opening up about our feelings when he's about to disappear back to London. I'm trying to be pleased for him, but all I can think about is my own sense of disappointment. Maybe it's for the best. I'm supposed to be here to work, after all, not get involved with someone. I need to push these thoughts out of my head and focus on my book.

If only it were that easy. As I head back into the garden, I can't help feeling that I've just missed out on something massive.

20

'Where are we going?' DI Harrison asked as DS Rogers took yet another turn.

'Armley Road,' he replied. 'I don't have all the details, but basically the homeowners were having some chimney repairs done, and the builders discovered a hidden alcove with a body in it. SOCO are there already doing their thing.'

Although the air conditioning was working flat out, DI Harrison still felt sweaty and her head was pounding as the migraine took hold. She wanted nothing more than to retreat to her bed, but she realised this was a crime scene that needed her full attention. She tried to ignore the pain, keeping her expression completely neutral as DS Rogers parked the car and they slipped on their protective overalls. She fought the rising sense of nausea by focusing on her breathing as the uniformed police officers lifted the crime scene tape to allow her and DS Rogers to pass underneath. A group of nosy neighbours were gathered but, after a quick scan, she made a point of ignoring them.

'It's in here, Ma'am,' Terri, one of the Scene of Crime Officers, told her unnecessarily as she entered the hallway. The house was at once familiar and strange. The décor was different, of course, but the layout brought back so many memories. Even if she hadn't known exactly where the body was, the flashing from the camera would have led her to it.

'The builders started to take down this wall,' the photographer explained, indicating the hole they'd obviously punched with their sledge-hammers. 'They found a bag behind it and opened it. I suspect they were hoping for buried treasure, but they got a body instead. I'm just going to do a couple more pictures in situ and then we can bring it out. Did you want to have a quick look before we do that?'

'Thanks, Geoff.'

It wasn't just the migraine that was causing DI Claire Harrison's legs to shake as she crouched down to inspect the hole. Behind her, DS Rogers was engrossed in discussion with Geoff about the crime scene. She looked into the hole in the wall and there was the body bag, instantly recognisable despite its thick coating of dust.

'Hello, Darren,' she whispered.

I lift my eyes from the screen, aware of someone approaching. I've been trying to focus on my work in an attempt to blot out all my conflicted feelings about Finn, Angus and everything else. Although it hasn't been completely successful, I've still managed to lose track of the time and I'm surprised to see, glancing at my phone, that it's nearly six o'clock. My mind's been such a whirlwind that I haven't even remembered to set the alarm to make me get up and move, and I can feel the stiffness in my neck as I raise my head after nearly four hours of staring at my laptop.

'Hiya,' Finn says softly. 'I thought I'd find you here. How's it going?'

'OK. You? All packed and ready?'

'Yeah. I've just settled up with Hugh and I'm about to leave for the airport, but I wanted to come and find you first to say goodbye properly.'

I study his face, trying to see if I can read anything into his expression, but I can't.

'I've really enjoyed getting to know you, Laura,' he continues. 'And I can't thank you enough for what you've done. You've literally saved my show, which means you've saved my career too.'

'It was nothing,' I tell him. 'I'm just glad I could help.' Why is this conversation so stilted?

'You did more than that, trust me.'

'Well, you helped me out of a few plot holes too, so I guess we're even.'

He smiles. 'Thinking of which, there's definitely something weird going on with the others. Gina and Lynette were in the library when I came out, and it looked like they were being nice to each other.'

'Lynette's helping her with some Tudor sex.'

'Not a phrase I think I'd ever have expected to hear before coming here. It's been an eye-opener, that's for sure. I'll miss our walks.'

'Me too.'

'Tell me if this is too presumptuous, but I'd like to keep in touch, is that OK? Can I give you my number?'

'Of course you can. I'd like that.' I hand over my phone and he types in the details. When he's done, I open WhatsApp and send him a series of emojis including smiling face, prayer hands and crossed fingers.

'That's for luck tomorrow,' I tell him. 'Also, you've got my number as well now.'

'Thanks. For everything. And good luck with the Double-Doubles. I feel like I'm abandoning you.'

I get to my feet and wrap him in a brief hug. 'I'll be OK. Don't worry about me. Go and sell your show. Who knows, I might even watch it.'

'If I sell it, I'll invite you to see it being filmed, how about that?'

'I'd like that. I've never been to a TV studio before.'

'I'll see what I can do. Right, I'd better get going.'

I watch as he disappears up the path and into the house. My emotions are conflicted. Should I have told him how I feel? Maybe this is fate telling me it wasn't meant to be. Maybe I've been misreading the signals all along, and this is for the best. It doesn't feel like it's for the best, though, and I'm dreading telling Liv. She's bound to have plenty to say on the subject.

* * *

'So, he just upped and left?' Liv's voice is predictably cross when I tell her the next morning. I'm out walking on my own. It feels weird without Finn next to me, but I was awake and didn't fancy lurking around the house. 'Thanks for digging me out of a hole but I'm off?'

'I think you're being a bit harsh. It seems like these pitching slots are super rare, so you don't mess about if you're offered one.'

'Hm. Just seems like very bad karma to me. Angus pitches up here, upsetting the status quo, and somehow your new guy gets summoned back to London on the very same day? Who have you been upsetting?'

'Nobody. I'm sure there's nothing supernatural going on, Liv. It's just the way these things pan out sometimes. Anyway, enough of my woes. Tell me about Donna. How was the drink?'

Her smile is so wide it tells me all I need to know before she opens her mouth.

'It went well then,' I observe.

'Brilliantly. Honestly, I just felt like we connected on so many levels. It turns out she did quite a bit of travelling when she was younger as well, and we think we might actually have been in Cambodia at the same time. What are the odds of that, eh?'

'So you'll be seeing her again?'

'Tonight. She's coming round for dinner.'

'I'll give you this, Liv. You don't hang around, do you?'

'What's the point? If I like her and she likes me, let's not waste time playing games.'

'Well, I just hope you have more success than me.'

'Mm. I will admit to being disappointed for you. This Finn guy sounded promising. At least you've got his contact details so you can stay in touch. Maybe he's more of a slow burn, and something will happen when he invites you to the filming.'

'If he invites me. He hasn't even sold the show yet, and there won't be any filming to invite me to if he doesn't.'

'Then you invite him to your book launch.'

'I don't have book launches, as you know. The closest I get is the glass of champagne Ruby gives me when I go to her shop to sign the first batch of a new novel. I'm starting to wonder if I imagined the whole connection. He's definitely been odd since we kissed. Maybe he didn't like it, and he's secretly relieved that he's got this excuse to leave early.'

'I don't think so.'

'Uh-oh. Is this a Liv "certainty" coming on?'

'No. But he didn't back off because he thought you were a pity party, did he? He backed off because, and I quote, you were out of his league. That's a pretty powerful statement.'

'I still think that was an odd thing to say. I mean, I'd understand if I looked like Kendall Jenner, but I don't.'

'Beauty is in the eye of the beholder, Laura. You're obviously his type. And I bet even Kendall Jenner is wracked with insecurity about some aspect of her body. It comes as part of the whole "being female" thing.'

'Maybe he was trying to say that I intimidate him in some way. Nobody wants to feel like that.'

She laughs. 'Apart from your frank exchange of views with Angus yesterday, I don't think anyone could call you intimidating.'

'He hasn't bothered you again?'

'No. I think he got the message loud and clear. So, what's your plan for the rest of the retreat then, now you don't have Finn to entertain you?'

I sigh. 'I don't know. Keep my head down, I guess. I did wonder about coming home early too, but I've paid for the two weeks and I am making good progress with the book.'

'There's only another five days. I'm sure even you can tolerate the witches for that long. What does Finn call them?'

'The Double-Doubles.'

'Yeah, them. Steer clear of the cauldron, don't accept any food or drink that they might have put potions in and I'm sure you'll be fine.'

'Thanks. If I ever want encouragement, I know where to come.'

When I reach the bridge that Finn and I have used as our turning point, I stop and lean against the parapet, breathing deeply and taking in the view. I am surprised how much I'm missing him already, and he's only been gone for a few hours.

'*Toute seule?*' a voice says from next to me, and I turn in surprise to see the same old lady we met on our first walk here together.

'*Oui,*' I tell her.

'*Où est ton copain?*' She must sense my incomprehension, as she tries again. '*Ton petit ami?*'

She's obviously talking about Finn. '*Il est parti,*' I tell her, hoping that my schoolgirl French is enough to make myself understood. '*Il est allé en Angleterre. Travail.*' I shrug my shoulders in a kind of 'That's life, but what can you do' way that I hope is suitably Gallic.

She sighs and pats my hand, and I feel the need to try to clarify the situation with her, which is odd given that I don't know her at all and my French is surely not up to the task. What was the word she used?

'*Ce n'est pas mon copain*,' I tell her. '*C'est juste un ami*.'

To my surprise, she bursts out laughing. Oh, shit. Maybe I've said it wrong and told her something that sounds totally inappropriate instead. That would be just my luck.

'*Oh, chérie*,' she breathes once she's calmed down. '*Je suis une vieille dame et j'ai vu beaucoup de choses dans ma vie. Pensez-vous que je ne peux pas reconnaître deux personnes qui vont ensemble?*'

This is too much, and I have to admit defeat. '*Je suis désolé. Je ne comprends pas*,' I tell her after wracking my brains for the words.

'You and this boy. You belong together,' she says in heavily accented English. 'I saw it in, *comment le dit-on*, how you were.'

'You speak English?'

'A very little. Like your French, I think, *hein*? But we do not need to speak the same language to understand love. *L'amour, c'est un langue universal, non?*'

'You think Finn and I are in love?'

'*Bien sûr*. You may not see it yet, but it is there. *C'est comme une graine. Il suffit de l'arroser et de le regarder grandir*. Like a plant, you know? Some plants, they grow very quickly but are not strong. *Les Arbres*, trees, they grow more slowly but they last. You and your friend are like that.'

I smile at her, unsure what else to do. '*Merci*, I think,' I tell her. She's read way more into the situation than can possibly have been there, given that Finn and I had only just met when we saw her last, but I don't have the heart to tell her that I think she's probably mistaken. I have no idea what kind of relationship Finn and I will have going forwards, but the more I think about it, the more I think that yesterday was probably our moment, and we missed it.

I'm philosophical as I make my way back to the house. Maybe I just let myself get carried away because I enjoyed spending time with Finn so much. Would our bubble have translated into the real world? We're both creative people, I suppose, but is that a good thing in a relationship? Part of the reason that Angus and I worked as well as we did was that he was the steady one, with a solid job that allowed me to take risks and pursue my writing dream. Liv may believe it's always better to regret something you did than something you didn't do, but maybe, sometimes, it's better this way around.

21

It's impossible not to pick up on the atmosphere as I make my way in to breakfast. The seating arrangement has changed, for one thing. Gina and Lynette are sitting next to each other, chatting quietly, and Suzie has been forced to move down to make room. From her facial expression, she's far from happy about that. To be fair, Grace doesn't exactly look ecstatic either, and she hasn't even been bumped from her usual spot. Next to her, Tess is quietly sipping a cup of coffee and seemingly ignoring the torrent of non-verbal tension in the room.

'Is it all right if I sit next to you?' I ask Suzie.

'Come to join the mortals now your little playmate has left?' she replies sarcastically.

'On second thoughts, maybe I'll sit at the end where I normally do,' I tell her, backing away. I'm not in any mood for barbed remarks today.

'No, it's fine,' she says with a sigh. 'Sorry. I expect you're missing Finn, aren't you?'

'A little, yes.'

'Come,' she instructs. 'Sit next to me. Gina's obsessed with her new friend, so I could use some conversation.'

'Thanks a lot!' Grace complains. 'You make it sound like I've been completely ignoring you as well.'

'Of course you haven't,' Suzie soothes her. 'But I'm aware none of us have really given Laura a chance, and I'm just wondering if perhaps we should, that's all.'

Grace's facial expression is enough to tell me what she thinks of that idea, and it's not positive. I'm also a little suspicious of Suzie's motives, so resolve to keep my guard up.

'I've never asked you what you write,' I say to her as I take my seat and Cara, used to our preferences by now, places a steaming coffee in front of me.

'I'm working on a saga,' she tells me.

'Like Gina's?'

'No, twentieth century. Basically, it follows three generations of the same family through the pre-war era, and then the two world wars, showing how they're affected by the tremendous social upheaval that took place during that time.'

'Wow. That sounds like a big project.'

'It is, particularly as I don't get that much time to work on it when I'm at home. These retreats are literally the only opportunities I get to immerse myself fully in it. I love my family, but they are time hogs. How do you manage it?'

'My family consists solely of a dog,' I tell her with a smile. 'As long as she gets her walk, she's pretty easy.'

She leans in conspiratorially. 'I probably shouldn't admit this in front of Gina, but I've read all of your books and I love them.'

This does catch me by surprise. 'Really?'

'Oh, yes. Who can resist a gritty murder plot? Tell me though, why write as a man?'

As I explain the publisher's rationale to her, I become aware that the other conversation around the table has stopped.

'That's ridiculous,' Gina declares crossly when I've finished. 'My husband reads lots of books written by women.'

'She's right,' Tess tells her. 'Your husband is an exception, I fear.'

'Really? Maybe I should resubmit my book as Gerald,' she muses.

'But you've already got a publisher lined up,' Grace reminds her. 'You've made it.'

To her credit, Gina does have the grace to look a little uncomfortable, and I notice Lynette's mouth twitch up. They may have buried the hatchet, but it seems there is still a little bit of residual rivalry there.

'Yes, the great Florianus,' Lynette says, flashing a grin. 'You were lucky to land a deal with them, weren't you?'

'I was, but there's never any harm in aiming higher,' Gina says, evidently trying to deflect Lynette. 'Florianus are lovely, but quite small in the grand scheme of things. And, with Tess's edits and your, umm, more *florid* scenes, it might be worth me scoping out some bigger players for a wider audience.'

Lynette obviously feels she's pushed her sister as far as she dares without hostilities breaking out once again, as she focuses back on her breakfast.

'Actually, I do have some news on that front,' Tess says to Gina. 'I know you've found the edits hard, but I was having a chat with a friend of mine last night, and I happened to mention your book. She's an agent and she's offered to have a look at the first three chapters with a view to submission if you're interested. She has a number of authors contracted to the big five, so it might prove fruitful.'

Gina looks like all her Christmases have come at once. 'Really?'

'Yes. Don't look so surprised. It's a good book. It just needed slimming down a little. Nobody's making any promises here, but it's got to be worth a try, unless you're completely tied into this Florianus crowd.'

'No, not tied at all,' Gina tells her, beaming. 'I have complete freedom.'

'Then that's something to consider. Now, how is everyone else getting on? Suzie, Grace, anything to show me?'

'No,' they chorus.

'And Laura has her own editor, so it looks like another quiet morning in the garden for me. If any of you need me, you know where I am.' She pushes back her chair and heads in the direction of the bedrooms.

'That's amazing news,' Grace says sycophantically to Gina as soon as Tess has left the room. 'I'm so pleased for you. Maybe, if they're not going to be publishing you, Florianus might be looking for another author. You don't happen to have the details of their submissions department, do you, Gina?'

Gina looks uncomfortable, clearly trying to find a way out of this hole without revealing Florianus's secret, to Lynette's evident delight.

'They're, umm, rather specialised in what they publish,' Gina says after a brief pause. 'I'm not sure you'd be a good fit.'

'I'm happy to take my chances,' Grace persists.

'That's as may be,' Gina replies, her tone now frosty. She's obviously keen to shut this down as quickly as possible. 'But I think they're currently closed to submissions. They literally only opened for a few days and, by all accounts, they were swamped. I guess I was just lucky.'

'That you were,' Lynette observes drily, earning herself a sharp look from her sister. Maybe the hatchet isn't totally buried after all, and this is just a temporary ceasefire.

'All I'm saying is maybe you could put in a word,' Grace says, clearly unwilling to let it go.

'I'm really not sure that would do any good,' Gina replies curtly, pushing back her chair and standing up. 'You need to find your own feet in this world, Grace, not rely on others to pull you up. Lynette, shall we?'

As the two sisters leave the dining room together, Grace leans across the table to Suzie and me.

'I know we've been friends for ages,' she murmurs crossly, 'but she's been completely up herself since she got this deal. I don't mind saying that I'm really starting to hate her. "You need to find your own feet, Grace."' She parrots Gina's voice. 'Well, fuck off, Gina.'

I'm unable to keep my eyebrows from shooting up. Until now, I'd thought Suzie and Grace's loyalty to Gina was unwavering.

'Don't look like that, Laura,' Grace continues. 'You can't possibly like her either. She's basically dismissed your writing as doggerel from the moment you arrived.'

'I don't really have any opinions either way,' I lie, causing Suzie to snort with laughter.

'Good try,' she says. 'But I can smell the bullshit. I'm still not completely sure what it is about you that winds her up so much. I mean, you've done nothing to antagonise her beyond being successful, but she can't seem to forgive you for that. I'm with Grace. I think Gina might need to find herself some new friends unless she gets over herself. This whole Florianus thing has gone straight to her head.'

* * *

DI Harrison felt...

What? What did DI Harrison feel? Come on, Laura. The body of the man she murdered and, with the help of her now deceased father, bricked up in an alcove twenty years ago has just been discovered. She's going to be all over the place, worrying about whether there's any evidence she might have over-looked that could tie her back to Darren, and reliving his past abuse. So what did she *feel*?

With a sigh, I delete the words. It's no good. I can't concentrate today. It's nothing to do with the shift in power dynamics among the Double-Doubles, although it was nice to have a semi-civilised conversation with Suzie and Grace for a change. I can't get Finn out of my head. I never asked him what time his pitch was, but all I can think about is him getting ready for it. He'll be going over his presentation, running his hand distractedly through his hair in the way he does when he's absorbed in something. His eyes will be alight with enthusiasm and it wouldn't surprise me if his mouth is twitching, half forming the words as he reads through the text of his submission. I really hope he lands it. Picking up my phone, I open WhatsApp and send a short message.

> Thinking of you today. Good luck. xx

I watch the screen for a while but, although I can see it's been delivered, the ticks don't turn blue. He's probably in the zone, or maybe he's already in there. I try to picture the scene. A large room full of corporate types in grey suits, with Finn in the middle, pitching for all he's worth.

'Just keep the speed down,' I murmur, as if he could actually hear me. 'They won't follow you if you get carried away and talk too fast.'

It's become clear to me that I'm not going to get anything done until I hear from him. I need something to distract me, so wander in the direction of the house.

'Everything OK?' Cara asks as I approach the terrace, where she's laying out the usual sumptuous array of pastries.

'Yes. I think I'm going to go out today. Hugh recommended a couple of places to visit when I arrived, but I'll confess I can't remember what they were.'

'The obvious one is Cordes-sur-Ciel,' she tells me. 'But I'd avoid that. Pretty as it is, it's a terrible tourist trap and parking is a nightmare. If I were you, I'd head for Castelnau-de-Montmiral. It's gorgeous and much less touristy. If you're feeling brave, you could continue on into Gaillac for lunch. There are a number of good restaurants there. I'll give you a list if you like.'

'Thanks.'

I can't resist helping myself to a pastry while Cara grabs leaflets and writes down addresses on a piece of paper. I wonder briefly whether I should invite Tess to come with me, but decide in the end that I'm not feeling especially sociable. I'd rather just let my mind wander where it wants as I take in the scenery, and having to make conversation will feel like a chore. Hopefully, I'll get some inspiration and be able to concentrate when I get back.

Oh, who am I fooling? I know exactly what I'm going to be thinking about all day, and it's not going to be Claire's predicament.

God, I hope I do hear from Finn. I never asked him to tell me how it went, and he might be so caught up in what he's doing that he forgets to let me know. As I bundle my stuff into the car, I send him another message.

> Let me know how you get on. xx

Right, enough now. Stop harassing the poor boy, Laura.

22

Although Castelnau-de-Montmiral was gorgeous, just as Cara described, Gaillac proved to be rather busier, traffic-wise, than I was prepared for, and I sighed with relief when I finally found a parking space where I could abandon the car and continue my exploration on foot. I haven't heard anything from Finn, but my stomach is growling with hunger so I'm currently trying to find a bistro that Cara said is one of her and Hugh's favourites. According to her, the *Tartare de boeuf Limousin* is to die for but, although I'd consider myself reasonably adventurous where food is concerned – you can't be a wallflower about these things in Liv's house – I'm unsure whether a plate of raw beef is going to do it for me today. However, Cara assured me that they've tried a number of things there, and they've all been excellent, so I'm going to treat myself.

As I follow the instructions from the navigation app on my phone, I can't help feeling a tinge of pride. Here I am, finding my own way about in a foreign country and, so far, nothing has gone wrong. The hire car is still the same shape as when I picked it up. I'm definitely feeling more confident with it, and I'm now making my way through the narrow streets like a local, albeit one with a disembodied English voice shouting directions from her pocket.

The restaurant, when I get there, is exactly what I was hoping for. The menu is written out on large blackboards leaning against the windows, and a number of diners are already seated at the outdoor tables. I listen carefully and the only language I can hear is French, which is a plus, I reckon. If the locals eat here, it must be good. A waitress is bustling backwards and forwards with carafes of wine, baskets of fresh bread and plates piled high with all manner of delicious-looking food. At the tables, the customers appear to be in no rush, savouring their lunches as they debate whatever the issue of the day is. As if on cue, my stomach growls again, loudly this time.

Thankfully, my French extends just far enough for me to explain that I'd rather sit outside – *à l'extérieur* got the message across – and to navigate the menu. I was initially tempted to try the *Andouilette* sausages and messaged Liv to ask about them, but her response that they could be challenging, aroma-wise, was enough to put me off so I've gone for a chicken dish instead. As I wait for my food to arrive, I tilt my head up towards the sun and enjoy the hubbub of conversation around me, so I don't immediately notice my phone pinging to tell me that I have a new message. When I do pick it up, I'm excited to see that it's from Finn.

> Pitch went really well, thanks. The channel seem enthusiastic about the concept and they're going to take it to the next stage. They absolutely loved the idea of the rogue item. I should hear more in a week or so. How are the Double-Doubles? Xx

I'm smiling as I type out my response.

> There's trouble in paradise. Suzie and Grace are pissed off with Gina, who seems to have dumped them like hot bricks in favour of Lynette, of all people! I've taken myself off for the day to leave them to it xx.

The ticks go blue straight away and I can see he's typing a reply.

> Uh-oh. Let's hope nobody has poisoned anyone else when you get back. I wouldn't put it past any of them... Enjoy your day out. How's the book coming along?

What to say to that? I couldn't concentrate because I was thinking about you? Honest, but I don't want to spook him, so I opt for a more neutral reply.

OK. Darren still in the wall, but I'll get him out later, and then there will be the inevitable autopsy.

Foul play suspected?

He couldn't have bricked himself up in there.

Good point. This is why I'm not a crime novelist xx.

I'm trying not to read anything into the kisses on the end of his messages, but it's hard not to. Does he normally end all his texts like that, or is he flirting with me? To be fair, I've been sending him kisses too; perhaps he's just replying in the same way because he thinks that's what I expect. Thankfully, before I can go any further down this particular rabbit hole, my food arrives. I take a quick snapshot and send it to him with a brief message.

Got to go – lunch has just arrived and it smells amazing. Really pleased the pitch went well. Hope you have celebrations planned – keep me posted xx.

His reply is immediate.

Looks fab. Can practically smell it from here – enjoy! No celebrations until it's in the bag – don't want to jinx it. Hopefully, we'll be able to celebrate together once you're back xx.

* * *

By the time I get back to L'Ancien Presbytère, late that afternoon, I've analysed Finn's message from pretty much every conceivable angle. On the one hand, he could just be inviting me to celebrate as a friend who helped him out of a hole, but I have to confess I prefer the narrative where he wants it to be something more. After a delicious lunch, I had a happy time wandering round Gaillac before taking a circuitous route back to the house via Cordes-sur-Ciel. It turned out to be exactly as Cara had described; rammed with tourists and not a parking spot to be seen, so I didn't try to stop. It was pretty though.

As I pull up outside the house, I spot an unfamiliar car in the driveway. My first, brief, thought is that maybe Finn has hotfooted it back for the rest of the retreat, before I realise that he'd need to be a time traveller to have got here that quickly. The mystery only deepens when I walk out onto the terrace to be confronted by an apoplectic-looking Gina.

'*There* you are!' she exclaims furiously. 'Where the hell have you been?'

'Good afternoon to you too, Gina,' I say mildly. 'Is something the matter?'

'Of course something's the matter,' she fumes. 'Do I have to remind you that this is supposed to be a writers' retreat, not a holiday park for all and sundry? It was bad enough with Finn and his silly TV show, but this is beyond the pale.'

So much for Lynette keeping that a secret as well, then. Still, at least Finn managed to escape the flak. I can't for the life of me work out what it is I'm supposed to have done to upset her now, though.

'Sorry, Gina,' I say, trying to keep my voice level in the hope that it might calm her down a little. 'I'm not following you.'

'Oh, don't play the innocent with me,' she scoffs. 'It's obvious that you're behind this. What's the matter with you? Can't you focus unless you have someone fawning at your feet, hm?'

The irony of that statement is evidently lost on her, but I'm still no closer to uncovering what's going on, so I try again.

'Gina,' I say firmly. 'What are you talking about?'

'*Him*,' she practically yells as another person joins us and my jaw drops. I'm momentarily incapable of speech. This can't be happening, and I try blinking to see if maybe my eyes are playing tricks on me, but nope. The newcomer smiles warmly as he approaches.

'Hello, Laura. Surprised?'

'Angus,' I hiss. 'What the bloody hell are you doing here?'

'See?' Gina interjects. 'I knew you were behind this. Well, I'm going to be having a word with Hugh and Cara, you mark my words. You've caused nothing but trouble since you've arrived, and this is too much.'

She's right. The combination of Angus being here and her having yet another go at me is too much, and my temper deserts me.

'Oh, for God's sake, Gina! Just fuck off, would you?' I yell, making her start. If I wasn't so completely livid, it would actually be funny. Her mouth is working furiously, but no sounds are coming out.

'In all my life, I have never...' she eventually manages, before turning on her heel and fleeing.

'She seems an absolute charmer,' Angus observes drily. 'You might want to work on your interpersonal skills a bit though. I'm not sure "just fuck off, would you" is in the top ten phrases of how to win friends and influence people.'

'Shut up,' I tell him furiously. 'What are you doing here? How did you even find out where I was?'

He says nothing, but simply smiles enigmatically. Dear Lord, I've never wanted to punch someone so much.

'Well?' I demand after a few moments, when it's become clear he's not going to say anything.

'I can't shut up *and* tell you how I found you,' he says. 'You have to choose one.'

'Now is really, *really* not the time to be a smart arse. Tell me why you're here and how you found me. Did Liv tell you? I'll bloody kill her if she did.'

'No. I tried to get it out of her, but she wasn't giving anything away. I know she's your best friend and everything, but she's a bit of a Rottweiler sometimes, isn't she? Anyway, finding you was the easy part,' he says as if discussing nothing more important than the weather. 'Do you know how many writing retreats for English people are running in France at the moment? One. So it didn't need Sherlock Holmes to work out where you might be. As to why I'm here, I'd have thought that would be similarly obvious. I've come to win you back.'

'You've *what*?'

'Look, I know it was me that left and, at the time, I really thought it was the right thing. We seemed to be stuck in a rut and I wasn't happy in my job. But the truth is that barely a day went by on that ship when I didn't miss you, Laura.' He grins. 'Well, mainly Meg, of course, but also you.'

I stare at him, trying to take in what he's saying. His joke about loving the dog more than me was a common one in the old days, but it's just adding to my sense of disbelief now.

'As soon as the cruise was over, I came straight back to Margate to try to put things right,' he continues. 'I bought flowers and everything. That was awkward, I can tell you. I'm not sure who was more surprised when I knocked on the door of our flat – me or the woman who answered. It never occurred to me that you would have moved out.'

'What did you expect me to do?' I ask incredulously. 'Did you honestly think that I'd just gone into some form of suspended animation while you were away, like the fucking mice in *Bagpuss*?'

He stares at me blankly. 'I have no idea what you're talking about.'

'It's a children's story. Bagpuss is a stuffed cloth cat who lives in a shop, and the mice are part of a mouse organ. They come to life when Bagpuss does and go to sleep when he does. There's also a rag doll called Madeleine and a wood-pecker called Professor Yaffle – what now?'

'You're not making any sense. Have you been spending too much time in the sun?'

'If I'm not making any sense, it's because nothing about you being here makes sense. I thought I made it perfectly clear that I didn't want to see you again.'

'You were very fierce,' he admits. 'But that's what gave me hope, don't you see?'

'How?'

'If you no longer cared about me, you wouldn't have been so angry,' he says, smiling so beatifically you'd think he'd just discovered the meaning of life.

Once again, I'm rendered speechless. There's so much wrong with what he's just said that I literally have no idea where to start unpicking it.

'Let me get this straight,' I try. I feel like I'm drowning and I need some-thing, anything, firm to grasp on to. 'You decided, all on your own, that I was no longer what you wanted, disappearing pretty much overnight.'

'Bit dramatic, Laura. You make it sound like I ran away to join the circus or something.'

'You did. Only you ran away to sea instead of the circus.'

'We did talk about it.'

'No. You told me the night before you left and abandoned me to deal with the fallout.'

'OK, we'll have to agree to disagree on that.'

'No, we won't. It's what happened. Anyway. While you were playing *Pirates of the Caribbean*, or whatever the hell you were doing, you suddenly decided, equally out of the blue, that you wanted to come back home?'

'I missed you.'

'How many opportunities did you have to tell me that?'

'I'm sorry?'

'You could have called, messaged, emailed, whatever.'

'There isn't any reception at sea.'

'It's a cruise, Angus. I'm no expert, but don't they stop at ports on a fairly regular basis? And don't these ports have internet?'

'It seemed too personal for a call. I wanted to talk to you face to face.'

'Bullshit. You either didn't miss me at all, or you were too cowardly to pick up the phone and call. Neither exactly shows you in a good light, does it?'

'I did miss you,' he repeats mutinously. 'And you were the one who blocked my number.'

'Not for two bloody months. You had plenty of opportunities to get in touch. Anyway, for whatever reason, after months of complete radio silence, you somehow thought everything would just magically go back to how it was if you rocked up at my door with a bunch of wilted petrol station carnations. Talk me through that plan.'

'They were expensive, from that florist next to the bookshop, if you must know.'

'Oh. Well, that changes everything!' I exclaim sarcastically. 'Still way too little, way too late.'

'I thought, if we just had an opportunity to talk—'

'We did talk, Angus. On the phone. And I told you to get lost. I think I was pretty clear.'

'Yes, but like I said, you wouldn't have been so angry if you didn't care. So I tracked you down and, when Hugh told me a room had come free, I knew it was meant to be. Fate, you know? So I booked my tickets and here I am. I'm sorry I hurt you, but I'm here now and I promise you I'm not going anywhere again. I'll do whatever it takes to win you back, Laura.'

Dear God, he actually means it, I realise as I look into his face. How the hell am I going to get rid of him?

23

'You're kidding!' On the screen, Liv's face is a mask of horror.

'I wish I was,' I tell her. 'He was waiting for me when I got back from my sightseeing trip.'

'What on earth was he thinking?'

'He somehow got it into his head that me telling him to piss off and never contact me again actually meant that I still loved him.'

'That's some seriously fucked-up logic. How does that even work?'

'According to him, I wouldn't have been angry if I didn't still care about him.'

'Delusional, but you've got to admire his persistence, I suppose. What are you going to do?'

'I don't know! That's why I called. I need advice, urgently.'

'Hmm. OK, how did you feel when you saw him?'

'Shocked, mainly, then angry. Why?'

'And why do you think you were angry?'

'Because life here is difficult enough without Angus coming in and stirring the pot. Honestly, I thought Gina was going to have a coronary.'

'Which one is she?'

'Ringleader, snotty cow.'

'Oh, yes. What's it got to do with her?'

'She's on her high horse because Angus isn't a writer and this is supposed to be a writing retreat. Plus, he obviously let on that he was looking for me, so not only does she think he shouldn't be here in the first place, she's blaming me for it.'

'I'd tell her to piss off. What?'

I grin. 'I kind of did, but it was a bit stronger than that. I'm not sure she's speaking to me now.'

'Good for you. Interfering old bat. It's not your fault Angus is there. I mean, it kind of is, but you didn't invite him, did you? And if the criteria for staying were that strict then the hosts should have told him he didn't meet them and turned his booking down.'

'I think we can assume Gina and I aren't going to be besties. I'm not convinced she doesn't blame me for Finn being here as well.'

'I thought he was flying under the radar.'

'So did I, but it turns out Lynette would make a sieve look watertight. Those two are thick as thieves at the moment, so I guess Lynette had no compunction about throwing Finn under the bus. At least he wasn't here to cop the flak.'

'Have you heard from him?'

'Yes. The presentation went well and he's optimistic.'

'And how did that make you feel?'

'He put kisses on the end of his messages.'

'Did he now?'

'Yeah, but then so did I, so maybe he was just responding in kind.'

'But you hope not.'

'I did like it.'

Her mouth curves into a smile. 'Does Angus know about Finn?'

'Of course not! It's none of his business.'

'Aha!' Her smile widens as her face lights up in triumph.

'What?'

'There's an "it" between you and Finn.'

'Sorry, I'm not following you.'

'I asked if Angus knew about you and Finn. You said *it* was none of his business. Ergo, there's an *it*, which is a thing, between you and Finn.'

'You know I said I was after some advice?'

'Yes.'

'I'm kind of regretting that now.'

'Nonsense. I should be charging you for this shit. Freud has nothing on me. So, do we agree that there is something between you and Finn?'

I sigh. 'I don't know.'

'OK, let's rephrase it. Can we agree that you'd like there to be something between you and Finn, at least?'

'I don't know that either. I mean, I really like him, but maybe it's not meant to be anything more than friendship.'

'Sorry, but that's a coward's answer.'

'No, it's a realist's answer. I don't know enough about him to work out if we'd be compatible, and I don't want to get burned again.'

'And yet the kisses on his texts, which may be nothing more than force of habit, have made you all gooey.'

I sigh. 'They have.'

'I'm going to leave that with you to think about. Back to Angus.'

'Must we?'

'I think we can both agree that he's your most pressing problem, given that he's literally there in your face.'

'Maybe I don't need to do anything, just wait for Gina to murder him.'

'She might murder you if she thinks you're responsible for his arrival.'

'What a mess.'

Liv grins. 'I don't know. You were after inspiration, weren't you? Take me through the cast of characters on this retreat again.'

I'm relieved by the distraction. 'So we've got Gina at the top of the Double-Doubles, which are made up of her, Suzie and Grace.'

'The loyal acolytes,' Liv agrees.

'Not so loyal, actually. They both admitted to me this morning that Gina's getting up their noses.'

'Interesting. Go on.'

'Then there's Tess, the retreat leader. She's pretty much neutral in all this.'

'Swiss Tess, we'll call her. Next?'

'Lynette. Gina's sister. They traditionally hate each other, but seem to have overcome their differences to work together on Gina's book. Then there's me, and now bloody Angus.'

'Sounds like the perfect backdrop for an Agatha Christie novel. What's the one where everyone dies?'

'*And Then There Were None*,' I tell her.

'That's it. So, Angus realises you don't want him back because you're in love with Finn and he murders you in a fit of jealous rage. Unfortunately, Lynette sees it and tries to blackmail him, so he poisons her. Gina is unsure whether she's more outraged by the death of the sister she hated for so long but is now strangely reconciled to, or the fact that Angus isn't a writer. Either way, she stabs him to death with a fountain pen.'

'I'm not sure a fountain pen is a very good murder weapon. I guess you could stab someone in the eye with it and blind them, but I don't know if you could inflict a fatal wound.'

'Something else, then. She bashes his head in with the ancient typewriter she insists on using for her writing. Meanwhile, one of the Double-Doubles has been plotting to murder Gina, because she's dumped them in favour of Lynette. I'm thinking poisoning, but we've already used that, haven't we.'

'It is considerably tidier than shooting, stabbing or bashing someone's head in with a typewriter though. No blood to clear up, unless the victim coughs some up, of course.'

'Which one of them is the murderer?'

'Grace, I reckon,' I tell her. 'She was the first to break ranks.'

'Excellent. Suzie can discover the body, have a change of heart and turn on Grace. Who's left?'

'Swiss Tess. Nobody hates her.'

'We need a mastermind. It could be her. Maybe she's got some secret vendetta against all of you.'

'What about Finn? He was here at the beginning, after all.'

'Good point, but I'm sure there are lots of options. Maybe he ingested something before he left that's going to kill him later. Or he's in cahoots with Tess – a stooge. No, this is it. He hears about you and dies of a broken heart.'

'You've still got some loose ends,' I point out. 'Cara and Hugh, who own the house.'

'Oh, bugger. OK. Swiss Tess hasn't killed anyone directly yet, so maybe she polishes them off simply so there are no witnesses. Unfortunately, she bungles it and Hugh doesn't die straight away. As he's lying on the ground in agony, she uses the opportunity to do a load of monologuing about how she pulled the strings and why she wanted everyone dead.'

'Monologuing?'

'Yes, it's compulsory. Villains always have to reveal their secret plan in a monologue just before the hero turns the tables.'

'We don't have a hero though. Everyone's dead or dying.'

'Exactly. She thinks Hugh is incapacitated and his movements are merely him writhing in pain, but he's secretly trying to get to the sideboard, where he's got a gun concealed. She's so busy with her monologue that she doesn't notice what he's up to and so, with his last few gasping breaths, he lifts the gun and shoots her in the forehead.'

'Impressive. I like it.'

'You can have it for your next book. The usual fees apply.'

'Which are?'

'Oh, I don't know. My name in the acknowledgements as your muse, a case of wine...'

'My muse?' I can't help laughing now.

'Yeah, why not? I've always fancied being someone's muse.'

'Talking of which, how is the lovely Donna?'

'She's fine.'

'Mmm-hmm?'

'What?'

'You've clammed up, Liv. That means one of two things. Either it's all imploded spectacularly and you're trying to avoid talking about it, or you've fallen so hard that you're already thinking about what to wear for your wedding. I'm guessing, given that you seem to be in a pretty good mood generally, that it's the second.'

Now it's her turn to sigh, and I laugh again.

'Oh dear,' I observe. 'You have got it bad.'

Our conversation is interrupted by a soft knocking at my door.

'Hang on,' I say to Liv. 'Back in a mo.'

I place the handset on my bedside table and cross the room to open the door. My visitor is neither a surprise nor welcome.

'I'm on the phone,' I say to Angus. 'Go away.'

'Who are you talking to? Liv?'

'Yes, not that it's any of your business.'

'Are you talking about me?'

'No. Funnily enough, neither of us find you that interesting. Was there something you wanted?'

'I thought we could talk.'

'Well, we can't. I'm busy.'

'Later then?'

'Angus, there isn't anything to talk about.'

'Have you thought about what I said earlier, at least?'

'I really haven't,' I lie. If I give even the slightest hint that Liv and I have been discussing his arrival and picking it apart, he'll take that as a positive sign and I need to shut that down. I know it sounds cruel, but it would be worse to let him think there's a possibility of us getting back together, only to dash his hopes later.

He sighs expressively. 'I'll see you at dinner. Maybe we can talk then.'

'I doubt it. Look, I've got to go.'

I think the message might just be starting to percolate through, as he does look a little crestfallen as I close the door. My brief pang of guilt is swiftly swept aside by the voice from my bedside table.

'Bloody hell. Talk about needy,' Liv says dismissively.

'You heard?'

'Of course I heard. I'm on loudspeaker. I might as well be standing next to you.'

'So you see the problem.'

'No. I can see the ceiling. The problem was in the doorway. What are you going to do?'

'Isn't that where we started? I guess I just have to keep repeating the same message until he gets it. Anyway, stop changing the subject. Donna. Spill.'

'Fine. Yes, she's amazing, OK? We connect on so many levels. I think it helps that we've both seen a lot of the world. She gets me, does that make sense?'

'Don't I get you?' I ask, unable to keep the hurt out of my voice.

'Of course you do, but I'm not having sex with you, am I?'

'Things have moved on then?'

She harrumphs, evidently irritated at being caught out so easily. 'They might have done,' she says cagily.

'And?'

'And what? I'm not giving you a blow-by-blow account, Laura. Even by my admittedly low standards, that's too much information.'

'Is it good, that's all I want to know. Are you happy?'

'It is very good, and I am very happy. As is Meg, since you didn't ask. Having two of her favourite human beings together in the evenings is like whatever the doggy equivalent of catnip is. The only problem is that she does get terribly jealous. If Donna and I start to cuddle, she doesn't like it at all.'

I smile. 'Don't worry. She was just the same with Angus and me. Barking, then trying to get in between to separate us. We used to have to shut her out of the bedroom if we wanted to have sex, and then she'd quite often spend the whole time whining on the other side of the door.'

'That sounds familiar.' Liv laughs. 'If you're interested, we've solved it.'

'Really? How?'

'Firstly, don't leave the room together. She knows something's up and will be out of the door ahead of you if you do that. So, after some experimenting, we worked out that the best approach was for one of us to leave the room while the other sets up the distraction before following.'

'Distraction?'

'Nature documentaries on TV. She absolutely loves them. Stick David Attenborough and some wildebeest on there and she's transfixed. To be fair, she quite likes farming programmes too, although we had to stop her from watching *Countryfile* because she tried to join in whenever there was a sheepdog doing something, and her claws were scratching the TV stand. We did try her on *Clarkson's Farm*, but there's too much machinery and not enough animals to hold her attention. What?'

'If you've tried all those programmes already, that seems like an awful lot of sex in a short time.'

Liv blushes slightly, catching me by surprise. I don't think I've ever seen her blush before. 'We've discovered that we're very compatible sexually as well as emotionally,' she admits coyly.

'I'm delighted for you,' I tell her, embarrassed myself now. 'I'm not sure how I feel about you experimenting on my dog though.'

'It's not experimentation, it's entertainment. It was Donna's idea, actually. She said that not all dogs have the brainpower to interpret the images on TV, but she reckoned Meg, being so bright, would be able to do it and she was right.'

I laugh, pleased that we've defused the slightly awkward moment. 'Flattery will get you everywhere. Tell me Meg is a genius and I'll let you do whatever you like.'

The conversation flows easily for another twenty minutes or so. After we finish, I lie on the bed and reflect on what's been said. I'm not sure I found her advice about Finn and Angus terribly useful, although I have to admit I did enjoy discussing the 'murder at the writers' retreat' plot much more than I perhaps should have. Although we obviously both found her revelation about her sex life with Donna a bit too much information, I am genuinely happy for her, because I don't think I've ever seen her this excited about someone before. It does present me with a problem though. Despite her assurances, I'm certain I'm going to be playing gooseberry to the two of them, and that's going to be awkward.

The other disturbing result of our conversation is that it stirred up memories of Angus and me trying to find ways to have sex without alerting Meg and, though I hate to admit it, they weren't completely unpleasant. He may have been a lazy lover, but he's familiar, and that's much less frightening than the prospect of having sex with someone new for the first time.

24

I managed to avoid Angus pretty successfully last night, and I'm congratulating myself on that fact as I get myself ready for my morning walk. To be fair, I don't think anyone was really in the mood for talking. Gina spent most of the evening staring flintily at either Angus or me and I don't think I'm exaggerating if I say that we'd both be feeling pretty poorly right now if looks really could kill. Suzie and Grace were also silent, presumably still coming to terms with the fact that their leader cast them aside so casually. Tess was wisely keeping her own counsel, and so the only person making any attempt at conversation was Lynette who, among her other failings, seems to be completely incapable of reading the room. Even Cara and Hugh were muted. I felt for Cara, actually, as she'd pulled out all the stops with some absolutely fabulous *Moules Marinières* that Gina took one look at and flatly refused to eat, followed by a *Boeuf Bourguignon* that Hugh informed us included the vital steps of adding brandy, igniting it and then extinguishing the flames with a good bottle of red wine. His attempt to lighten the mood fell on deaf ears, however, and we all headed our separate ways as soon as the meal was over. Angus did make a vague attempt to corral me, but I think he read my expression and wisely decided to leave it.

It's another beautiful morning and I'm looking forward to some solo time as I close the front door carefully behind me and tilt my face towards the sun.

My conversation with Liv is still occupying my mind, so I'm planning to use the walk into town to process it a bit.

'I was hoping to catch you.' Angus's voice makes me jump.

'How did you know I'd be here?' My irritation is plain.

'I was chatting to that hippy woman yesterday, and she told me you normally went for a walk before breakfast.'

'Did she?' Bloody Lynette and her runaway mouth. A thought suddenly comes to me, and I don't know why, but it makes me feel slightly guilty.

'What else did she tell you?' I ask.

He hesitates, which I'm fairly certain tells me all I need to know but, for some reason, I want to hear him say it.

'Go on. Spit it out,' I instruct him.

'She said that you were friendly with the guy who was in my room before me and you used to walk with him every morning. Is that true?' He sounds hurt, which is pretty rich, when you consider what he did.

'Finn and I are friends, yes. What's it to you?'

'Friends, or more?'

I can feel my temper starting to fray. How dare he?

'Angus,' I begin, trying to keep my voice level. 'That really is none of your business. You ceased to have any right to know anything about me or my life the moment you walked out of our front door.'

To my surprise, this doesn't have the intended effect at all. Instead, his expression turns earnest.

'I see what this is,' he says. 'And I totally understand.'

'I'm sorry?'

'You're using this guy to punish me. It's no more than I deserve and, for what it's worth, I forgive you.'

Once again, he's so far off beam that I don't even know where to start. Unfortunately, he obviously interprets my silence as agreement, because he continues his frankly delusional speech.

'I did the wrong thing, Laura,' he's saying as I continue to stare at him. 'I wasn't happy, I explained that, but I should have stayed and worked on our relationship rather than running away. I know there's nothing I can say to take away the pain I caused you, but I was a mess. I needed time to reflect and work out what I really wanted, and I know now that it's you. I'm not expecting us to just pick up as if nothing was wrong, don't worry. I had some sessions with the cruise therapist and she explained how I'd need to take things slowly and allow you to move at your own pace. I broke your trust, and that doesn't come back overnight. I want you to hear that I understand, and I'm prepared to be patient.'

I can't take any more. 'Which part of this are you not getting, Angus?' I demand furiously. 'You left. You didn't just break my trust, you took everything I thought I knew, everything I felt was safe, and smashed it to pieces with a sledgehammer. You can say sorry all you like, but it's not going to change that. Now, if you don't mind, I have a walk waiting for me.'

'I'll come with you.'

'I don't want you to come with me!'

'I know you don't, but what kind of man would I be if I just let you wander off on your own in a foreign country? Anything could happen.'

'Have you seen this place? Nothing is going to happen, and I don't need your protection, or whatever you think this is.'

'Still coming with you.' His stubborn expression is instantly familiar, and I realise any further argument is just going to be wasted breath on my part.

'Fine,' I huff. 'Keep up and don't be annoying.'

He smiles. 'I can promise the first, but there are no guarantees on the second.'

Thankfully, he does seem to have heard me, as the first part of the walk passes without him interrupting my thoughts with his idiotic ramblings. I'd still much prefer him not to be here at all, but I'm grateful that he's stopped spouting nonsense, at least. One thing that he said is niggling at me though, and in the end it's me that breaks the silence.

'You saw a therapist?' I ask.

'I did.'

'But you hate therapists. You always dismissed therapy as navel-gazing bollocks for needy people who are too lazy to sort their own lives out.'

'Yeah, I know. I was wrong about that too. I've been wrong about a lot of things. Laura—'

I hold up my hand to stop him. 'You've answered the question. Please stop speaking now.'

When we reach the bridge, I'm almost amused to spot the old woman shuffling towards us. Of all the days to bump into her again, it would have to be the day that I've got Angus in tow.

'*Bonjour, madame,*' I say politely as she approaches.

'*Bonjour, mademoiselle.*' She pauses to look Angus up and down. '*Un nouveau copain?*' she asks, curiosity written all over her face.

'*Non,*' I tell her firmly. The last thing I need is for her to think that Angus is my boyfriend. If she starts one of her rants about true love, it's just going to add fuel to the fire.

'*Bon,*' she replies, before leaning in to whisper in my ear. '*Je ne l'aime pas.*'

I can't help smiling as I reply. '*Je ne l'aime pas aussi.*'

She puts her hand on my arm as she corrects me, speaking slowly so I can catch the words. '*Tu ne l'aimes pas non plus.*'

'What was that all about?' Angus asks after I've bid her farewell and she's shuffled off. The temptation to tell him that she's a self-professed expert on love and relationships who took an instant dislike to him is almost overwhelming but, true as it might be, I'm feeling slightly more charitable towards him than I did when we left the house, so I decide to spare his feelings.

'She's someone I bump into occasionally,' I tell him instead. 'We were just passing the time of day and talking about the weather.'

'You sounded really sexy talking French like that,' he says. 'You should do it more.'

'Angus?'

'Yes.'

'No. Just no. OK? You don't get to call me sexy any more.'

'It's a compliment.'

'I don't care what it is. It's inappropriate and weird.'

'I know you're angry with me,' he continues, unwisely in my opinion given that I'm actually managing to be reasonably civil towards him at the moment. 'But we did have ten years together, Laura. You can't just rewrite history and wipe them out. Ten years in which we saw each other naked more times than either of us could count. Ten years of intimacy. That happened, whatever you feel about it now. I think that entitles me to pay you a compliment without you jumping down my throat.'

'Argh!' I cry, clapping my hands over my ears. 'Please, just stop.'

'Making you uncomfortable, am I?' A faint smile is playing on his lips. I used to love it when that happened. It was like a secret mini-gesture just for me. His smile is very slightly lopsided and I used to find it sexy as hell.

'I don't want to talk about... naked stuff,' I tell him. 'It's giving me the ick.'

He roars with laughter. 'Naked stuff?' he repeats. 'What are we, seven?'

'Shut up, Angus.'

'Sex,' he replies, still laughing. 'Intercourse. Our two naked bodies coming together, instinctively knowing what the other wants and craves. Don't tell me you can't picture it and it's not a good image, because I won't believe you. We were good, weren't we?'

'Whatever. I'm not joining in your personal porno movie.'

'Naked stuff,' he breathes again in amusement. 'Bloody hell.'

Thankfully, we lapse back into silence as we embark on the return journey, but I can tell something is playing on his mind.

'What?' I ask eventually.

'Have you ever heard of Kintsugi?' he asks.

Uh-oh. I haven't a clue what Kintsugi is but, if he's been seeing a therapist, he could have been up to all kinds of batshit crazy stuff. I bet it's some kind of weird chanting meditation thing, where you align your chakras or whatever, and he's going to try to suck me in to doing it with him as some kind of totally messed-up bonding exercise.

'I'm not into that kind of thing,' I tell him. 'I can just about cope with Liv and her Pilates.'

He grins. 'You think it's a type of Yoga, don't you?'

'Isn't it?'

'No. It's a Japanese art form. The most literal translation of the word is "golden repair". They take broken pottery, use a special lacquer to glue it back together again, and then cover the repair with gold. The philosophy behind it centres around embracing the beauty of imperfection, that an object can become even more valuable after being broken and repaired.'

'I see.'

'There was a talk about it on the cruise. Really interesting, actually.'

'I'm delighted that you're taking the opportunity to expand your cultural horizons. Was there a point to this?'

'Yes. It's us, don't you see? It was your allusion to the hammer that made me think of it. You're right. Our relationship was a beautiful clay pot full of love. When I left, it was like dropping the pot on the floor. It broke and all the love leaked out of it. That's where we are now. But, if we apply Kintsugi, not only can we repair the pot and refill it over time, but it could end up being an even more beautiful pot than we had before.'

I sigh. 'Angus, that is a lovely analogy, I'll grant you, if a little bit woo-woo. But this pot is more than broken, that's what I'm trying to get across to you.'

'OK, tell it your way,' he suggests.

I think for a moment.

'Humpty-Dumpty is probably better.'

'What?'

'All the king's horses and all the king's men couldn't put this shit together again.'

He looks at me incredulously. 'That's all you've got? I give you a beautiful analogy, even if I do say so myself, involving intricate Japanese craftsmanship, and you come back with a sodding nursery rhyme?'

'It does the job, doesn't it?'

Now it's his turn to sigh. 'You're not prepared to give me any kind of second chance, are you?'

'No. There's another saying that applies here, actually.'

'Do I want to hear it? Is it another nursery rhyme?'

'Nope. It's a metaphor. The horse is dead, Angus. Stop flogging it.'

We're almost at the turning to L'Ancien Presbytère before he speaks again.

'What about this other guy. Finn, is it?'

'What about him?'

'Are you together? I know you said it's none of my business, but it would help me to understand why you're so sure we don't have a future.'

'We aren't. Like I told you, we're friends.'

He stops and turns to me, making me stop as well. He looks at me for so long that I start to feel uncomfortable.

'You'd like it to be more,' he states eventually.

'I don't know. Maybe, maybe not. I mean it though. Whatever happens, it's got nothing to do with you.'

He starts walking again, albeit slowly.

'Here's what I don't understand,' he says as the house comes into view. 'I'm a known quantity. You know we work well together as a couple. You were happy, weren't you? I'm offering you all of that back. You, me and Meg. We can find another flat and have our old lives again, only better. I don't know this Finn, but neither do you, really. You're putting someone you've spent a few days with above ten years of solid relationship? Risky, don't you think?'

'You're coming at it from the wrong angle. Yes, we had ten years and yes, they were broadly happy, at least I thought they were. But that's not what this is about. I may have known you, loved you, for a long time, but you shat the mat in spectacular style. There isn't a Kintsogo—'

'Kintsugi,' he interrupts.

'Whatever. The pieces are too small to be glued together. The pot isn't worth the effort. Actually, that reminds me. Can I ask you a question?'

'Of course.'

'Did you resent me earning more than you?'

'Of course not! I was delighted that you were doing so well and achieving your dreams.'

Unfortunately, this is where me knowing him so well lets him down. He may be saying the right thing, but I saw something quite different flash across his eyes. Liv was right, and my resolve strengthens further.

'Look,' I begin. 'Let's say I believed everything you've said – I know you do – and we got back together. I'd just be waiting for the inevitable moment when it all got too much for you again and you disappeared. Yes, Finn might be an unknown in comparison, but at least he doesn't come with a history of heart-break and disappointment.'

Angus's shoulders sag. 'OK, I get it,' he says. 'For what it's worth, I truly am sorry. If I could go back and change it, I would.'

'I know. But you can't, and I'm not sure you should. Whatever you feel now doesn't change what drove you to leave in the first place, and part of that was me. I don't regret our time together, and maybe I'll come to feel fond of you in time. But it can never be more than that. We both need to move forwards, not backwards.'

He looks completely defeated now. 'You're right,' he says miserably. 'I'm sorry. Do you think we'll be able to be friends, at least?'

'I don't know,' I tell him honestly. 'I'm not ruling it out, but sometimes a clean break is better for everyone. There is one thing you can do to improve the chances though.'

'Oh, yes?'

'Stop bloody apologising all the time! It's getting really annoying.'

He laughs, as I knew he would.

'You're right. I'm sorr— Oh, bollocks. I'll try.'

It's all I can do not to breathe a sigh of relief. I think he's finally got the message.

25

'Victim is male, around twenty-eight to thirty years old. I'm sure it will come as no surprise when I tell you this is homicide,' Alicja, the pathologist, told DI Harrison and DS Rogers matter-of-factly as she led them through to the post-mortem examination room. Despite living in the UK for over thirty years, her English still carried a strong Polish accent.

'We kind of figured that, given the location of the body,' DS Rogers replied with a half-smile.

'Hm.' Alicja's stony-faced expression gave no clue about whether she'd picked up the hint of sarcasm in DS Rogers's remark. Normally, DI Harrison would take pleasure in the exchange; DS Rogers was famed at the station for his ability to mimic the severe Alicja. However, she'd barely slept a wink last night, waking several times to find her sheets drenched in sweat. Eventually, she'd given it up as a bad job and got up at around four in the morning, with the result that her headache was still very much present and she was feeling tired and drained today.

As the station's leading murder detective, with a stellar track record, DI Harrison had seen her fair share of dead bodies over the years, but she was still unprepared for the sight that met her when Alicja pulled back the sheet. Darren's body was effectively reduced to a skeleton, with the occasional clump of hair and a few scraps of material that she could just recognise as being remnants of the clothes he was wearing when she and her dad had bundled him into his improvised sarcophagus. Beside her, DS Rogers recoiled, covering his mouth with his hands.

'If you are going to vomit, please use a cardboard receptacle from over there,' Alicja told him unsympathetically, causing DS Harrison to wonder for a moment whether she knew she was the object of his ridicule. Normally, she'd make a mental note to follow up. There's nothing guaranteed to make a detective's work more difficult than a hostile pathologist. Today, however, any tension between Alicja and DS Rogers was so low on her list of things to worry about that it simply didn't register.

'OK,' Alicja continued, pulling a laser pointer from her lab coat pocket and aiming it at the back of Darren's skull. 'There are hairline fractures here, consistent with victim being struck with a blunt object.'

'Like a hammer?' DS Rogers asked from his vantage point pretty much as far away from the body as it was possible to be without leaving the room.

'No,' Alicja replied dismissively. 'Hammer would cause a different pattern. This is something wider, like the flat side of a spade. Something like that. Anyway, victim did not die from this.' She smiled mirthlessly. 'Very nasty headache. No more.'

'So what did kill him?' DI Harrison forced herself to ask.

'This.' Alicja moved the pointer to Darren's neck. 'Look closely,' she commanded. 'Can you see these marks here? Abrasions consistent with knife wounds. Victim has them on both sides. Whoever stabbed him did so many times, with considerable force.'

'So probably another male?' DS Rogers asked, evidently trying to score at least some points for deduction.

'Would have to be very small man,' Alicja observed. 'Angle of blade is upward, meaning assailant was shorter than victim. Victim is only one hundred seventy-five centimetres. Attacked by midget, maybe, but more likely that assailant was female.'

'But you mentioned considerable force.'

Alicja sighed in the way that people do when they have to explain something to an imbecile. 'Assailant was probably very angry woman, DS Rogers. Angry women are surprisingly strong, you know?'

'A crime of passion?' DS Rogers continued, seemingly desperate to redeem himself now.

'Vot do I know? My job is simply to work out how victim died. Your job is to work out who and why, isn't it?'

'Fine.' DS Rogers was looking distinctly unsettled now. Alicja had definitely wiped the floor with him today. 'Have you been able to calculate, based on the wounds, roughly how tall the assailant would have been?'

'Of course. I am scientist. These wounds speak to me as clearly as you do, DS Rogers. Assailant is around one hundred sixty centimetres tall.'

'What's that in real money?'

Alicja sighed expressively again. 'One day, English people will learn to use proper measurements, like grown-ups. Conversion chart is on the wall there.'

DS Rogers crossed to the chart and examined it. 'Five foot four inches. About your height, Ma'am.'

'It's a very common height for women,' DI Harrison observed testily. 'I think we'll need more than that to secure a conviction, don't you?'

'Yes, but it's a start. So far, we know we're probably looking for a woman, around five foot four and possibly of a similar age to the victim. If it's a crime of passion, she might have been his wife or lover. Do we have an ID for the victim?'

'Not yet,' Alicja replied. 'Is only matter of time though.'

And so the game began. Piece by piece, the puzzle would start to come together and the net would begin to close. As the senior investigator, DI Claire Harrison was somehow going to have to solve a murder she herself had committed, without implicating herself in the process.

Life was so fucking unfair sometimes.

'I thought you might like some coffee.' I look up to see Angus with a slightly anxious expression on his face, carefully setting a cup down on the table. 'I'm not disturbing you, am I?'

'No,' I tell him, glancing at the countdown timer on my phone. 'You've timed it perfectly, actually.'

'Great. Do you mind if I bring another cup over and join you?'

'As long as you don't start on about us getting back together again.'

'No.' He smiles ruefully. 'That ship has sailed. I get it.'

'Slightly unfortunate analogy,' I can't help pointing out.

'You're right, sorry.'

'Stop apologising for everything!'

He holds up his hands in surrender. 'Sorry for being sorry. Back in a moment.'

I watch him as he heads back towards the terrace, where the coffee and pastries have been laid out. For a moment, I feel sorry for him. Despite every-thing, I do still care for him and I don't like being the reason for his evident unhappiness. But, I remind myself fiercely, nothing has actually changed. He may say he wants to come back and give it another try, but that look that flashed across his face when I challenged him told me that he definitely has a problem with me earning more than him and, if he can't even admit that, we're just going to end up back in the same place.

'I also brought you one of Cara's delicious-looking pastries,' Angus tells me when he returns, setting down a plate in front of me. 'Do you know, if it wasn't for the fact that everybody else here seems to hate me, I'd be loving this. It's such a beautiful place, and the food is superb.'

'I don't think anyone hates you.'

He laughs. 'Nice try, but it's obvious that the snotty woman absolutely loathes me, and you've made it perfectly clear you'd rather I was a million miles away. The others seem broadly indifferent, I'll grant you, but the overall mood is hostile.'

'I wouldn't worry about Gina,' I reassure him. 'Despite her going on about you not being a writer, I think her main beef is actually that you're connected to me. If you think she's anti you, that's nothing compared to the way she feels about me.'

'What have you done?' He smiles. 'Apart from telling her to fuck off, of course.'

'I have no idea. According to Lynette, her sister, she hates me because I'm already published, but I can't believe anyone would be that petty.'

'Sometimes other people's success can be hard to swallow,' he observes.

'Are you speaking generally, or from personal experience?' I ask. Maybe he'll open up and be truthful this time.

There's a long pause while he takes a mouthful of his pastry, and I do the same. It's soft, buttery and very moreish, but I find I'm not enjoying it as much as I normally do. I'm waiting to hear what he has to say, and I have the distinct impression I'm not going to like it.

'Personal experience,' he admits eventually. 'Look, Laura. I know I said the money didn't matter earlier, but that wasn't strictly true. Don't get me wrong, I'm absolutely delighted that your career took off in the way that it did. If anyone deserves to be a roaring success, you do. But it did leave me feeling a bit left behind sometimes, if I'm honest.'

'Why?'

'Because it put you in a different league from me, don't you see? If you fancied going out for dinner, you'd just book a table for us in that fancy restaurant at The Mermaid hotel. I'd have to save for weeks to be able to afford to take you there. It felt... unbalanced somehow and it made me feel inadequate, because I couldn't keep up.'

'Oh, Angus. I'm so sorry. I never meant to make you feel that way. I guess I just wanted to share, and it never occurred to me until Liv brought it up.'

'What did she say?' he asks, his voice a little sharp.

'Pretty much exactly what you've just said. Honestly, I didn't have a clue.'

'Of course you didn't. It's one of the many things I love about you. I totally get that this is a "me" problem – the therapist made that clear.'

'I still can't believe you saw a therapist.'

'Me neither. Anyway, have you had any more thoughts about Finn and what you're going to do?'

'No, and I'm not talking to you about Finn. That's just too weird. What's next for you, do you think? Back to Glasgow?'

'Bloody hell, no. I think I'll contact the cruise line when I get back. They were pretty happy with me, so I don't think I'll have any trouble getting more work from them. Are you sure I can't see Meg before I go?'

'I'd prefer it if you didn't. She was so unhappy when you left the first time. Weeks went by before she stopped hanging round the door and whining at the time when you'd normally get home. I know she'd be delighted to see you, but she's just starting to settle and I don't want to set her back.'

'I understand. Perhaps you can tell her you saw me and that I send her all my love.'

'I'll certainly do that.'

He drains his cup and stands. 'Right. I'll leave you in peace.'

'What are you going to do?'

'To be honest, I didn't expect things to go this way, so it didn't occur to me to book flexible flights, which means I'm stuck here for the duration. I've got the hire car though, so maybe I'll do some sightseeing. Don't worry, I'm not going to be in your face all the time. I'll see you later, yeah?'

'Yeah, OK.'

I'm surprised to notice how relieved I am when he walks away. I'm glad that he's got the message and has stopped trying to persuade me to go back to him, and I feel more at ease in his company than I was expecting, but him being here is still a distraction I definitely don't need. The fact that his presence has riled Gina up even more is also not particularly helpful, although she's been keeping her distance since our contretemps yesterday. Is it too much to hope that maybe she's got the message as well?

And then, of course, there's Finn. I still don't have a clue what, if anything, to do about him. I haven't heard any more from him, not that I was expecting to, but he's definitely got under my skin and, the more I think about it, the more I feel there's unfinished business there.

26

It's the final morning of the retreat and I'm ready to go home. Although it's lovely here, and I can't fault Hugh and Cara's hospitality, I need to get away from Gina and her death stares. She hasn't spoken a word to me since I stood up to her in the garden, but she positively oozes hostility every time we have to share a space. I'm sure the fact that I've become more friendly with Suzie and Grace since their revelations the other morning hasn't helped, but I'm frankly tired of her and whatever her problem with me is.

The good news is that Angus has kept his promise and hasn't made any more attempts to persuade me to go back to him. In fact, I'd go as far as to say we're being very grown-up and amicable at the moment. He's sensibly decided that I'm not at risk of attack on my morning walks and left me to take them alone. In theory, I was using the time to concentrate on the plot of my book, but the reality is that I spent them daydreaming about Finn. My favourite fantasy is one where our kiss at the waterpark ends in the bedroom, and I have to say I have rather enjoyed the images. The only downside is that my mind became so Finn focused that it fooled me into thinking I actually saw him a couple of times. The first Finn doppelganger was thankfully unmasked before I made a fool of myself. He looked just like Finn from the back, but the moment he turned to greet someone else, it was clear it wasn't him. The second time, I actually called out before I realised I was trying to get the attention of a total stranger. That one did take a bit of unravelling, as it turned out my French was nowhere near good enough to explain to a confused local that I thought he was someone else.

After our usual delicious breakfast, I pack my bags, double and triple-checking that I haven't left anything behind, before going to look for Cara so I can say goodbye.

'Is everything all right?' she asks me when I find her in the dining room.

'Absolutely. I just wanted to thank you for looking after us all so well. I think I'll have to stay away from the scales for a while.'

She beams. 'Thank you. It's been a real pleasure having you and I hope you found inspiration.'

'I did. Who knows, I might even come back.'

'Do. Can I ask you a question before you leave?'

'Of course.'

'Hugh and I have tried not to pry, but we're naturally curious and can't help ourselves. When you first arrived, you seemed to be getting on very well with Finn.'

'Yes,' I say, suddenly unsure where this is going or whether I'm going to like it.

'And now you seem to be getting on well with Angus.'

'He's my ex,' I tell her firmly.

'He's still keen on you though.'

'I think we've ironed that out. Was there a question?'

'More of an observation, now I come to think about it. I'll admit I'm no relationship expert, although I flatter myself that I landed a good one with Hugh, but we both felt there was a spark between you and Finn that isn't there with Angus.'

'Angus and I are definitely in the past,' I agree. 'I'm not sure Finn felt the spark though.'

'Oh, he did. He's nuts about you, it's obvious from the way he kept finding ways to be with you or sit next to you at mealtimes. You two were thick as thieves. I think he's just a little shy and not sure how to make his move.'

'He got spectacularly burned in his last relationship,' I agree. 'I think that makes him cautious.'

'And you?'

'Angus walked out. That's a hard thing to come to terms with but, in a weird way, him flying out here to try to win me back has been cathartic.'

'It's helped you to see more clearly.'

'Yes. He thinks he wants me, but he doesn't really. Part of him craves adventure, which is why I think he signed up for the cruise line, but he also likes stability. If he could do his cruise job knowing that I was waiting patiently for him when he got home, that would be his dream scenario. The only problem with that is I'm not prepared to be a part-time partner, and I'd always be worried that he'd just walk out again. We were good for each other once, but now it's time to move on.'

She smiles. 'Then you're ready.'

'For what?'

'For Finn.'

I sigh. 'I'm not sure it's as simple as that, even if the old lady in town thinks it is.'

'What old lady?'

'I've met her a few times on my early-morning walks. She was convinced Finn and I were a dream couple, and she took against Angus the moment she set eyes on him.'

Cara laughs. 'Madame Laurent. She's a real local character. She fancies herself as the town matchmaker and, to be fair, her record is impeccable. If she thinks you and Finn are made for each other, I'd take that on board.'

'No pressure, then.'

'Look, all I'm saying is what we saw, and it seems Madame Laurent saw it too. Yes, Finn might need handling with kid gloves while he learns to trust again, but it seems everyone who's observed the two of you feels the same.'

'I don't know. I've only just got myself back on track after Angus left. Maybe I'm better off as I am for now. Apart from anything else, I'm on a deadline and can't get distracted until I finish this book.'

'If you ask me, you're already distracted. Can I give you a piece of advice?'

'Can I stop you?'

'No, probably not. If you do nothing, this will wither and you'll always wonder whether you missed an opportunity. Find a way to meet up with him once you're back. I think that will help you decide what to do next. Oh, and Laura?'

'Yes?'

'*Bonne chance.*'

* * *

The house is empty when I get home. Although that's to be expected as Liv
will be at work and Meg's presumably at doggy daycare, I feel a pang of disappointment nonetheless. I've been pondering Cara's words for most of the journey, and I feel the need to talk to someone. Although I ended up sitting next to
Angus on the plane, he wisely kept his own counsel and didn't try to make
conversation all the way, like he normally would have. He did tell me he'd
secured another contract with the cruise line, leaving in a week or so, and he's
going to spend the time in between visiting his parents in Glasgow, which I'm
sure they'll enjoy. He's also agreed to pay the back rent on the storage unit and
take it on going forwards, which I'm quite pleased about.

After unpacking and putting a load of washing on, I'm still feeling unsettled, so I decide to wander in the direction of Maison Olivia. The day is almost
over, Liv should be packing up soon, and I'm definitely in need of her
company.

'Laura!' she yells when I stick my head around the pâtisserie kitchen door.
'Welcome home. I'd hug you only I'm covered in flour. What time did you get
back?'

'Not long ago.'

'You've timed it perfectly. I'm just about to close up and go to collect Meg. I
told her you were coming home this morning and she seemed pleased,
although Donna tells me she's absolutely loving her time at daycare. She's the
life and soul of the place, apparently.'

'And how is the lovely Donna?'

'You can find out yourself, when she comes over later.'

This draws me up short. I've been so focused on the situation with Angus
and Finn that I haven't really given any more thought to the prospect of
playing gooseberry to Liv and Donna. Liv must be able to read my expression
as she immediately moves to reassure me.

'It'll be fine,' she says. 'I'm not going to suddenly drop you like a hot brick
just because I'm in a new relationship. Trust me.'

'I just don't want to get in the way. If you need me to start looking for somewhere else to live—'

'Of course I don't! I've really enjoyed having you living with me and the
great thing about Donna is she isn't needy or jealous, so she's not going to get

all funny if I want to spend the occasional evening just with you. In fact, she wasn't going to come round tonight, but I persuaded her because I want you two to get to know each other. Is that all right?'

I smile. 'I should have known you'd be ahead of me on this. I'd love to meet Donna properly, especially as it sounds like she's already a big part of your life.'

Liv grins. 'Either that or I was just using her to keep me entertained while you were away. I guess we'll find out this evening.'

'I think the expression on your face when you talk about her makes it pretty obvious, Liv.'

'It's too early to say she's the one, but...'

'You're hopeful. Wow, I've never seen you fall for someone this fast before.'

'I know, but I can picture us five or ten years from now and it doesn't frighten me. This is the first time that's ever happened. With Trevor, even looking a week ahead used to terrify me. Thinking of which, what's going on with you? Managed to unravel the tangle you found yourself in yet?'

As I begin to fill her in on everything that's happened since we last spoke, it feels like a weight is lifting from my chest. She listens carefully when I tell her what Cara said and, although she doesn't exactly come down on Cara's side, she does agree that I need to make contact with Finn, even if it's just to discover that he's not interested, so I can close the door and move on.

'I need an excuse though,' I complain. 'Otherwise it just looks weird.'

'Simple. You're just checking in to see if he's heard anything from the TV people. Then you can tell him you're home and see what happens.'

'I guess that might work, although I'm pretty sure he'd have messaged me if he'd heard.'

'Just do it. Remember the mantra?'

I sigh. 'It's always better to regret something you've done rather than something you haven't.'

'Exactly. Sometimes my own wisdom amazes me. Right, I've got to shut up shop. Are you coming to collect Meg with me? She'll be delighted to see you.'

'Of course.'

* * *

It's a while before we're ready to leave. Liv tidies and cleans the kitchen until everything is put away in its place, gleaming immaculately, while I help Bella tidy up the shop.

'How are your elderly lovers?' I ask her while we work.

'Good,' she enthuses. 'They're in here twice a week, regular as clockwork, and I think he's staying over sometimes.'

'Based on?'

'He's very particular about his appearance. Always clean-shaven with his clothes pressed just so. But he's looked mildly dishevelled a couple of times recently. I think he's got as far as staying over, but not as far as planning to stay over.'

'I'm not following.'

'Let's assume he comes down the night before to take her out to dinner or whatever. Planned sleepover would mean he'd bring an overnight bag with a change of clothes. But that carries assumptions about the stage of their relationship that she's perhaps not ready for. So he comes, theoretically prepared to catch the last train home, only she always invites him to stay. So it feels spontaneous even though they both know what's going to happen, and it's less pressure on her. The downside is that he can't bring overnight stuff, so he's unshaven and a bit crumpled the next day. I'm currently trying to work out if that's part of her thing, that she prefers him a bit rough and ready.'

'Bloody hell, Bella. Are you sure you're not reading more into this than there is?'

'I might be, but it keeps me entertained.'

I smile at her. I did enjoy most of the retreat, despite Gina and her attitude, but it's really nice to be home.

27

'We have an ID on the victim,' DS Rogers informed the team at the morning briefing. 'His name is Darren Enticknap and he was the owner of the property at the time of his death, which was recorded as suicide.'

'Why? Surely someone must have reported him missing, at least?' The voice belonged to DC Carpenter, who'd joined the team from uniform six months earlier. Normally, DI Harrison liked her; she was keen and eager to make her mark. Today, she just wanted her to go away.

'It seemed an open and shut case, from what I've been able to find out,' DS Rogers told her. 'The victim left a note saying his girlfriend had just left him, his car was discovered by the coast, which explains the lack of a body, and he was apparently about to lose his job.'

This was news to DI Harrison. She couldn't remember Darren saying anything about that. She tried not to shudder as she thought what he would have been like at home all day with nothing to do except find fault with her.

'Any luck tracking down the girlfriend?' she asked, hoping above all for a negative answer.

'Not so far, Ma'am,' DS Rogers replied.

'She's got to be the prime suspect, hasn't she?' DC Carpenter interrupted. 'Aren't most murders committed by people known to the victim?'

'The majority, yes,' DS Rogers agreed. 'So I agree that the girlfriend is pivotal. I spoke to the neighbours, but most of them moved in after the events we're interested in, so didn't know anything. However, one older resident said she did remember him. She was a bit hazy about it, but seemed to think the girlfriend was blonde and called either Claire or Sandra. The only useful piece of information she divulged was that she was certain she worked in the Pig and Whistle pub.'

'Would you like me to follow that up?' DC Carpenter really was being irritatingly keen this morning.

'That would be difficult, as the Pig and Whistle closed fifteen years ago.'

'I could contact the tax office?' DC Carpenter persisted. 'They must have PAYE records.'

'Good idea, assuming the staff were on the payroll and not simply paid cash in hand. Follow it up, but don't waste too much time on it if it proves to be a dead end.'

'Good work, everyone,' DI Harrison told them, keen to wrap this up as fast as possible. For the time being, things seemed to be going her way. Although she had been on the payroll at the pub, she was fairly certain that the tax office only kept five years of historical PAYE records so DC Carpenter wouldn't find anything to link her to the Pig and Whistle. The neighbour might be a problem though. But DS Rogers had said she was hazy, so that probably wouldn't come to anything either. She just needed to sit tight and hold her nerve.

'Have you texted him yet?' Liv's voice from the other side of the door startles me.

'I'm working. Go away,' I reply testily. I know she'd say she's only got my best interests at heart, but Liv seems to have turned the idea of me contacting Finn into some kind of personal crusade.

'You aren't working,' she replies, sounding completely unruffled by my grumpy tone. 'I'm willing to bet a fiver that you haven't written a word in the last hour.'

Beside me, Meg stirs in her sleep, half opening one eye and regarding me balefully. Although she was delighted to see me when I got home, I think she's pissed off with me now because she's worked out that me being home means no more doggy daycare.

'Stop that,' I tell her. 'I said I'd talk to Donna about it later, OK?'

'Has she still got the arse with you?' Liv calls.

'You might as well come in,' I tell her with a sigh.

'I bring offerings,' she announces as she opens the door. 'Fresh coffee and a rather nasty piece of millionaire's shortbread.'

'The coffee is welcome, but you can keep the shortbread. I'm trying to be good after thoroughly overdoing it while I was away.'

'Suit yourself. It's disgusting anyway. How people eat this stuff is beyond me. There's no balance of flavour, nothing to excite the palate. It's just layer after layer of sugary sweetness.'

'Why did you make it then?'

'Donna likes it.'

'Wow.'

'What?'

'It must be love if you're prepared to do that.'

Liv grins. 'It's a two-pronged attack, if you must know. Give her what she likes to keep her sweet, but also try to educate her palate at the same time.'

'Poor woman.'

'Oh, she's OK. Do you like her?'

'I've already told you I like her, Liv. She's a good match for you and I can see why she makes you happy.'

'Yes, I know. I just want to make sure that you're still all right about her though. You don't feel left out?'

'I'm fine.' In truth, Liv has been so keen to make sure I don't feel like the third wheel that she's overcompensated if anything. 'Just relax. I like her; I think she likes me. The only person who's unhappy with the current state of affairs is Meg here, and I'm going to fix that.'

'I told Donna that you were thinking about sending Meg back to daycare, and she's delighted.'

'I think it's the right decision. I just resent paying for other people to look after Meg when it should be my job. But I get that she's mainly Collie and needs more stimulation than I can provide. I don't know, Liv. I feel like I've failed her a bit.'

'Nonsense. You're doing everything you can for her. Top dog mum of the year, that's you. Anyway, have I won the bet?'

'No, because I didn't accept it.'

'Only because it would have cost you a fiver.'

'Fine. No, I haven't written anything for the last hour.'

'Just message the boy, will you? Put us all out of our misery.'

'That's not the reason I haven't written anything.'

'Bollocks. You've been sitting here trying to decide and procrastinating as usual. Just do it.'

'Argh. OK. You've worn me down. I'll message him now, OK?'

'Good.' She settles herself on the bed.

'What are you doing?'

'Watching.'

'Umm, no? These things are private.'

'They are for normal people, but you need supervision.'

'Oh, for God's sake,' I growl, snatching up the phone. To be honest, the message is easy because I've spent so long thinking about what to say, not that I'm going to admit that to Liv. Having tried lots of different options, I've gone for something that I hope sounds casual enough not to frighten him, while making it clear I'm expecting him to reply.

> Hi Finn. Just checking in to see whether you've heard anything from the TV people? I'm back in the UK – escaped the Double-Doubles!! xx

'There. Happy now?' I say, showing her the screen once I've sent it.

'Ecstatic. I'll be even more ecstatic when he replies.'

* * *

'He hasn't replied,' I complain later that afternoon. I've given up trying to write anything as I've been fixated on my phone.

'Has he seen it?'

'Nope.'

'Maybe he's in meetings or something.'

'Or maybe he lost his phone and this isn't his number any more. Or maybe it was stolen and I'm actually messaging the new owner in China or wherever the phone is now.'

'Maybe he's been eaten by a shark, or abducted by aliens,' Liv observes wryly.

'Stop taking the piss.'

'Stop acting in such a pissworthy manner then.'

'I'm not sure that's a word.'

'It is, even if I've just had to make it up to describe you. Anyway, I expect he's just busy. Relax, he'll get back to you, I'm sure.'

As if on command, my phone beeps to let me know I have a new message.

'Is it him?' Liv asks, leaning forwards as I pick it up and unlock it.

'Yes.' I'm suddenly aware of my heartbeat, which has definitely quickened.

> Hiya! You must be a mind reader as I was just about to message you. Been in meetings all day with the TV people but the result is… they've gone for it! Show will be called 'Winning Bid' and recording starts in a couple of weeks. Believe I owe you a studio tour and dinner if you're still interested. xx

'Hmm,' Liv observes, reading the screen over my shoulder.

'What?'

'I can see why you'd think he wasn't interested. I mean, it's not very enthusiastic, is it?'

I turn to look at her.

'I'm kidding, you idiot. Give it to me. Let's see. "Just about to message you"; "I owe you a studio tour and dinner"; two kisses. I'm with Cara. He's nuts about you.'

'You can't deduce that from a short message.'

'Of course I can. You'd better reply quickly though. If he's half as much as a ditherer as you've been, he'll be paralysed with self-doubt, wondering if he's overplayed his hand.'

Before I can come up with a suitable riposte, we're interrupted by the ringing of the doorbell and Meg barking furiously.

'Yes, all right,' Liv tells her as she goes into the hallway. 'It'll be Auntie Donna come to see you, I expect.'

Meg's tail is thrashing so hard when she spots Donna that I feel a slight pang of jealousy. I know she loves me, but she's been a bit more muted with me since I've been back, reminding me a little of how she was when Angus first left. To see her so full of joy at the sight of someone else isn't easy.

'Hi, Laura,' Donna says to me, after she's kissed Liv hello and made a huge fuss of Meg. She obviously spots the look on my face because she continues quickly. 'Don't worry. Dogs are lovely, but they're not terribly diplomatic.

Meg's excited to see me because she knows me and associates me with fun. It doesn't mean she loves you any less, I promise.'

'Bloody disloyal, that's what I call it,' I reply. 'I'm the one that buys her dog food and provides a roof over her head. Miserable animal.'

Donna smiles. 'You don't mean that.'

'No, probably not. It wouldn't hurt her to be a little more appreciative sometimes, though.'

'The thing you have to remember about dogs is that they live completely in the moment,' Donna explains. 'One of my owners is a computer programmer and he described it brilliantly. Apparently, in computer programs, you have a concept called If... then... else. So if condition A is true, one thing will happen, but if it isn't then something else will. Dogs totally don't get this. So Meg doesn't think "If I show how pleased I am to see Donna, then Laura will get upset". She's just "Oh, wow. I'm excited to see this person and I want to show it". Think how she was when you turned up to collect her from daycare last time. She couldn't get enough of you.'

She's right, I realise. Meg was just as delighted to come home from daycare as she was to see Donna just now. I need to stop expecting her to be capable of human emotions.

'Laura's a bit all over the place because of a boy,' Liv tells Donna with a wink.

'It's not that,' I retort. 'It's just...'

'It so is that,' Liv replies with a laugh when I run out of steam.

'Well, let's get your dog sorted, and then that'll free up your mind to deal with the boy,' Donna says kindly as we head into the sitting room. 'Any chance of a cup of tea and a piece of that delicious shortbread, Liv?'

Thankfully, Liv is standing behind her as her exasperated eyeroll is far from subtle.

'Of course,' she manages to say without a hint of sarcasm. 'You go and chat to Laura and I'll bring it in when it's ready.'

'Shall I let you in to a secret?' Donna says as we settle ourselves on the sofa and Meg climbs up between us. 'I'm not actually that fussed about million-aire's shortbread. I mean, it's nice and everything, but it's not my favourite.'

'Why get Liv to make it for you then? You know she doesn't like it?'

Donna grins. 'It's a comparatively minor character flaw in me for her to focus on. All the time she's trying to wean me off the shortbread, she's not noticing all my other major flaws.'

'I'm really not sure that's how it works, Donna. Maybe stick to dog psychology.'

'Perhaps you're right. Anyway, I do appreciate it because I know it's not her thing, but she does it because she thinks it makes me happy. I probably ought to let her off though. Her pastries are to die for, aren't they?'

I smile back at her. 'I really hope that's not a euphemism.'

She tilts her head back and laughs. 'I'll have to think about that. Now, let's talk about young Meg here.'

By the time we all make our way up to bed some hours and a bottle of wine later, I'm feeling much happier about Meg's situation, and any final reservations I had about Liv and Donna's blossoming romance have also melted away. Donna is easy company, it's lovely to see Liv so happy and there wasn't a single moment where I felt excluded. In fact, the evening has been so much fun that it's only as I'm climbing into bed that I realise with horror that I never messaged Finn back. Hurriedly, I grab my phone and, after re-reading his message, send a reply.

> Congratulations!! I knew they'd go for it. Studio tour and dinner both sound amazing. When did you have in mind? I'm flexible xx.

28

'Not that one,' Liv says firmly as I come down the stairs for the second time.

'Why? What's wrong with it?' I smooth the dress I've put on for my dinner with Finn. To my surprise, he suggested coming down to Margate rather than meeting in London. He's obviously done his research too, as he's booked a table at The Mermaid, arguably one of the best places to eat in the town at the moment.

'Too floral. You look like a housewife from the fifties, not a siren.'

'Oh, for goodness' sake.' I turn on my heel and stomp back upstairs.

'Put the yellow one on,' Liv calls after me. 'You always look great in that.'

'He's seen the yellow one. I wore it in France.'

'He's a man. He won't remember, trust me. And put some better underwear on too. You need to maximise your assets.'

'It's just dinner, Liv,' I call from my room as I pull the floral dress over my head, dumping it on the floor with the pile of other rejected outfits. Who am I kidding, I think as I unfasten my bra and start rummaging in the drawer for the push-up one I bought on a mad whim last year. I realise it's not going to work as soon as I find it, however. With a growl of frustration, I put the original bra back on and yank the yellow dress down over my body.

'Better,' Liv observes from the sofa when I reappear. 'The bra still isn't helping you though.'

'Yeah, well, the only one that does is black, and that's not going to work with this dress, is it.'

'OK, fine.' She sighs expressively and turns to Meg on the sofa next to her. 'What do you think, Meggie? Do we sign Mummy off to go to meet this man looking like that?'

Meg is obviously uninterested in fashion as she doesn't even look at me, instead opening an eye to peer at Liv, wagging her tail briefly in the hope that being spoken to means something good is going to happen to her, and then closing it again with a soft sigh when she realises it isn't.

'You'll do,' Liv says encouragingly after a moment. 'Stop biting your lip though.'

'It's normal to be nervous. I haven't been on a date since, well, I can't remember. What if I've forgotten what to do?'

'It'll be fine. It's not like you're meeting a total stranger. This is the guy you spent hours just chatting to when you were away. If nothing else, you should be able to do that, no?'

I know she's right, but that doesn't alleviate the knot of nerves that's formed in the pit of my stomach. Thankfully, before I can wind myself up any more, the doorbell rings, setting Meg off as usual.

I'm not sure what I'm expecting to feel as I open the door and see Finn standing there. Excitement? Relief? Like me, he's made an effort, wearing a dark blue jacket over a white shirt and chinos, with polished brown brogues underneath. Like me, he looks a little nervous.

'Hi,' he says, making no move to embrace me.

'Hi yourself.' I smile at him, but it doesn't feel natural at all. Why isn't this working? Is it because I'm struggling to reconcile the smartly dressed man in front of me with the casual guy I hung out with in France? Maybe it's the fact that he's in my space now, rather than the comparatively neutral ground of L'Ancien Presbytère. Whatever it is, something's not quite right and, from the way he's behaving, he feels it too.

'Nice dog,' he observes, bending down to stroke Meg, who is busily sniffing him. 'Meg, isn't it?'

'That's right. Well remembered.'

'And this must be your housemate, Liv,' he continues as she appears behind me. 'I'm Finn. Lovely to meet you. I've heard a lot about you.'

'Nice to meet you too,' Liv replies warmly. I'm not looking at her, but I can sense her sizing him up. 'I hope Laura said only good things about me.'

Finn smiles, but again it's not the easy smile I'm used to seeing. 'She did.'

'Good,' Liv tells him firmly. 'She'd be looking for a new home for her and her mangy dog otherwise.'

Normally, I'd be straight in with some riposte, but I just feel self-conscious, so an awkward silence falls.

'I guess we'd better, umm...' Finn offers.

'Yes,' I agree hastily. 'See you later, Liv.'

'I won't wait up!' she calls after us. Finn doesn't quite flinch at the implication, but I can tell it hasn't helped. We haven't even made it to the end of the road and this is already firmly in disaster date territory.

'So, how have you been?' Finn asks as we make our way along the sea front towards The Mermaid. This is one of my favourite parts of Margate. A lot of people are sniffy about it and, to be fair, the area round the beach is a little run down, but I always like to imagine what it must have been like in its heyday, when the trains down from London would have been packed with people excited by the prospect of a holiday by the sea. So, for a moment, I don't register that he's spoken.

'Sorry, what did you say?'

'I was asking how you'd been.' He stops and faces me. 'Are you all right? You seem a little distracted.'

'Sorry. I was just admiring the view.'

He looks around and, from the expression on his face, he's not impressed by what he's seeing. It feels like a rejection of my hometown and I'm a little irritated.

'I'm fine. How are things with you?' I ask, keen to get the conversation, such as it is, back on track.

'Busy,' he replies. 'I'd forgotten how much work goes into taking a show from concept to reality. But it's coming together really well and the production company have started recruiting contestants, so we should be ready to start filming soon.'

'It must be so rewarding, seeing your ideas come to life in that way.'

'No more rewarding than seeing your book in a bookshop, I'm sure. How's that coming?'

'Yes, good. I'm confident I'll hit the deadline.'

'I'm pleased for you.'

We lapse into silence again as we continue to walk. I don't know what he's thinking about, but my mind is in turmoil. The truth is that the book has hardly progressed at all since I've been home, and I'm in a complete panic about the deadline. In France, I'd have been honest and told him that, so why did I lie? Something's definitely not right here, and I can feel my mood plummeting.

'Tell me about this hotel,' Finn says, finally breaking the silence. 'One of my colleagues lived around here until recently and, when I mentioned to her that I was taking you out to dinner, she told me I absolutely had to book a table at The Mermaid.'

'It is good,' I tell him, relieved to be on safe ground conversationally at least. 'In fact, it's my go-to for any kind of celebration. Angus and I came here a few times.'

No sooner are the words out of my mouth than I'm regretting them. His face falls.

'I'm so sorry,' he says. 'I never thought that this might bring up painful memories for you. Look, let me ring them and say something's come up. We can get something else.'

'It's my fault. I shouldn't have said anything. Don't worry, there won't be any painful memories dragged up. I'm over him, and the food really is superb. I'd challenge even Cara to match the standard of cooking.'

'Would you go back to L'Ancien Presbytère, do you think?'

I consider the question for a moment. 'Yes, probably. Preferably with a friendlier crowd though. What about you?'

'Yes. I did enjoy it, even with the Double-Doubles giving me the evil eye all the time.'

Although I'm pleased that talking about our time in France seems to have loosened us up, there's still an elephant in the room, namely Angus. Do I tell him that Angus came out after he left? I want to be honest, but I don't know how Finn would react and I don't want to cause any more awkwardness than there is already. Thankfully, I'm able to shelve my dilemma, for the time being at least, when we arrive at The Mermaid. Despite the nerves about seeing Finn, and the uncomfortable walk here, I'm starving and I desperately hope my stomach isn't going to start rumbling as I peruse the menu.

'You're right, this is good,' Finn observes as we take the first mouthfuls of our starters. Frankly, I'm grateful for the distraction of the food. Although the conversation does seem to have eased a little, it's still not flowing naturally, and I'm no closer to deciding whether to tell Finn about Angus. I don't know why I'm finding it so hard; all I need to do is reassure him that I had no trouble rebuffing him. I just feel weirdly guilty about it, for some reason, as if Angus and I were sneaking around behind his back.

'That was lovely, thank you,' I tell him when we arrive back at Liv's house at the end of the evening. He's been a perfect gentleman and walked me home, even though it's out of his way because we walked straight past the station on the way here. I have enjoyed his company, but I can tell we're both disappointed with the way the evening has turned out.

'Do you want a coffee or anything?' I ask, more out of politeness than a genuine desire for him to come in and prolong things.

'No, thanks. I need to get to the station before the last train leaves.'

'Of course.' I reach up and kiss him chastely on the cheek. 'It was lovely to see you. Thanks for coming down.'

'It was the least I could do. I'll be in touch with some dates for you to come and see the show being filmed, if you'd still like that.'

Would I? I'm so depressed about how this evening has gone that part of me just wants to crawl under the covers and forget Finn ever existed.

'Yes, that would be great,' my mouth says without asking my brain first. Typical Laura, I think. You'd rather put yourself through another excruciating non-date than risk offending him. I just don't get it though. Why didn't this work?

* * *

'Only one set of footsteps,' Liv's voice calls from her room as I make my way up the stairs. 'Disappointing.'

'It was a fucking disaster,' I reply morosely as I cross the landing. I've barely taken another step before her bedroom door bursts open and she emerges, wrapping me in a hug without seeming to break her stride.

'In. Now,' she commands, manhandling me towards her room. 'Tell me what happened.'

'It was just really, really awkward,' I tell her as Donna moves her legs to make room for me to sit down on the side of the bed. 'We barely had three words to say to each other.'

'Hmm. Why do you think that is? You told me you never stopped talking when you were in France.'

'That's exactly it. Maybe it just doesn't translate here.'

She thinks for a long time before speaking again. 'I do have another theory, if you're interested.'

'Go on.'

'You go to France. You meet him. You like him. Yes?'

'Yes. Nothing new there.'

'Then this old woman turns up and starts babbling at you about true love and all that.'

'I'm not sure where you're going with this.'

'Bear with me. Basically everyone around you, including some random mad old woman and me, I'm ashamed to say, has been on your case about how you need to get together with Finn. Maybe we just put too much pressure on you.'

I take a moment to digest what she's saying. 'Maybe. But that doesn't explain why he was so stilted. I'm sure I'd have relaxed if he'd been more like his usual self.'

'Yes, but think about it. These things go two ways, don't they? Maybe his mates have been pressurising him just as much as we have. We've all loaded so much expectation on the two of you that it was frankly impossible for you to live up to it.'

I smile ruefully. 'Are you seriously trying to tell me that you believe yourself to be responsible for screwing up my love life?'

'Not all by myself, no. But I think I may have contributed, and for that I'm sorry.'

'Wow.'

'The question is, how do we fix it?'

'Talk to him?' Donna suggests. 'That's usually what people say, isn't it?'

'Yes,' Liv agrees. 'But I'm not sure that's the best approach in this instance.'

'If you say "just get naked and jump his bones", I'm going to bed,' I tell her.

'I wasn't going to say that. You need to recreate the situation where you were comfortable with each other.'

'Go back to France? How on earth am I meant to persuade him to do that?

Besides, the retreat is over and Cara and Hugh probably have a new bunch of guests. That's before we even get to the cost.'

'No. It's not about the place. It's about you. You both need to rediscover the people you were out there. Maybe you just need to take the pressure off yourselves and let this grow organically. So, talk me through a typical day.'

'Well, we'd walk into town in the morning.'

'Yeah, that won't work in the current circumstances. Next?'

'We'd have coffee together mid-morning and chat about how we were getting on.'

She thinks for a while. 'Do you know where his office is?'

'No idea.'

'Bugger.'

'I could ask him?'

'No. He's like a car with a flat battery; we need the surprise to jump start him.'

'I'm not turning up to his office looking like a stripper or anything, Liv.'

'I wasn't proposing that either. Stop being so prickly. You're going to surprise him with a coffee and a delicious pastry, that's all. The tricky bit is where and how. If you can't go to him, we need a way to lure him back down here.'

'And your plan is?'

'No idea. Leave it with me though.'

29

DI Harrison knew something was off the moment she walked into the morning briefing. If the stares of her colleagues weren't enough to unsettle her, the presence of the DCI in the room definitely was. A formidable man with an equally formidable waistline that he put down to 'networking lunches', he pretty much never got involved in the day-to-day running of a case, especially one as relatively straightforward as this.

'Good morning, everyone. Chief,' she said, trying to keep her voice level. 'Let's get straight down to it, shall we? DS Rogers, we'll start with you.'

'Actually, Detective Inspector,' DCI Venables interrupted. 'I wondered if I might have a quick chat with you. Are you able to spare me five minutes in my office?'

'I'd prefer to get this done, Sir,' she replied, trying to buy time to work out what on earth he'd want to talk to her about. 'Then we can release the team to their work.'

'I'm sure DS Rogers can deputise for you, just this once. DS Rogers?'

'Umm, yes, Sir. That will be fine.'

Feeling thoroughly outmanoeuvred, DI Harrison followed the chief to his office.

'Take a seat, Claire,' he said wearily, settling his considerable frame into the chair behind the desk, causing it to creak ominously.

'Sir, I have to object to DS Rogers running the meeting. This is my case and—'

DCI Venables held up his hand to stop her. 'I'm taking you off the case, Claire,' he said simply.

'Why, Sir? I don't understand.'

DCI Venables sighed deeply. 'Certain information has come to light, which changes things somewhat. Am I right in thinking you visited the crime scene yesterday?'

'Yes, but I followed all the correct protocols. I wouldn't have disturbed any evidence.'

'I'm sure you wouldn't. It just so happens that your arrival coincided with one of the neighbours, a Mrs Jones, returning from a shopping trip. I'm not going to insult your intelligence, Claire. She says she recognised you as the victim's girlfriend. She was surprisingly adamant about it, despite the twenty-year gap.'

'Oh, come on, Sir!' Claire tried to sound as if the idea was totally absurd even as the panic rose in her chest, threatening to squeeze the breath out of her. 'Is this the same woman who was so hazy before? She's unreliable at best, attention-seeking at worst.'

'That may be true, and I hope it is. But, as of now, we have to treat you as a suspect. I'm therefore suspending you from duty on full pay until further notice. I'm sorry, Claire, but you know how much scrutiny the police force is under these days. We have to be seen to be doing everything exactly by the book. I'm sure it will all turn out to be nothing, so just enjoy a bit of time off, OK?'

'It's no good,' Liv says, barging into my room a week after my date with Finn. 'I've been wracking my brains and can't think of a way to get Finn down here without him smelling a massive rat. I had it all worked out in my head, you know? He comes into the pâtisserie, looking a little nervous. He sees you behind the counter with a coffee and slice of *Tarte Normande* ready to go, the string music swells and *voilà!*'

I laugh in spite of myself. 'I never had you pegged as such a romantic.'

'Oh, yes. In the wilder versions, you've got a bit of flour on your nose, which he gently wipes away before kissing it. We're talking full-on romcom here. Anyway, I've failed. Sorry. I'm pissed off too, because I'm sure a slice of my *Tarte Normande* would persuade him he never wanted to leave Margate again.'

'You tried, and that's the main thing.'

'Have you got any ideas?'

'Nope. I messaged him the day after we went out for dinner to say thanks, as you know, and got a pretty vanilla response.'

'You could demand to see him. Say you need to talk.'

'I think that would spook the hell out of him. Maybe it wasn't meant to be, and we should just let it go.'

'Nonsense. That matchmaker woman clearly saw something.'

'Is this the same matchmaker woman you accused just a week ago of putting too much pressure on me?'

'Yes, but we have to consider the possibility that she did have a point. All that kissing—'

'Two kisses.'

'—and your romantic morning walks. You didn't shoot people down when they suggested there could be more, which means you were open to it. I just wish there was a way to get you two back together.'

'It'll happen if it's meant to be, Liv. In the meantime...' I indicate my laptop.

'Oh, yes. I'll leave you in peace. Don't forget Donna's bringing Chinese takeaway tonight. I think she does it deliberately to wind me up. She knows as well as I do that the stuff we get here isn't a patch on real Chinese food. Did I ever tell you about the street market I worked at in Chonqing?'

'No, but you can tell us both later. I need to get this done.'

'Of course. Sorry. Do you want a cup of tea in a minute?'

'That would be lovely. Thank you.'

I'd like to be able to say that the book is providing a welcome focus since my disastrous dinner with Finn, but progress is still agonisingly slow. However hard I try to concentrate on the plot, I keep finding myself disappearing down a rabbit hole of analysis, replaying every snippet of our stilted conversation and trying to work out what I could have said to bring about a different outcome. I did definitely feel something on that day when we kissed each other, but it's the memories of us wandering into Saint-Antonin-Noble-Val, chatting about everything and nothing, that I daydream about most of all. I mean, Angus and I used to chat, but it was usually about boring domestic things or the dog. Finn seemed interested in everything about me, as I was with him. He had a way of making me feel like I was the only other person in the world when we were talking. Damn it. I miss him.

As I'm sitting there, staring at the screen, I can feel something shift inside me. This isn't Liv's problem to solve, or Finn's, or anyone else's for that matter. The fact is that I need to see him again, if only to bring closure. I grab my phone and bash out a message to him.

> Are you working today?

To my relief, the ticks go blue and his reply comes back quickly.

> Staring at set design concepts at home. Why?

I'm smiling as I type.

> Four o'clock. Time for a cup of tea and a delicious biscuit.

> OK...

> Have you got delicious biscuits?

> I think there are some chocolate digestives in the cupboard. They might even be in date...

> Here's the plan. We're each going to make a cup of tea and get a biscuit. I'm going to video call you in ten minutes, and I expect to hear all about the show. OK?

The ticks go blue but he's not typing. Shit, have I overplayed this? Just as I'm beginning to think this was a really bad idea, his reply comes through.

> See you in ten *smiley face emoji*

'I thought you were in the thick of it and I was bringing you tea?' Liv looks confused when she walks into the kitchen to find me fiddling with the teapot.

'Yes, but I reached a good break point,' I lie. 'Anyway, you're always making the tea. Time I made it for you for a change.'

She looks at me suspiciously for a moment before smiling. 'Fine. Just make sure you warm the pot and use the timer. I'll know if it's over brewed. There are some Madeleines in the tin there. I'll have one of those as well.'

'Great. Why don't you go and make yourself comfortable and I'll bring it over when it's ready.'

'I assume you're joining me?'

'Not today. I've got a call I need to go on.'

Another suspicious look. 'Really? You never mentioned it just now.'

'It's a last-minute thing.'

* * *

By the time I've made the tea and reassured Liv for a second time that nothing weird is going on, honestly, nearly fifteen minutes have passed. I practically run into my bedroom, shutting the door behind me and stabbing the call button on my phone.

'Hiya,' Finn says as the call connects. 'This is a surprise. What brought it on?'

'It's partly an apology,' I tell him.

'What for?'

'For my part in whatever happened when you came down here. I thought that doing something that we did every day while we were in France might give us the opportunity to reset our friendship.'

He sighs. 'It's me that needs to apologise,' he says. 'I was really looking forward to seeing you, but then I just kind of froze. I can't explain it, and I've been trying to find a reason to get in contact and say sorry. But then I thought maybe this was what you wanted, and then it all got in a mess in my head.'

'Me too. God, what a pair.' As if choreographed, we each take a sip of our tea. I can't help studying the background on my screen, trying to get a feel for his home.

'So, tell me about the show,' I prompt after a moment, before things can get awkward again. 'Have you got the set design there?'

He smiles. 'I have, but it's top secret so I'm not sure I can show it to you.'

'Worried I'm going to sell the idea to the competition?'

'You can never be too careful but, as it's you...' He picks up the phone and switches to the rear camera so I can see his screen, which is one of those massive things that pretty much spans his entire desk.

'This is a 3D rendering,' he tells me as the phone wobbles momentarily. 'Sorry, just grabbing the mouse so I can show you around. So, the contestants will stand at the podiums here, and there is a display on the front of each one showing their prize fund. Then this massive screen facing them here is where the auction items will be displayed, and this is where the really clever stuff happens.'

'Go on.'

'We're going to be using virtual reality. So the contestants will have VR headsets they can put on, and then they can handle the objects in the virtual world, turning them over to look at them from different angles and so on. Whatever they see will be shown on the screen here so the studio audience can follow along. For viewers at home, we'll just cut to the VR feed.'

'Impressive.'

He turns the camera so I can see his face again. 'It is, isn't it? I wish I could take the credit for the idea, but it actually came from one of the brainstorming sessions at the beginning.'

I can feel myself relaxing as he talks me through the rest of the concept. I'm still not really up on game shows, but I feel a connection to this one after all the time we spent on it together. However, while I'm excited to see it coming to life, I'm more pleased that my idea seems to be working.

'How's the book?' he asks when we've been through everything to do with the show. We've covered a few other topics too, and I'm surprised to see that nearly an hour has passed.

'Top secret. I'm not sure I can tell you anything.'

'Hold on, that's not how it works!'

I laugh. 'I'm joking. If I tell you now, we won't have anything to talk about at teatime tomorrow, will we?'

He grins. 'That's an excellent point. I might have to buy some better biscuits though. These digestives are definitely past their best.'

'Hold off if you can,' I tell him. 'I think I might have an idea about that. Give me your address. I want to send you something.'

* * *

'Everything OK?' Liv asks when I join her downstairs. 'Did you sort whatever it was?'

'I did, thank you, but I need to ask a favour.'

'Go on.'

'You know how you're the best pâtissière in Margate?'

'I sense I'm being buttered up for something I'm not going to like. Yes?'

'The point is you're brilliant, and therefore you must know other brilliant pâtissiers. Who's the best one in London?'

'If it were me, I'd go to Jean-Luc. Why?'

'I want to send someone some Madeleines.'

Her eyebrows shoot up. 'Do you now? Am I allowed to know who?'

I grin. 'Finn, if you must know. I think we might have made a breakthrough. That was him I was just talking to.'

By the time I've explained my idea for us to meet virtually for tea every day, recreating a little bit of what we had in France and hopefully setting the scene for our next real-life encounter to be much less awkward, she's fully on board and it's all I can do to stop her from ringing Jean-Luc to demand he drop whatever he's doing to go and bake Finn some Madeleines this instant.

'I'd still prefer it was me making them,' she says when we've placed an online order for delivery the next day. 'But Jean-Luc is one of the best, and I'll send him a threatening text tomorrow to make sure he's on his A-game.'

For the first time since our disastrous dinner, I feel at peace as I climb into bed that night. Even if this is as far as we go, it's really nice to be speaking to Finn normally again.

30

'This isn't working, is it,' I say exasperatedly. Although we haven't managed to have a teatime catch-up every day, we have managed to meet quite a few times over the last couple of weeks. On screen, Finn's face is concerned.

'If I'm going to be brutally honest with you, I don't think it is. Sorry. It seemed like such a good idea to begin with.'

I sigh. 'So what now? Chuck it all in the bin? It feels like a waste, having come so far.'

'Can I make a suggestion?'

'Yes, anything.'

'You could limp on, trying to make this work, but I can sense your heart isn't in it. I get that you've invested a lot, but deep down you know this isn't going to make you happy. So yes, painful as it is, I'd scrap Claire attempting to murder the neighbour and focus on the PAYE evidence.'

'There isn't any. HMRC only keep five years.'

He smiles. 'Actually, I did some research on that for you. They do have older records, but the process of obtaining them is much slower.'

'Really?'

'Yup. So maybe the neighbour caves under the pressure of a formal police interview and says she can't be 100 per cent sure that Claire is the girlfriend, even if she did look familiar. But then the DC – what's her name?'

'DC Carpenter.'

'Yes, her. She's been tenacious and got the PAYE records linking Claire to the pub.'

'That only links her to the Pig and Whistle though, not the murder scene.'

Finn laughs. 'Am I writing this book, or are you? The point is that the time-line matches and it corroborates the neighbour's evidence.'

I think for a moment. 'I still think we'd need something more, but the PAYE records could unlock that too.'

'Go on.'

'They wouldn't just link Claire to the pub, they'd provide a record of everyone else working there at the same time.'

'Pauline?'

'Bingo. Pauline would definitely recognise Claire, even twenty years on. She confirms that she was living with Darren and that's the missing link. Have I ever told you that you're a genius?'

Finn's smile widens. 'You may have said it once or twice. Before we wrap up, are you still on for tomorrow?'

'Absolutely. Wild horses wouldn't keep me away.'

'OK. I'll send you all the details. I'll already be in the studio when you arrive, but the security people know they're expecting you and will have a pass waiting for you. They'll also call me to come and get you.'

'I can't wait.'

'I just hope you aren't bored rigid.'

'I think that's extremely unlikely.'

* * *

I'm awake long before the alarm goes off at six thirty the next morning and I'm relieved to see, on peering out of the curtains, that the weather has decided to be kind even though we're heading into autumn. I've given myself plenty of time to make sure I'm looking my best for today, but I have the kind of hair that frizzes into an unmanageable mess at the first sight of a raincloud, so the clear blue sky is welcome.

Liv and Donna are already fully dressed and sipping on cups of tea when I pad into the kitchen. This isn't a surprise; Liv has always been an early riser and generally gets to Maison Olivia shortly after seven, even though they don't open until nine, and Donna has to do what she calls 'the school run', collecting dogs from the houses of those owners who've paid for the privilege.

'All set for your big day?' Liv asks. 'How are you feeling?'

'Nervous, but in a good way this time.'

'Explain.'

'So, when we went to The Mermaid, I was nervous because I didn't know if we'd have anything to talk about, or if the friendship we'd cultivated in France would translate back to the UK.'

'You were anxious.'

'Yes. Whereas now I'm nervous because I'm seeing Finn face to face, but also looking forward to it. I'm not worried because I know I'm going to have a good day.'

'You're excited.'

'Exactly.'

'You'll have a blast,' Donna assures me. 'These places are amazing. Did I ever tell either of you about the time I was on *Blankety-Blank*?'

'No,' Liv tells her. 'And it'll have to wait, sorry. Laura's got to get going.' She turns to me. 'Are we expecting you back for dinner?'

The question catches me completely by surprise. Finn hasn't mentioned anything about dinner, but then again he hasn't given any indication that the visit today is time limited.

'I don't know,' I reply. 'Can I text you?'

'Of course. If I don't hear, I'll assume it's good news and you're not coming home.'

'That's a terrible idea,' Donna counters. 'If you don't hear anything, it might be because Finn's taken inspiration from one of her books, chopped her up and left her in a ditch.'

Liv grins. 'I may only have met him for a couple of minutes, but I think that's extremely unlikely. She'd be more likely to look the wrong way crossing the road and be mown down by a bus. Country mouse up in the big smoke and all that.'

'One,' I interject crossly, 'I'm perfectly capable of crossing the road, thank you. And two...'

'Yes?' Liv asks when I dry up.

'Actually, you might have a point there. I'm not exactly a country mouse but I'm certainly no city slicker. Shit, do you think everyone's going to be looking at my outfit and judging me?'

'No, and this is anxious Laura talking. I can guarantee you that nobody in London is even going to look at you, let alone give you enough mental processing to judge you. They're all far too wrapped up in their own lives.' She shudders. 'I hate London, now I come to think about it.'

'I've never heard such bollocks!' Donna exclaims. 'Honestly, Laura, you should have seen her when we were in Chinatown. She was like a pig in clover, snuffling out the best restaurants like truffles.'

'Can you hear that?' Liv asks her.

'What?'

'That sound. You need to listen carefully, but I'm pretty sure I know what it is. It's the sound of similes screaming in pain.'

'Oh, do shut up. I thought you were being serious there for a minute.'

Normally, I'd sit at the kitchen table and enjoy their good-natured banter, but Liv is right. I need to get going.

'I'll see you guys later. Thanks for taking Meg in today, Donna.'

'It's nothing,' she replies. 'Actually, scratch that. It's not nothing. You'd normally be paying handsomely for the privilege, so make sure it's worth my while, OK?'

I've been over this journey so many times using the planners that I think I could do it from memory, but I still consult my phone several times to double check I'm going the right way. I may not be a country mouse, exactly, but it's a long time since I've been to London and even longer since I've had to navigate around the place on my own. I've decided to treat myself and go on the high-speed train to St Pancras, which gives me a fairly straightforward two-Tube trip to White City. According to the map on my phone, the studio is just across the road from the station, so it shouldn't be that hard to find.

While I may be prepared in terms of the route, I'd forgotten how hot, stuffy and crammed the London Underground system is. By the time I step out into the fresh air at White City, my shirt is clinging to my back, my face feels uncomfortably flushed and I'm sure the combination of heat and humidity has undone all my careful work on my hair this morning. Despite Liv's predictions of doom, I make it across the road unscathed and even get through the ridiculous automated revolving door without trapping any limbs or my bag in it.

You know those alternate reality scenes in films, where a character steps through some kind of portal into a totally different world? That's what the studio lobby feels like. Outside, it's all heat, bustle and noise. I can see it through the large windows. It takes me a moment to figure out what the lobby reminds me of before it comes to me. It's cool and quiet as a tomb, only one with lots of space, gleaming floors and really nice chandeliers. I mean, it's not totally silent; I can hear a phone ringing on the reception counter, but it's so muted as to be barely audible. Even the people are silent. There's a faint clack-clack of heels on the floor as a woman crosses to the security gates, and a man is standing in the corner, having a whispered conversation on his mobile phone, but they're both kind of swallowed by the overall silence. For a moment, the rebellious streak in me fills me with the urge to shout, 'Good morning, everyone!' at the top of my lungs, just to prove to myself that I'm still alive. Instead, I make my way over to the reception desk, where a blonde woman who doesn't look old enough to have left school regards me with interest.

'Hi,' I say quietly. 'I'm Laura Spalding, here to see Finn Robertson.'

'Oh, yes,' she replies. 'We're expecting you. I'll give him a call and let him know you're here. There are a couple of security things I need to do, but if I time it right, we'll get those finished just as he arrives.' She picks up the phone on the desk and presses a couple of buttons.

'Can you tell Mr Robertson that his VIP guest has arrived?' she says. 'Thank you.'

'VIP?' I ask.

'Oh, yes. He was very clear that we were to extend you every courtesy. Now, can you just look into the camera there for me for a second? Perfect.'

After a few keystrokes, the printer next to her quietly comes to life and spews out a card with my picture and a QR code on it. She folds it expertly and slots it into a plastic wallet attached to a gold lanyard with 'VIP' embroidered on it at regular intervals.

'This will get you through security,' she explains. 'All you have to do is scan the QR code. When it comes to the lifts, you'll need to scan it on the reader first. It will then allocate you a lift that's going to the floors you're authorised to visit. Any questions?'

'Umm, no.' To be honest, I didn't understand a word of what she's just said about the lifts, but hopefully Finn will be able to explain it better.

All I need now is for him to arrive.

31

_____

'There you are!' a familiar voice exclaims, and I turn to see Finn hurrying towards me from the direction of the barriers. 'How was your journey?'

'I made it,' I tell him with a smile. 'I'll take that.'

'I never doubted you would,' he says, wrapping me in a warm hug that instantly reassures me today is not going to be a repeat of the last time we saw each other. 'Your navigation skills put mine to shame. I can't tell you how excited I am that you're here. I've got so much to show you. Shall we?'

To my surprise, he reaches out and takes my hand. It's a nice sensation that reminds me of our first morning walk together. I can feel myself being swept up in his enthusiasm as he leads me across to the barriers, where he shows me how to scan my pass to get through. This is more like it. This is the Finn I'm used to, and I can feel the happiness bubbling up inside me.

'It's only the third day of filming, but everyone's really excited about the show and the contestants seem to be loving it,' he says as he scans his pass on a reader by the lifts. 'Lift number six. Over here.'

'The reception lady was trying to explain the lift system to me, but I didn't get it,' I confess.

'It's pretty simple. Our studio is on level two, so the only floors I'm allowed to access are level two, this level and the basement, where the canteen is. When I scan my pass, it knows that, and will allocate me to a lift that isn't going to visit any other floors.'

'But surely you could just get in another one anyway?'

'I could, but I wouldn't get very far. You have to scan your pass to get out of the lift lobby on every floor, and it won't let you if you're not authorised to go there. Worse, you could end up stuck, because your pass won't let you summon a lift from somewhere you're not supposed to be, so you have to wait for someone to come along and take pity on you.'

'Blimey, sounds more like a villain's lair than a TV studio.'

'Security is very tight. Production companies are understandably paranoid about their intellectual property, so they don't want random strangers wandering in and possibly stealing it.'

'But aren't they all working for the same channel?'

'Oh, no. This is a shared space. Production companies rent studios as and when they need them.'

In true British tradition, we fall silent and stare at the floor number display while we're inside the lift, despite being the only people in here. I'm very aware of Finn's hand still holding mine. It may only be a small act of intimacy, but it's making my heart thump hard in my chest.

'We're in the middle of the second show of the day,' he continues once we're out of the lift and have navigated another set of security barriers.

'You film more than one a day?'

'Yes. Five, to be precise. It's a tall order, but one of the things audiences like is to see contestants more than once, so we start with five in each show. We replace the person who gets to the final every time, but keep the others. It gives a sense of continuity through each week. A lot of shows do it.'

'I assumed you put them up in hotels for the week or something.'

'Nothing so flash. We do ask them to bring changes of clothing so it looks like time has passed between each show and we offer them a room the night before because it's an early start, but they're only here for a day.'

'Sleight of hand.'

'Sleight of TV.' He opens a door into a room that looks like the bridge of a spaceship and ushers me inside. 'This is the control room,' he says softly. 'It's the best place to watch the action from and we can speak, but we'll have to keep our voices down because the people in here are talking to the presenter via his earpiece, the camera operators and so on, so we need not to distract them.'

As if on cue, a man sitting at the spaceship desk leans forward to a microphone and says, 'He's a philatelist, Elliott. Ask him about that. Make it sound like you don't know that it's stamp collecting and imply it might be something a bit smutty instead. Camera 3, standby to capture Elliott's expression when the contestant explains.'

I watch as one of the large screens on the far wall zooms into the presenter's face, just as he phrases the question, raising his eyebrow in a manner that's very slightly suggestive, without going into full-on clown mode.

'You got Elliott MacIntosh to present?' I ask. 'I've heard of him. Isn't he the poster boy for just about everything at the moment?'

Finn shrugs, feigning nonchalance, but the smile on his face betrays him. 'Apparently, he adored the concept and couldn't wait to get involved.'

'You're loving this, aren't you?'

'Of course,' he murmurs. 'I'm literally seeing my baby, our baby, come to life. Come over here. I've arranged for a couple of chairs so we can watch in comfort. I might have to abandon you periodically, but I'll be here as much as I can be.'

It doesn't take long before I'm completely caught up in the action. There's so much going on, and being able to hear the commands from the control room played out seamlessly on screen just makes it all the more magical. Every so often, everything stops and runners rush on to the set to add or remove props.

'The audience at home will be watching an ad break during these bits,' Finn explains when I ask about it. 'You can cover all manner of sins with an ad break.'

By the time the head-to-head comes around, I'm leaning forward in my chair willing the contestants on. Neither of them correctly identified the rogue item, which was a painting in round three, so whichever of them wins will have the disappointment of seeing their prize halved.

'Welcome back,' Elliott says, smiling warmly into one of the cameras. 'Before the break, we said goodbye to Sandra, but Richard and Sarah have played a superb game so far and are ready for their next challenge, the head-to-head. In this round the objects sold for a value of between ten and twenty thousand pounds, so there's the possibility of adding up to twenty thousand pounds to your prize fund. Sarah, that would more than pay for your new kitchen. What else would you spend the money on?'

'I'd take my mum on holiday somewhere hot,' Sarah replies. 'She's done so much for me, it would be lovely to do something nice for her.'

'What a kind thought,' Elliott almost simpers. 'Of course, the final prize amount hinges on whether the winner has correctly identified the item that didn't belong in its category, so the stakes couldn't be higher. OK, first to play is the person with the lowest prize fund and that's you, Richard. Here's your first item.'

Unfortunately for poor Richard, his guesses are miles off and Sandra pretty much wipes the floor with him, securing her place in the final. After bringing in the props for the last segment, filming resumes with Elliott reminding the audience once again that her final prize amount depends on whether she picked the correct rogue item. She hasn't, of course. All the contestants missed the rather ordinary-looking painting with the initials WSC in the corner, which meant it had been painted by Winston Churchill and was actually worth a fortune. Sandra leaves with enough money for her new kitchen though, which seems to satisfy her.

'Right, lunch break,' Finn announces as the runners appear to start setting up for the next show. 'Are you hungry?'

'I am.'

'The canteen here is excellent,' he tells me as we head back towards the lift. 'I'll warn you that it's easy to get carried away.'

He's not wrong. When we get down into the basement, I feel like I've stepped into the buffet of a luxury all-inclusive resort. There are different counters for salads, sandwiches, hot food and desserts. This presents me with a dilemma. I still don't know whether Finn is planning anything for this evening, in which case I definitely want to stick to something light, or whether I'm going to be on the train home as soon as filming finishes. It seems pushy to ask, so in the end I play it safe with a salad and some fruit.

'Very restrained,' Finn observes as he takes out his debit card to pay for his lunch. 'You don't pay, by the way,' he explains. 'Part of being a VIP.'

'You're not exactly pushing the boat out yourself,' I tell him, indicating the sandwich and apple on his tray.

'If I had the full lunch every time, I'd probably end up having to join a weight loss programme,' he says with a laugh as we make our way over to a booth in the corner. 'Can I tell you a secret?'

'Yes.'

He leans forward conspiratorially. 'I'm having to watch what I eat, because there's a woman who keeps sending me madeleines.'

'Really? What kind of person would do something like that?' I reply, entering into the game. 'I've read about these people who want to show their love through food but overdo it. I think they're called feeders. Is she one of those, do you think?'

He pretends to consider the question. 'I've never thought about it that way. You think she's sending me biscuits because she's secretly in love with me?'

'I don't know,' I say, recklessly seizing the opportunity of the game we're playing to drop him a real-life hint. 'I would suggest you're very clear with her. If you like her, then tell her that. If not, then you need to let her down gently before she gets too attached. You don't want to end up like the poor guy in *Misery*, chained to the bed by a deranged fan, do you?'

'Hm.' He's giving nothing away and I'm starting to wonder if I've taken it too far. 'Good advice. I'll certainly think about it.'

* * *

The afternoon's filming was interesting, especially as one contestant actually managed to identify the rogue item correctly and potentially double their prize pot. Unfortunately for them, they were then knocked out before the final and didn't benefit. Instead, Geoff, a data scientist from Market Harborough, saw his fund halved but waltzed off twelve thousand pounds richer. Finn came and went, dealing with issues as they arose, so I didn't think anything of it when he disappeared halfway through the filming of the final episode of the day. It soon became awkward, however, when filming wrapped up and there was still no sign of him. Eventually, one of the production crew approached me to explain that he was going to see me out because, unfortunately, Mr Robertson had been called away but had asked him to apologise on his behalf.

I know it's not Finn's fault that he was called away, but I'm feeling flat as I head into the Tube station. I'd hoped that we'd be able to go for a drink, or even something to eat, but we didn't even get the chance to say goodbye. Just to make things worse, fate decides now is the ideal time to play tricks on me with another Finn doppelganger. The Tube is rammed again, so I've found myself pressed up against the door leading to the next carriage and, at one point, I catch the briefest glimpse through the window of a guy who I could have sworn was Finn, apart from the fact he was dressed much more smartly. My view is blocked almost immediately by another passenger and, by the time I get to St Pancras, I've convinced myself that I was just seeing things. Great, that's the first sign of madness, isn't it?

32

My mood is bleak as I step onto the platform at Margate and start making my way towards the exit. It only sinks further when I realise that I've been so busy being disappointed about the way the day ended that I've completely forgotten to message Liv to let her know that I'll be home for dinner after all. Maybe I'll pick up a ready meal and a bottle of wine. It feels like a ready meal and bottle of wine kind of night. To make matters worse, it seems like the phantom Finns are here too; I stop dead as, for a moment, I could swear someone is calling my name.

'Bloody hell, careful,' an angry voice says as a solid mass bumps into me, almost knocking me off my feet.

'Sorry,' I tell the man, but he's already gone, obviously in a hurry to get home like everyone else here. I shake myself and resume my walk to the exit. Hearing things is probably the second sign of madness. At this rate, I'll be a fully paid-up lunatic by the time I get home.

'Laura!' the voice calls again, more clearly this time. 'Over here.'

I turn my head and blink. The spitting image of Finn that I saw on the Tube is standing near the exit, calling my name and waving. I hesitate for a moment, waiting for him to disappear like the other phantoms, but either this is a prolonged psychotic episode, or Finn really is here in Margate.

'Finn?' I ask when I reach him, unable to keep the incredulity out of my voice. 'What are you doing here?'

His grin is so wide that it's threatening to split his face in two. 'I'm here for an evening engagement.'

'Oh,' I say, swallowing the pang of disappointment. Of course he wasn't coming here for me. 'Is this related to whatever you were called away for?'

'Very much so.'

He's beaming at me, but I can't work out why.

'You don't look very pleased to see me,' he says after a moment.

'I am. I'm just confused.'

'Let me explain. I wasn't called away at all. I needed time to change and get into position.'

'For what?'

'To see where you went. Although I hoped you'd come back here, there was a possibility you might have made arrangements to meet up with friends or do some sightseeing in London this evening, and that would have derailed my plan.'

'You *followed* me?'

He does at least have the grace look a little bashful. 'Not exactly. I just needed to be certain that you were coming back home.'

'Why? You're not making any sense at all, you know that? So far, we've got a bogus thing that you're called away to deal with, and some A-grade stalking so you can implement some mystery plan. I'm not reassured, Finn.'

He looks at me quizzically. 'It's a surprise, don't you see?'

'No.'

'My evening engagement is you, if you're free.'

I stare at him, totally nonplussed now. 'So you effectively blew me out earlier, only to hotfoot it down here to surprise me? We could have just gone for a drink in London.'

'We could, but there's something I need to do, and that can only happen here.'

I narrow my eyes. 'Was that you on the Tube? Why the change of clothes?'

'This is a more suitable outfit for the surprise. It gave me a hell of a shock when your face appeared at the window. I think the woman next to me thought I was mad, because I was trying to hide behind her. I don't think I'm cut out for surveillance work.'

'This all seems very elaborate and I'm still not completely comfortable that you followed me. What's supposed to happen now?'

'Wait and see. We need to grab a taxi from the rank.' He must sense my hesitation, because he smiles. 'Don't worry, I haven't forgotten.'

He's making less and less sense. Either that or I genuinely am going mad and this is all some sort of terrible dream.

'Haven't forgotten what?'

'That you're a martial arts expert.'

I surreptitiously pinch my thigh as hard as I can to try to wake myself up. This must be a dream and it's just too bizarre for me. Unfortunately, nothing changes apart from the fact that I now have pain in my thigh.

'Who told you that I was a martial arts expert?' I ask, bewildered.

'You did, on the day I arrived at the retreat. As you climbed into my car, you told me quite clearly that you were a martial arts expert so it would end badly for me if I tried anything on.'

A vague memory bubbles up to the surface and I start to laugh. Finally, something in this frankly unbelievable scene is making sense.

'What's so funny?' Finn asks.

'I lied,' I tell him.

Now it's his turn to look confused. 'Why?'

'In case you were a murderer.'

'Did I look like a murderer?'

'They come in all shapes and sizes. How was I supposed to know?'

'So you're not a martial arts expert.'

'I've watched *The Karate Kid*. Does that count?'

'The original, or the remake?'

'Both.'

'I'm not sure it does. Anyway, I promise not to murder you in the taxi if that helps you feel safe about getting in one with me.'

I look at him. He's Finn at full wattage right now, and I feel a bit like one of those moths that just can't help being attracted to the light. He may not be Henry Cavill, but his personality is like one of those cartoon magnets, causing objects miles away to break free and fly towards them.

'I'll get in a taxi with you,' I tell him.

'Great.' He takes my hand and leads me outside. Most of the other people from our train are long gone now, and the taxi rank is empty. Thankfully, one pulls in as we make our way over and Finn holds the door open for me.

'My lady,' he says, bowing deeply. I scoot across the seat automatically, expecting him to follow but, to my surprise, he closes the door. What the hell is he playing at now?

'Can you take us here?' he says, showing the driver something on his phone. I lean forward to try to see it, but Finn has angled the screen so it's impossible.

'Of course. Hop in, mate.'

The door opens again and I'm relieved when Finn slides in next to me.

'Where are we going?' I ask.

'Wait and see.'

'I'm not good at cloak and dagger.'

'You're a crime writer,' he counters.

'Did you say you were a writer?' the cabbie interjects. 'Would I have heard of you?'

'I doubt it,' I tell him. This is my default response as it just saves awkward questions.

'I read a lot of crime,' the cabbie continues. 'Have you heard of Larry Spalding? I bloody love his books.'

'Do you?' Finn asks, a mischievous smile playing on his lips. 'What would you say if you had Larry Spalding in the back of your cab?'

'Probably nothing,' the cabbie says with a laugh. 'I had Tracey Emin in here once. I knew who she was, obviously, but I was so busy trying to work out if she'd be offended if I said I loved her work that I ended up keeping my trap shut. Missed opportunity or what, eh? Anyway, I don't know what Larry Spalding looks like, so he might have been in the back of my cab already for all I know.'

'I don't think Larry would mind you chatting to him,' Finn says, clearly loving this now. 'He's quite a down-to-earth person on the whole.'

'Do you know him?' The cabbie is clearly impressed.

'I've met him a few times,' Finn tells him. 'He's a lot of fun, actually.'

'Well, if you see him again, tell him that Alan the cabbie from Margate is a super fan. I'll give you my card if you like. If he's ever in the area and needs a taxi, you know.'

'I'm sure he'd love that.' I can see Finn is struggling not to laugh now, and I'm torn between wanting to punch him in the leg and laugh myself.

'Right. Here we are,' the cabbie announces as he pulls up outside a familiar building.

'The Mermaid?' I ask.

'I'll explain in a minute,' Finn tells me as he pays the cabbie and makes a show of storing the business card in his wallet.

'You are a very bad man,' I say as the taxi pulls away.

'Nonsense. I probably made his day.'

'Hm. Are you finally going to tell me what this is all about?'

'It's simple. Last time we came here, things didn't exactly go the way we planned.'

'That's one way of putting it.'

'I fucked it up.'

'That's another way of putting it, although I certainly wouldn't say it was all your fault.'

'I felt it was my fault. I was kicking myself all the way home. I'd spent so long rehearsing what I was going to say, and then the bloody words failed me at the crucial moment.' He shudders. 'It makes me cringe just thinking about it now. And then, I wanted to contact you and say I was sorry and could I make it up to you, but it just felt like I'd ruined everything. Then you got in touch with your teatime idea.'

'I thought I'd lost you as a friend.'

I swear I see a flash of something that looks like disappointment cross his face, but it's gone so fast and tonight has been so odd that I'm starting to doubt my own judgement.

'Anyway. So we could have gone out for something to eat in London, but I felt like dinner here would always be hanging over us. So, I thought we'd come back and try again.'

I'm stunned. Nobody has ever put this much thought into arranging something for me before, and it's all I can do not to cry as I think about how much planning he must have done. Without hesitation, I reach out, take his face in mine and plant a huge kiss on his lips.

'What was that for?' he asks when I finally release him.

'To say thank you for all of this. To say sorry. But mostly because I wanted to.'

'I see.' A smile breaks on his face as I feel his hand gently lifting my chin, and then his lips are on mine again. I close my eyes, just enjoying the sensation. It's not one of those hungry kisses, where you can feel the other person's tongue practically trying to force your teeth apart. There isn't any tongue at all. It's also not one of those kisses that are so crushingly hard you wonder if your lips are slowly bruising, nor the kind that's so soft you wonder if it's actually happening at all. It's the kind of kiss you want to carry on forever, so you can just lose yourself in it. There's no doubting the message behind it, and my body is receiving it loud and clear. At least, until a thought comes to me that makes me start to giggle.

'What?' Finn looks confused as he breaks the kiss.

'*Goldilocks and the Three Bears*,' I tell him. 'Your kiss reminded me of that story.'

'Before you go any further, I need to inform you that you hold my entire masculinity in the palm of your hand right now. If you're going to tell me that kissing me is like kissing a bear, I might never get over it.'

'Relax. It was more the beds. One was too hard, one was too soft, and the other... The other was you. Just right.'

'Really?'

'I'd need to sample a few more to be sure, but I'm confident.'

'There are plenty more where that one came from,' he assures me, before grinning again.

'What?'

'I'm changing your nickname. Luggage Laura doesn't fit any more.'

'Who am I now then?'

'Lovely Laura,' he says simply. 'I think it's appropriate, don't you?'

'I think I can live with it. Now, I'm starving. Did someone mention dinner?'

33

A YEAR LATER

'Remind me why we're doing this?' Finn asks as he pulls on his jacket. It's the same jacket he wore for our first date, the one that went so wrong, but that thought barely enters my head before it's replaced by a much better one; namely how good he looks in it.

'Because we're shameless voyeurs. Because I'm never going to have a book launch like it, and because Lynette invited us.'

'Does Gina know we're coming?'

'I sincerely hope not. If we play our cards right, she might never even know we were there.'

'I've booked us dinner at Fortnum & Mason afterwards. I thought we might need a treat to get over it. Meg's staying with Liv and Donna overnight, so it won't matter if we get back late.'

Of course he has. One of the things about Finn that I love the most is how he always tries to add something special to everything we do. From surprising me at Margate station so he could recreate our first date the way it should have gone – it was very nice, thank you – to remembering to organise care for Meg when he's planning another surprise for me like tonight, his attention to detail is immaculate.

Of course, the fact that everyone else around me adores him too also helps. Liv said a few months ago that I looked so happy she was seriously considering building a sex dungeon, kidnapping him and locking him in there until she found out what his secret was. I'm not sure Donna was wildly impressed with that idea, even if Liv was joking. Even my father likes him, despite some dark remarks at the beginning about 'two creatives with no guaranteed income' being a recipe for disaster. Honestly, sometimes I think that man would make Eeyore look chirpy. Mum, typically, keeps asking loaded questions about hats and possible wedding venues, but we're in no rush. It'll happen when we're ready.

Despite a lot of extremely nice kisses on the evening that we'd both say marks the start of our 'proper' relationship, I'd describe us as more of a slow-burn couple. Finn didn't stay the night until we'd been together for over a month, by which time my whole body was a screaming mass of tingling nerve endings just waiting for the spark to go off. Put it this way: not only have I had no need to open the boxes that were under my bed since that night, I'm also very glad Liv was staying at Donna's, although it would certainly have cured her of thinking I was in any way sexually repressed. After nearly eight months and a lot of discussion about whether we should live in London or Margate, we decided Margate was better for Meg and we moved into our house four months ago. Sometimes I still pinch myself when I see it, as it seems incredible that we're homeowners rather than renters. But I've loved putting our mark on the place. There are four bedrooms, which gives us a study each (we quickly worked out that shared working space was not for us), plus our room and a spare that we haven't managed to invite anyone to stay in yet. Our most frequent visitors are Donna and Liv, and they're only a ten-minute walk away, so it's easier for them to go home at the end of an evening.

'Mm. You look good,' Finn says as I slip the cocktail dress I've bought for the occasion over my shoulders and wriggle it into place. 'Can you stop doing that though, please?'

'What?'

'Wiggling your bum like that. It's doing things to me that could make us miss the event completely.'

'What, like this?' I ask with a smile, exaggerating the movement.

'Argh! Enough. I'll wait for you downstairs.'

'I won't be long. Bit of make-up and a necklace and I'll be ready.'

'I'll ring the taxi company now then.'

'It's a nice afternoon. We could walk to the station.'

'You're wearing heels.'

'Good point.' This is what I mean about his attention to detail.

* * *

The train to London is pretty much deserted and the journey passes quickly. *Winning Bid* has proved to be a huge hit, to the extent that the network is talking about moving it into an evening slot to capitalise on its popularity. None of this has done Finn any harm financially, and they've also commissioned him to come up with detailed plans for a couple of other concepts they're interested in. I'm currently between books, having just handed in the sequel to the one I was working on in France, so any downtime like this tends to be spent brainstorming ideas either for the new shows or my next book, which is definitely going to be *Murder at the Writers' Retreat*.

'Bloody hell!' I exclaim when we reach our destination. 'I know the invitation said gala book launch, but this is next level. How much do you think that cost?'

Finn ponders for a moment. 'She's pretty much got the whole window of the bookshop. This is Piccadilly, so we can assume it wasn't cheap.'

'According to Lynette, she's funding this all herself. That makes sense. Even if I didn't hide behind my pen name, I don't think my publisher would pay for anything as lavish as this.'

'They ought to. You make them a fortune.'

A man in a dark suit is standing blocking the entrance, only moving aside once he's inspected our invitations. Inside, there's more of the same. Large floor-standing banners are dotted about, adorned with pictures of Gina above the front cover of her debut novel. Between them, tables are piled high with hardback copies of *The Lion and the Snake*.

'Champagne, orange juice or water?' The waiter proffers a tray and we each take a glass of champagne.

'I don't think I've ever seen Gina smiling before,' I observe as I look at one of the banners.

'It's probably trapped wind,' Finn says with a grin. Before we can dissolve into fits of giggles, however, a familiar face appears.

'How are you, Suzie?' I ask.

'Very well, thank you. I wasn't expecting to see you here. Does Gina know?'

'Lynette invited us.'

'That makes sense. Relations are better, but I think Lynette still can't help winding Gina up from time to time, and you being here is bound to piss her off. By the way, I absolutely loved your last book. I bought it on the day it came out and I think I finished it within a week. The body in the garden at the end was a brilliant twist. Grace and I think that it's Darren's previous girlfriend. If he turns out to be a murderer who was planning to kill Claire as well, does that make her actions self-defence and get her out of prison?'

I smile. 'You'll have to read the next book to find out.'

'Ladies and gentlemen,' a voice calls over the hubbub of conversation. 'If you could please take your seats, the evening is about to begin.'

'Is Lynette here?' I ask Suzie as we make our way towards an area where some seats have been arranged facing a wing-backed armchair.

'Yes, but she's keeping a low profile. This is very much Gina's night.'

'That seems a little unfair, given how she basically saved the book, from what I understand.'

'Yes, but you know what Gina's like. It's not all bad for Lynette though. If you buy a copy, have a look at the acknowledgements. The sun shines so strongly out of Lynette's arse it's amazing she can sit down without setting fire to the furniture. Oh, shit. Did I just say arse? Champagne always goes to my head.'

As soon as we're seated, the MC announces Gina, who walks out looking for all the world like she was on the red carpet at the Oscars. Her floor-length silver dress is glinting under the lights, her hair is set firmly in a very flattering style, and her face is flawless.

'Good evening, everyone,' she says in a voice I almost don't recognise, before I realise it's her normal voice but without the constant tone of disapproval I'm used to hearing. 'Thank you so much for coming to this event. I owe each and every one of you a debt of gratitude.' Her eyes sweep across the assembled guests, but I swear I see them narrow when they fall on me. To her credit, she doesn't falter.

'Most of all, I have to thank my husband, John.' She indicates a portly, red-faced man in the front row. 'He's been my rock throughout my creative journey, literally the oil that has greased the wheels of my writing.'

'He's also bankrolling the shit out of this,' Finn whispers. 'Probably red in the face from all the whisky he had to consume to get over the size of the bill.'

'Now, without further ado,' Gina continues, 'I would like to read you the opening chapter of Gina Atkinson's debut novel, entitled *The Lion and the Snake*. After this, there will be an opportunity for you to purchase your own copies and, of course, I'll be happy to sign them for you.'

I cast my eyes around the room as she begins to read. I spot Lynette first; she's also in the front row, sitting next to Tess. Suzie is next to us, but I can't see any sign of Grace.

'Isn't Grace here?' I ask Suzie in a whisper.

'Goodness, no. She and Gina had a massive falling out a while ago. Basically, according to Grace, she found a way to submit her manuscript to Florianus, only to get a scathing rejection letter.'

'That happens a lot in publishing.'

'Yes, but there were a couple of phrases in the letter that made Grace suspicious. So she looked at Companies House and discovered that Florianus only had two directors, Gina and her husband. That confirmed her suspicions that the rejection letter had been penned by Gina. Of course, when she confronted her about it, Gina hit the roof and I don't think they've spoken since.'

I let my gaze continue around the room. Unsurprisingly, there's nobody else here I recognise and I let Gina's voice wash over me as she reads on. At the end, there's a round of polite applause followed by the scraping of chairs as people get to their feet. Most of them are collecting copies of the book, I notice.

'Should we get one?' Finn asks.

'I kind of feel we should. We were there for part of its birth, after all.'

'Wait here. I'll go.'

I watch him as he grabs a book off the table and makes a beeline for the till, but then I'm distracted by a voice at my shoulder.

'You came then?' Lynette asks. 'I know you said you would, but I wasn't sure you'd follow through on it.'

'Of course we did,' I reply, turning to her. She's holding a half-empty glass of champagne and her face is flushed, making me believe this might be the latest of several glasses. 'It was very generous of you to let Gina have the lime-light tonight.'

She tries to lean forward conspiratorially, but it comes off more like a drunken sway. 'No real choice,' she confides. 'He who pays the piper and all that. I don't mind, really. This kind of thing isn't my vibe. Let's just hope she sells enough books to make it worthwhile, eh?'

'Are you still getting on?'

'Yes and no. She's still fucking irritating sometimes, but I get moments of satisfaction. You should have seen her face when we arrived to set up and your book was front and centre of the store. She wouldn't even touch a copy herself, demanding that the assistants come and move them.'

Thankfully, just as I'm trying to find a diplomatic response, Finn reappears.

'Here we are,' he says, giving me the book. 'Hello, Lynette. I'm afraid I'm going to have to steal Laura away as we have dinner reservations.'

'That was fun,' he tells me as we make our way towards the door.

'What?'

'I got it signed. You should have seen the look on Gina's face. I think she might have refused had there not been onlookers. I hope I got the message right.'

I open the book and read the inscription inside.

To Laura. With love from one author to another. Gina xx

I grin. 'It's perfect, although I think we might have to hang garlic above the bed for a while.'

'Serves her right for being so rude to the woman I love.'

'You didn't love me back then,' I remind him.

'I loved you from the moment you threatened me with your completely fictitious martial arts training,' he replies, bending to give me a quick kiss. 'I just hid it well.'

Knowing Finn, that's probably true. Sometimes I still wish we hadn't had so many false starts, but I've come to realise it's irrelevant. He's here now, he loves me, and I love him. Nothing else matters.

* * *

MORE FROM PHOEBE MACLEOD

Another book from Phoebe MacLeod, is available to order now here:
https://mybook.to/PhoebeBackAd

ACKNOWLEDGEMENTS

Thank you so much for reading this book, and I hope you enjoyed Laura and Finn's story, as well as Claire and Darren's. A few people have asked me lately if I had ever considered writing in other genres, and the only one that has ever appealed has been crime, so I really enjoyed the opportunity to play with that a little in this novel.

Writing a book where the central character was an author proved surprisingly challenging, as it made me realise just how little I know about the publishing industry. I need to say a huge thank you to Rachel, Tara, and all the other people who have helped me understand how different companies work.

Talking of Rachel, this proved to be another book where she had to go above and beyond, so thank you also for being such a supportive editor. Thank you also to Cecily for copy editing once again, and Jennifer for proof reading. I must, as always, also say a huge thanks to the rest of the Boldwood team for the incredible work you do, both in turning my manuscripts into such beautiful books, but also helping them to find their audience. I know I say this every time, but you really are the best publisher to work with.

Final thank yous, as always, go to my family, who continue to support and encourage me with my writing.

ABOUT THE AUTHOR

Phoebe MacLeod is the author of several popular romantic comedies including the top ten bestseller, *The Fixer Upper*. She lives in Kent with her partner, grown up children and disobedient dog.

Download your exclusive bonus content from Phoebe MacLeod here:

Follow Phoebe on social media here:

facebook.com/PhoebeMacleodAuthor

x.com/macleod_phoebe

instagram.com/phoebemacleod21

ALSO BY PHOEBE MACLEOD

Someone Else's Honeymoon

Not The Man I Thought He Was

Fred and Breakfast

Let's Not Be Friends

An (Un)Romantic Comedy

Love at First Site

Never Ever Getting Back Together

The Fixer Upper

My Not So Perfect Summer

Too Busy for Love

The Do-Over

Hook, Line and Single

Love, Accidentally

Happily Never After

Boldwood
EVER AFTER
x♡x♡

JOIN BOLDWOOD'S
ROMANCE COMMUNITY
FOR SWEET AND SPICY BOOK RECS WITH ALL YOUR FAVOURITE TROPES!

SIGN UP TO OUR NEWSLETTER

HTTPS://BIT.LY/BOLDWOODEVERAFTER

Boldwood

Boldwood Books is an award-winning fiction publishing company seeking out the best stories from around the world.

Find out more at www.boldwoodbooks.com

Join our reader community for brilliant books, competitions and offers!

Follow us
@BoldwoodBooks
@TheBoldBookClub

Sign up to our weekly deals newsletter

https://bit.ly/BoldwoodBNewsletter